MAGNUS POWELL
and the Shadow Squad

GREG HULME

Dedication

In memory of my friend Jason, a man with the warmest heart and the most contagious laugh.

Published by The Word Hutt, 2021.

Prologue

'Citizens of Great Britain, we are at war. Our enemies have released a deadly biological weapon into the atmosphere called the Andromeda Virus, which as of this moment, has now claimed the lives of over twenty million people across the globe. That number continues to rise daily at a commensurate rate. The virus attacks the lungs within thirty seconds of inhalation and can result in respiratory failure and death in a matter of minutes.

Prime Minister Andrew Harris has made an announcement this morning from Number 10 Downing Street saying that he has deployed soldiers overseas to fight back against these attacks. He has stressed how important it is that everyone stays inside, seals shut all windows and doors and wears oxygen masks to avoid inhalation or exposure to the virus.

Scientists at the University of Oxford say they are making progress with human trials on a new drug called Theraclusamin, which is extracted from very rare plants found on the ocean seabed. The drug is reported to combat the effects of the virus while doctors push to start human trials on a new vaccine. At a press conference, Doctor Harold Fox, Head of Fox Chemicals division, had this to say:

'Whilst the trials look promising, we must all stay vigilant. Every one of us must follow the government's protocol and stay inside to protect themselves and their families from inhaling this deadly pathogen.'

The Prime Minister has ordered a dispatch of thousands of delivery trucks with food and essential supplies for every household in the country. He also announced plans to build a city in the sky surrounded by two hundred square miles of airtight walls. It will be a safe haven for those who stick to the rules and remain virus-free.

However, many have expressed concern that there will not be enough space and resources within these walls to house what remains of the population and keep it from being overrun. Prime Minister Harris has said that with these new developments and scientific breakthroughs, he is confident he can get the country back on track as long as everyone adheres to the government guidelines. We must remain strong, and we must follow the rules.

To all who are watching, this cannot be stressed enough. This virus is the greatest threat to civilisation the world has ever encountered. Everyone has a responsibility to him or herself and everyone around them to stay safe and to stay inside.

This concludes today's public broadcast announcement. I'm Jonathan Cole.'

End transmission

The year is 2102. London has become a barren, desolate wasteland of empty streets, rusty broken down vehicles and rotting, moss-covered buildings as far as the eye can see. The streets and open fields that were once rife with natural life and beauty have now become littered with endless dust and debris.

Its remaining inhabitants have become confined to their airtight, underground bunkers, held captive by the lethal pathogen loitering in the air above ground. They are no longer considered free people. They are prisoners. The liberty they once took for granted is but a memory long forgotten, and all that now remains in the hearts of men and women across the land is fear and desperation.

The country has been separated into provinces in order to control the distribution of food and water. However, as the years have passed, shipments have been dramatically reduced, and resources have become finite. As a result, the population in Great Britain continues to dwindle, with many people intentionally exposing themselves to the omnipresent virus as a quick solution to end their constant suffering. Some consider it a blessing to die quickly than to carry on living in a broken world. However, high-tech military drones now roam the lands as a deterrent to those attempting to leave their bunkers.

A powerful tyrant who goes by the name of 'The Master' has overthrown the British government and has turned a blind eye to his suffering citizens in favour of more self-indulgent activities. Little is known about him, but much has been speculated. They say that he is a supernatural being, not of this Earth, cast down to carry out judgement over those who have lived a life of sin. They say he has magical powers that have the capacity to move entire buildings and tear people limb from limb without him even lifting a finger.

Whatever the truth about him may be, he now resides behind his impenetrable fortress in the sky - the newly built city of Arcadia, which lies ten thousand feet above ground and houses only the select few lucky enough to have been born into wealth and prosperity.

Within the walls of this city, the air is safe to breathe, and resources are plentiful. Anyone with enough money to buy their way in can share in the luxury and live something closely resembling a normal, happy lifestyle. However, this comes at a price. Under the Master's ruling, any member of the Elite lucky enough to be allowed entry to the city are thus forbidden to leave it under any circumstances. Those who do, risk their own life and the lives of their family.

Many outsiders have attempted to breach the walls of the city over its ten-year existence; they seek only to have the right to breathe clean air without the use of an oxygen mask, to eat good nutritious food, not in powdered form, and drink fresh, sustainable water captured straight out of the sky. However, with insufficient resources or firepower at their disposal, no one has ever come close to breaking through the gates.

All communication has been cut off from the outside world. With nobody fighting to protect the ever-decreasing population across the country, all hope seems to be lost for its remaining citizens.

- CHAPTER 1 -
BANISHMENT

Lightning strikes and rain thrashed down over the abandoned streets of London as a man dressed in a white armoured suit flew thousands of feet in the air toward the city of Arcadia. That man's name was Jethro Beckett. Then, in his mid-fifties, Jethro was considered a man of great importance within the confines of the Arcadian walls. He'd spent over twenty-five years as head of the combat training and weapons division for the Arcadian army and was well respected among his 'Elite' peers.

However, this particular evening he had been entrusted by his Commander to carry out a top-secret mission more dangerous than any he had ever encountered before. The mission required him to temporarily leave the city walls, the ramifications of which had potentially devastating consequences for him and his family.

As he made his approach to the glass border of the city in the sky, he could barely see through his helmet's visor as the heavy rain clouded his vision. Rain was not something he had a great deal of experience with, having spent so long inside a city with constant simulated sunshine. He decided, at that moment, that he needed to invent a device for his helmet that would stop rainwater impeding his vision in the future.

As Jethro propelled himself forward, he pushed a button on the left side of his helmet and began to speak into his built-in microphone.

'Commander. I'm approaching the border now. Open the doors.'

Seconds later, a cog shaped gate spun open at the entrance of the city, allowing Jethro to fly in through the circular gap. He landed safely on his feet as the airtight gate sealed shut behind him. Jethro stretched out his arms and legs and, within seconds, vast waves of piping hot air blasted at him from every angle. Jethro stood unfazed; his suit able to withstand the heat of red-hot molten magma.

After ten seconds, the air stopped blowing, and an electronic female voice was heard over the speakers:

'Decontamination process complete.'

Once his suit had been cleared, Jethro edged forward as the wall in front of him slid open to reveal a tall man dressed in a black suit and tie standing in front of him, looking noticeably apprehensive. His name was Tobias Campbell, a man in his late forties, who was recently appointed Commander-in-Chief of the Arcadian government. Naturally, this position demanded great respect from those who lived in Arcadia; however, he was not held in as high regard as he would have preferred. Many believed he was a lazy, arrogant and untrustworthy politician who lied and manipulated his way to the very top. However, Tobias was adamant that all the actions he had ever taken in government had been in the best interest of the nation and its people.

As he watched Jethro approach him, Tobias felt a strong sense of fear in the pit of his stomach. He cautiously looked around to check the coast was clear and began to speak.

'Is it done?' he asked with anxious impatience.

'Of course, it's done. I wouldn't be back here if it wasn't!' Jethro replied with obvious aggravation.

He pushed a button on his helmet, and it instantly folded into the back of his suit, revealing his face. He was a ruggedly handsome man for his age with a short, well-groomed beard and a black patch over his right eye.

'You were gone longer than I'd expected, Jethro,' said Tobias, his voice dropping to a more urgent tone as both men distanced themselves from the gateway.

'Well, I ran into some complications regarding the drones that *you,* Commander, failed to deactivate,' Jethro replied accusingly.

'Yes, well, I had some bigger issues to worry about.'

'What do you mean?'

Suddenly the two men's conversation was cut short by the sound of a high-pitched siren in the distance, which was getting progressively louder. Jethro looked up to see flashing red lights illuminating the sky, heading straight towards them with imminent haste. Both men stopped in their tracks as if their feet were magnetised to the floor.

'What's going on?' asked Jethro in a panicked voice.

Tobias didn't respond. In fact, he couldn't bring himself to look up from the ground.

'TOBIAS!' Jethro yelled out in anger.

The Commander finally looked up into Jethro's fear-stricken eyes.

'I'm sorry, Jethro....'

Tobias paused. He could barely form the words he wanted to say.

Jethro looked at him with utter contempt as the realisation of what was occurring around him finally started to sink in.

'You set me up,' he said, shaking his head, 'didn't you, you son of a bitch. YOU SET ME UP!'

Jethro lunged at the Commander and wrapped his hands around his neck. Tobias reached into his pocket and pulled out a cylindrical, electrically charged rod six inches in length. He pressed the rod against Jethro's chest, sending a huge surge of electrical energy straight through his body. Jethro flew back ten feet and landed in a heap on the hard concrete floor.

Tobias took out a gun from his inside pocket and pointed it directly at Jethro's head.

'I had no choice, Jethro. The Master found out about your absence from the city and ordered an immediate arrest upon your return. It was out of my hands,' Tobias stated defensively. However, Jethro wasn't buying it. He knew the lengths Tobias was prepared to stoop to in order to avoid taking responsibility for his actions.

'And how exactly did they find out I was gone, Tobias?' he asked accusingly.

Tobias didn't have time to answer him, as, at that moment, the flying vehicle with the flashing red lights and ear-splitting siren landed ten feet in front of them.

The vehicle's doors flew open, and ten of Jethro's white-suited soldiers came bounding out and surrounded him. Each soldier was holding a long metal staff equipped with an electrical charge at both ends. They aimed their weapons at the captain with excellent precision as he slowly rose to his feet.

'So, this is how it's going to be, is it?' said Jethro in disgust. He took a long look at the men surrounding him. He'd spent decades of his life training them to be soldiers with unmatched fighting prowess, only for them to turn on him within the blink of an eye.

'Don't make this difficult, Jethro,' said Tobias.

Jethro simply laughed and shook his head in disbelief. Suddenly he pulled a small, circular device from his pocket and threw it into the air. The device had an extremely powerful magnetic pull, which forced the weapons out of the soldiers' hands. One of the more stubborn soldiers refused to let go of his staff and went flying off along with it.

Jethro pulled out an extendable metal rod from his belt and began attacking his men with it. The soldiers tried to fight back, but they were no match for their captain's combat skills. He was able to read their every move with remarkable ease. Tobias attempted to aim his gun at Jethro as the fight proceeded, but the captain was moving far too quickly for him to lock on to his target.

Jethro was close to winning the fight when all of a sudden, his feet started lifting off the ground against his will. His arms stretched out wide, and he lay floating in the air, unable to move a muscle. His heart sank. He knew that only one thing could be causing this, and it definitely wasn't a malfunction in his suit.

Another door at the back of the vehicle opened, and out came a man sitting on a chair hovering four feet off the ground. He was wearing a dark, hooded cloak and a black mask with tubes linked to a breathing ventilator on the back of his chair.

Jethro's eyelids closed in dismay. Here was the man he definitely didn't want to see this evening. It was the Master, ruler of Arcadia himself.

Tobias and the wounded guards each took the knee as their leader hovered closer towards the scene. The Master stopped his chair in front of Jethro and started to speak in a deep guttural voice.

'Welcome home, Jethro. Pop-out to get a little fresh air, did you?' he said sadistically.

'Master, please forgive me. There were reports of more riots in the streets of London this week. I was running tests on some new technology to help ensure the safety of its citizens.'

Jethro couldn't get his words out quickly enough. He knew deep down that the lie he just told was not going get him out of trouble but revealing the truth would make things far worse.

'Do you honestly expect me to believe that, Jethro?' the Master responded coldly.

'It's the truth, my Lord. I swear it!' Jethro tried to sound as convincing as he could. 'The experiments would have been too dangerous to conduct within these walls.'

'SILENCE!' The Master boomed. Jethro immediately stopped talking.

'You know the law of this land, Jethro. No one is permitted to leave this city under any circumstances without my consent. Doing so risks the lives of every human being who resides within these walls, including your own family.'

Jethro's eyes grew wide in terror.

'Where are they?' he asked, sounding increasingly frightened.

'Oh, don't worry, old friend. They're right here.'

The Master held out his arm, and out of the back of the vehicle flew a lady in her mid-forties, with dark brown curly hair and gentle features. Next to her was a strapping, twenty-something young man with a handsome face and mousey brown spiked hair. It was Jethro's wife Maria and his son Hunter, both of whom were wearing similar armoured suits to his own.

'I wouldn't let them miss out on this moment,' said the Master, clearly smiling under his mask.

'Dad!' Hunter shouted. 'What's happening?'

'Jethro, help us,' Maria whimpered as both she and Hunter joined the captain's side, suspended in mid-air.

Jethro tried to fight back against the master's powers with all his might, but they were far too strong for him to overcome.

'Please, my Lord,' Jethro pleaded, 'punish me, not my family. They had nothing to do with this.'

'You should have thought of them before you left the city, Jethro,' the Master said, with unapologetic disdain, 'you've left me with no other option.'

'No. Please, my Lord,' Jethro cried out in terror. He knew exactly where this was going.

'I take no pleasure in this Jethro. You have been of tremendous value to me over the years, and you have served your country well. I wish it didn't have to be this way, old friend, but I cannot make preferential exceptions, even for someone as talented as you. May God have mercy on all of you,' the Master uttered, almost in a whisper.

With a flick of his finger, the masks concealed in the Beckett family's suits folded over their heads, and the gateway doors opened behind them.

Tobias looked away in shame. He couldn't bear to watch what was about to happen.

The Master stretched out the palm of his hand, and Jethro, Maria and Hunter were suddenly thrust through the gap in the wall at an incredible speed, and the gateway instantly closed after them. They continued to fly through the decontamination chamber and smashed through the gate on the other side.

The Master turned to Tobias, who once again bowed his head sheepishly.

'You did well, Tobias,' said the Master, stroking the commander's head as if he were some kind of pathetic lapdog, 'it's always good to know that I have people in my cabinet who understand what loyalty means.'

'Yes, Master,' Tobias replied, clearly intimidated by his omnipotent leader.

'It's such a terrible shame. Jethro was a very accomplished individual. It's going to be tough to find a replacement for him,' said the Master, almost melancholic in tone. There was no response from Tobias, whose legs were shaking uncontrollably under his own weight. He was desperately counting down the seconds until the Master would stop stroking his head with that dry, old, wrinkled hand of his.

'Well, I shall retire to my chambers. Good evening Tobias,' said The Master as his chair began hovering back to the vehicle.

'Good evening, my Lord,' Tobias replied, still unable to look up from the ground.

The guards quickly followed their Master into the vehicle as it took off back towards the city. Tobias glanced over at the closed gateway, filled with an enormous sense of regret.

Thunder and lightning crashed in the sky as the Beckett family hurtled towards the ground at an incredible speed.

'Push the red button on your chest!' Jethro called out to his wife and son through the communication device in his helmet. He had much experience with these suits, given that he was the technician who designed them, but his wife and his son had little to none.

Hunter pressed the red button on his chest, which instantly activated the rocket boosters located in various compartments in his suit. The boosters stabilised the pace of his fall and kept him suspended in the air. He looked down at his parents, who both continued to plummet at an almighty speed.

'Maria, push the button!' Jethro cried out to his wife. Maria was frantically pushing the button on her chest, but nothing was happening. The impact of crashing through the gateway had caused her suit to malfunction, and there was no power getting to the boosters.

'JETHRO!' she cried out in terror. 'MY SUIT'S NOT WORKING!' Maria became hysterical as panic began to set in. She started thrashing about in the air as they both continued to plunge at a hundred miles an hour toward the ground below.

'HANG ON!' Jethro shouted as he shifted his body into a vertical position and activated the boosters on the soles of his feet. This propelled him forward with greater speed, enabling him to get closer to his wife as she continued to fall. He reached out to try and grab one of her legs that were dangling in front of him, but he couldn't get a good grip.

The ground was only a few yards away when Jethro finally got a hold of Maria's right foot. He gripped it tightly as the boosters on his suit activated and abruptly stopped their fall mere feet from the ground. However, the sudden force caused Maria's body to violently jerk upside down, and her helmet smashed on the concrete floor, shattering the visor.

Jethro eased his wife to the ground as the boosters on his suit slowly faded out.

'Maria, Maria, are you okay?' he said with concern as he saw his wife writhing around face down on the ground. She didn't reply. Jethro could only make out harsh wheezing sounds that she was making as if she was hyperventilating. He quickly turned her over onto her back and saw that she had her hand over her face, desperately trying to cover the hole in her broken visor.

Jethro's heart stopped. He looked into his wife's fear-stricken eyes as she slowly began to suffocate.

'No! Maria stop! Stop breathing in! Please stop breathing in!' Jethro pleaded. However, he knew the damage was already done. A single breath of the toxic air was enough to cause terminal damage to the lungs. It was only a matter of minutes.

In that instant, Jethro felt completely helpless. His wife was dying right before his eyes, and there was nothing he could do to prevent it. He embraced her lovingly in his arms as the light slowly left her eyes and her body became limp. She was gone.

Jethro began to weep. His heart felt like it'd been ripped from his chest within a matter of seconds. How could he have let this happen? Maria was completely innocent in all of this. He let out an intense cry of agony and sorrow, which echoed through the empty streets of London.

Above him, Hunter was slowly lowering himself to the ground. He saw his father holding his mother's body in his arms as he landed.

'Dad? Is everything okay?' he asked innocently.

Jethro's heart stopped again, and his eyes closed upon hearing his son's voice. How was he going to explain to Hunter that his mother was dead? He gently lay Maria down on the concrete floor.

Hunter noticed the smashed visor on the ground and started putting the pieces together in his head. He quickly sprinted over to his mother's body.

'MUM!' the young man cried with anguish as he stood over her, desperately trying to shake her back to life. But it was no use.

Jethro pulled his son away from his mother and wrapped his big arms around him in a tight embrace. Hunter cried uncontrollably in his father's arms.

'Why, Dad? Why did this happen?' he asked, his voice shaking and overwhelmed by emotion.

'We were betrayed, son. None of this was ever supposed to happen.'

Jethro started breathing less heavily. He was beginning to think more clearly, and he knew he now had to be strong for his son.

'Hunter, listen to me. We're going to be okay. Do you hear me?' Jethro said as he pulled his son away from his body and held his shoulders tightly. He looked him deep in his weeping brown eyes, 'We have to be strong for your mother now. Do you understand?'

Jethro spoke slowly and calmly. However, Hunter simply shook his head. Nothing made sense to him. He understood the laws of Arcadia, which meant he knew his father must have done something unthinkable to justify their banishment from the city. He was determined to find out the truth.

'What did you do?' he asked, looking appalled at Jethro. He could see the fear growing in his father's eyes.

'WHAT DID YOU DO?' Hunter yelled at the top of his lungs. But Jethro couldn't bring himself to respond. He wanted more than anything to tell his son the truth, but he knew he would have to wait for the right time. This definitely wasn't that.

Jethro simply looked down at the ground avoiding eye contact with his son. Hunter shot his father a hate-filled look and turned away from him in disgust. Jethro knew his son had lost all respect for him in that moment. Maybe he deserved it.

He looked up at the city ten thousand feet in the sky.

In his mind's eye, he saw the faces of the men responsible for what had just transpired.

First, he saw the faces of his soldiers. The men he'd trained since they were young, all of whom turned on him without a moment's hesitation.

Then he saw Tobias, the Commander-in-Chief responsible for his absence from the city in the first place. The man who sold Jethro out in order to avoid his own implication.

Then finally, he saw the face of the Master. The man who, at one point, Jethro called his friend. The man responsible for the suffering of thousands of innocent lives. The man responsible for the death of his beloved Maria.

Jethro's blood began to boil, and his eyes turned red with rage. Lightning scorched the sky above them once more.

Somehow, someway, he was going to make every one of them pay.

CHAPTER 2

A BOY AND HIS ROBOT

Fifteen Years Later

The night was silent. A calm wind blew through the Akani kingdom, and heavy rain bounced off the forest leaves and splashed on the ground below. The sky had turned blood red as a raging fire burned in the distance, just a few miles away from Lord Foltran's dark, menacing-looking castle.

A crescendo of fast-paced footsteps could be heard in the distance as two bodies emerged in silhouette from the forest mist wearing thick, bulky armour and carrying large, cumbersome weapons. One of the bodies was Cultar, a heroic-looking man with a strong muscular build, long, black hair and a thick bushy beard. He was carrying his weapon of choice, a gigantic battle-axe with sharp blades on both sides capable of slaying a dragon with the thickest scaly skin.

His comrade was a female called Lariel. She had a thin, slender body with striking red hair tied in a ponytail and carried a long, thin sword that shimmered in the moonlight.

As they sprinted through the forest towards the Dark Lord's castle, it suddenly became evident that the two warriors were not alone. Hundreds of demonic creatures emerged from behind the rustling trees and surrounded the scurrying duo. The creatures' red eyes glowed in the shadows behind the trees, and their razor-sharp teeth chomped at the air in front of the fearless heroes.

Suddenly Cultar and Lariel stopped running as their path was cut off by demons flapping their wings and hissing in their direction. If the two warriors stood a chance of reaching the castle to defeat Lord Foltran and complete their quest, it was clear they would have to take care of these pesky demons first. They stood back-to-back in battle formation as the monsters continued to edge closer in a threatening fashion.

'I hate this part,' said Lariel, exasperated. Her voice was unexpectedly masculine and slightly robotic in tone.

'You always say that!' Cultar replied in a broken, teenage boy's voice.

'We wouldn't be in this mess if you hadn't read from that book,' Lariel barked accusingly.

Cultar rolled his eyes.

'And if you hadn't have tried to take a shortcut through Fangothra, I wouldn't have had to read the book, would I?' he said, exasperated. 'Look, let's just get on with this, shall we? We're nearly at the end.'

'Fine!' Lariel said begrudgingly.

The two warriors suddenly lunged ferociously at the demons, swinging their weapons and slicing through their enemies with ease. As each loathsome monster was hacked to pieces, they turned instantly to ash, leaving nothing but a clear blue wisp floating in the air.

'I swear there's more of these demons than there usually is,' Lariel said, casually slicing the wings off a savage beast.

'No, it just seems that way because you're getting slower!' Cultar replied with a wry smirk as he took out several screeching demons with one swing of his axe.

Soon the forest was lit up with blue wisps as the tenacious warriors continued to slaughter their enemies. Noticing the blue glow floating listlessly above them, Cultar lifted his axe high into the air, and the wisps began to gravitate towards it like a moth to a flame. At the centre of his axe's handle was a shimmering blue jewel designed to absorb the energy of the wisps and make the axe glow a faint turquoise colour.

Having successfully collected all the wisps, Cultar took a mighty swing of his axe and a blue energy field blasted from the blade and evaporated all the demons in its pathway.

'Yes!' he exclaimed with glee whilst punching the air with his fist. 'I love it when that happens.'

The two warriors seemed on the verge of victory when suddenly, Lariel was ambushed from behind by a flying beast, viciously biting the back of her neck. Cultar looked behind him to see Lariel struggling to defend herself. He immediately pointed his axe at the flapping demon and fired the blue beam at its head. Within seconds, the foul beast was obliterated into dust. Unfortunately, it was too late. Lariel's body went limp and fell to the floor.

Cultar rolled his eyes once again.

'Damn it, Andro!' he exclaimed with frustration. Suddenly the world froze, and a green holographic word popped up in front of them –

GAME OVER.

The lights flickered on to reveal a stark, square-shaped room six metres wide with plain, white walls and no windows or doors. The only items of furniture in the room were a single bed on one side and a washbasin on the other.

Sitting cross-legged in the centre of the room was a teenage boy dressed in thin, white pyjamas and wearing a white and blue helmet that came down over his eyes. Suddenly, the helmet began to move of its own accord and lifted off the young boys head. It hovered in front of him as two electronic green eyes appeared on the levitating helmet's face.

The boy's name was Magnus Powell, a fifteen-year-old who had a number of very distinctive facial features, which under normal circumstances might be considered slightly odd. The first being his exceptionally bald head. Since before he could remember, Magnus had been incapable of growing a single strand of hair on his entire body for reasons he could never explain. However, he considered this to be a blessing due to the fact that after all this time spent in captivity, any hair on his head would probably be wrapped around his ankles by now.

His second distinctive feature was his unnaturally pasty complexion. This was undeniably the outcome of a severe lack of exposure to natural sunlight as a result of his endless incarceration.

His last distinctive feature was a peculiar maroon coloured, firebolt-shaped mark on the skin surrounding his left eye, which stood out even more due to his abnormally white complexion.

All these features, combined with his short stature and skinny build, would probably make any normal human presume Magnus was either severely ill or mistreated in some way. Thankfully, he never had to worry about the prying eyes of regular folk, having been locked in this one room for the entirety of his fifteen-year life, with only his robotic friend Andro for company.

Having just lost, what he considered to be, a very important mission on one of his favourite games, Magnus sat with his arms crossed and glared at the robot hovering in front of him.

Andro emitted an awkward laugh.

'Sorry about that,' he said sheepishly.

'This always happens, Andro,' Magnus said, shaking his head. 'Just when we're about to complete the final mission, you find some pathetic way of getting yourself killed. I don't know why you insist on playing as Lariel.'

'I like her hair,' the robot confessed, looking slightly embarrassed.

'She's terrible! I can't remember the last time we even made it to the castle since you started playing as her,' said the disgruntled teenager.

'Well, at least we'll know for next time that the shortcut was a bad idea,' Andro replied, trying to sound optimistic.

'There won't be a next time. I'm sick of playing that game with you. You're terrible at it!'

The boy got up and stomped over to his bed.

'I'm sorry, Magnus. Would you like to play something else? How about Thunder Gods?' Andro suggested encouragingly.

'No.' Magnus replied dismissively as he lay down on his bed.

'Rising Dead?'

'No.'

'Sheep Tossing?'

'No.'

Andro shot him a look of deep concern.

'But you love Sheep Tossing.'

'No. YOU love Sheep Tossing! I think it's a stupid game,' said the teenager disparagingly.

'Oh,' replied the robot, somewhat dejected.

He thought back to a time when Magnus absolutely adored playing this game. It involved a farmer who gets lost in the woods and must throw his sheep at ravenous wolves to avoid getting eaten until he finds his way back to the farm. Magnus used to particularly enjoy the amusing bleating sound the sheep would make when they got tossed into the air. But it seemed the teenager had played the game that many times he'd fallen out of love with it.

Andro's thin, spindly metal arms escaped the confines of his plastic shell and began to rub his face as if deep in thought.

'Hmmm. How about a trip to the beach?' he suggested.

Suddenly a projector light shone out of Andro's head and bathed the room in breath-taking footage of an exotic, tropical beach with palm trees and blissful ocean waves.

Magnus rolled his eyes.

'No, Andro. Shut it off!' he said commandingly, getting progressively more agitated.

Andro closed the projector, and the beach scene disappeared.

'How about a joke?' The robot was really starting to clutch at straws by now.

'All your jokes are awful,' Magnus replied with a sigh, 'plus I've heard them all.'

'You've not heard this one. What does a pirate say on his eightieth birthday?'

Andro paused for effect as Magnus closed his eyes and shook his head in anticipation of an inevitably disappointing punch line.

'Ay, Matey!' Andro said in a stereotypical pirate's voice.

Surprisingly the joke actually made Magnus smirk.

'Okay, that's a pretty good joke, but the rest of your jokes are absolute garbage.'

Andro was silent for a few seconds and then got another bright idea.

'Would you like to learn some more sign language?'

'No!'

'Okay. How about a maths test?'

'Yes, I want to do a maths test.' Magnus replied with a blank expression.

'Really?'

'No!' Magnus said bluntly.

Andro hung his head.

'I don't want to do anything I've done a thousand times before, okay, Andro? I want something different.'

Magnus started to sound angry. He rolled onto his side and faced away from his robot friend.

Andro hovered next to Magnus' bed for a few seconds, not knowing what to say or do. He knew that teenage boys suffered mood swings now and again, but he had to admit; he was a bit out of his depth with this. Suddenly a loud horn sound echoed throughout the room, and a slot opened from the wall opposite Magnus' bed. A tray was pushed through the slot, and in an instant, it slammed shut again.

'Ah, hah!' Andro exclaimed joyfully. 'Dinnertime. This should cheer you up.'

Andro hovered over to the other end of the room. On the tray lay an empty cup and a bowl full of dark green powder. He picked up the tray and hovered over to the washbasin filling the cup with water and pouring it over the green powder. The powder converged with the liquid and began to grow into a thick, gooey paste, which to any normal person would likely appear distinctly unappetising. However, this was Magnus' favourite dish.

Andro filled the cup a second time with water and brought the tray over to Magnus' bed. He pretended to smell the food.

'Mmm, smells good,' the robot said eagerly, 'you'd better eat it before I get my hands on it.'

The teenager didn't respond and continued to face away from him.

'Magnus?' Andro said with mild trepidation, but once again, there was no response.

The robot was beginning to sense that his friend was deliberately ignoring him and wanted to be left alone. He placed the tray of food on the floor next to the bed and slowly hovered over to the other end of the room, looking distinctly dejected. He perched himself on his docking station and powered down.

Magnus was pleased that the silent treatment had worked. He loved his little robot 'partner in crime' dearly, but sometimes he did get on his nerves, especially when attempting to cheer him up. The worst part for Magnus was that he couldn't explain why he was getting so angry all the time. He'd spent every day of the last fifteen years locked in this room with nobody but Andro for company. They did everything together, playing games, watching old films, going on simulated holidays to incredible locations, studying and learning about the world, and they never had any issues before. But recently, Magnus was getting tired and frustrated with the same monotonous regime day in, day out, and he longed to know what life was like outside of the four white walls surrounding him.

He also started to become curious about the purpose of his life and the reason for his isolation. He wondered how he came into this world, where his parents might be, if they're even still alive, and if anyone would one day come to claim him as their own.

He'd watched old movies of people with beautiful, long flowing hair and wondered why he'd never grown so much as a follicle on his entire body.

Magnus would also question the origin of the large mark that covered his left eye. Was it a birthmark? Was it a skin defect? Had someone branded him as a baby?

He didn't even know what the hexagonal-shaped box with the blinking, green light attached to the ceiling of his room was for. Magnus would often stare at this blinking light for hours when he was having trouble drifting off to sleep and ponder what on earth it did. However, he was reluctant to touch it in case it shut off the air supply or something.

All these questions and more began to play on his mind long into the nights, and unfortunately, as knowledgeable and capable as his robot friend was, Andro could not provide definitive answers to any of them.

Magnus did count himself lucky, however. He couldn't fathom how much more miserable he'd be if he was locked in this room by himself. He started to think about all the things his robot did for him throughout his days locked in this inescapable tomb, from washing his clothes and bedsheets to playing games, educating him, and generally trying to make him feel positive. The boy had a lot to be grateful for.

Magnus turned over in his bed and saw Andro in power-down mode on his docking station. He suddenly felt a sting of guilt for being so rude to him moments earlier. He sat up on his bed and called over to him.

'Andro.'

However, the robot didn't respond.

'Andro!' Magnus repeated, this time more assertive. But there was still no response.

'Come on; I know you can hear me. Stop being such a big baby.'

One of Andro's eyes blinked on and then blinked off again a second later.

'Look, I'm sorry I yelled at you,' Magnus said with complete sincerity, 'I know you were just trying to cheer me up. I shouldn't have gotten angry.'

Both of Andro's eyes blinked on this time, looking distinctly less miffed.

'How about a game of Sheep Tossing?' Magnus suggested, trying his best to emulate Andro's upbeat tone from earlier.

Andro leapt off his docking station with great enthusiasm.

'Oh, yes, now you're talking. That's my favourite game,' the robot cheered.

'You say that about all the games in your system,' Magnus said with a chuckle.

Andro placed the back of his robotic hand close to his mouth speaker as if imitating someone whispering.

'I know, but this one's my number one favourite,' he said in a hushed voice.

'All right, if you say so. I get the first throw,' Magnus said as Andro assumed his place on the young boys head.

Before he could properly attach, however, Magnus felt a faint rumble vibrate through the floor in his room.

'What was that?' Magnus asked with a baffled expression on his face. Andro moved away from his head and had a quick look around.

'I'm not sure,' said the robot as he surveyed the room for anything untoward. Magnus stood up and listened to see if he could hear the rumble again; however, several seconds went by without a peep.

'Hmmm, it must have been a burst water pipe or something,' Andro said in a relaxed voice, 'I'm sure it's nothing to worry....'

Suddenly, Andro was interrupted by a violent shockwave, which shook the walls and caused the lights to shatter. The faint sound of a high-pitched alarm could be heard from outside as the room was consumed by darkness. Magnus fell to the floor in terror. Andro switched instantly into surveillance mode as he started frantically examining each and every wall from top to bottom using his red laser scanner.

'What's happening, Andro?' Magnus cried out, utterly petrified.

When he'd said he wanted something 'different' a few minutes ago, this was far from what he had in mind. Andro scanned the wall opposite Magnus' bed and observed it had several cracks in the brick.

'Something must have hit us from this side. I think it would be safer if you moved to the other wall, Magnus.'

Andro pointed at the wall opposite as the teenager swiftly followed his instructions. He curled up in a ball and leant up against the wall.

'Don't worry. These walls are reinforced with ten inches of thick concrete. There's no possible way anyone can break in,' Andro said with confidence.

This made Magnus feel slightly more reassured. The robot turned to face the wall again.

'If anyone does manage to get in here, they'll have to deal with me....'

Another shockwave cut him off again, except this one was louder and more violent than the last. The startled robot flew over to Magnus' side and attempted to nestle in behind him.

'So much for 'Mr Tough Guy',' Magnus said mockingly.

'I was designed for education and entertainment purposes; I'm not a battle drone, nor have I any desire to be one,' Andro retorted as he continued to budge in behind Magnus.

A few seconds passed, and another bang shook the room, making dust fly down onto Magnus' head. The teenager's heart was beating at a million miles a second in his chest. Every muscle in his body tensed up as if a thousand volts of electricity were shooting straight through him. He'd never felt fear of this magnitude before, and he seriously pondered whether he and Andro were going to make it out of this alive.

Magnus embraced his robot tightly to his chest and clenched his eyes shut. He heard another bang, which this time caused his eardrums to hurt and make an excruciating high-pitched ringing noise. He clasped his hands over his ears in the hope it would relieve his pain, but it provided little comfort for him at all.

Suddenly he felt a large crash shake the room as if the whole building was coming down around them. Magnus could see a bright light trying to penetrate his eyelids from the wall opposite. The sound of the siren was starting to grow again as he slowly began to regain his hearing. He shakily opened his eyes and saw beams of light shimmering through the dust and debris floating in the air.

Whoever was trying to break in had successfully blown a large rectangular crater in the thick concrete wall in front of him. Magnus had spent his whole life pondering what lay behind the walls of this small, isolated room. It seemed he was about to find out.

- CHAPTER 3 -
PRISON BREAK

Magnus squinted his eyes to try and see more clearly through the thick, dusty fog that by now had engulfed the entire room. Without thinking, he took a sharp intake of breath and immediately regretted it. He started coughing uncontrollably, and his breathing became short and sharp as the back of his throat gradually filled with tiny dust particles.

As the fog began to clear and Magnus was finally able to catch his breath; he could see several large, towering figures standing in silhouette at the entrance of the gaping hole in the wall. They were wearing black, armoured suits that covered their bodies from head to toe. Each individual's suit looked identical except for one specific detail - the fluorescent lights shining from the visors on their helmets were each a different colour.

One of the masked intruders, who had a bright blue light shining from his mask, put his hand in his pocket and pulled out a small torch. He ignited the torch and immediately shone the light directly into Magnus' eyes, temporarily blinding him. The frightened teenager lifted his arm to block the light, and in doing so, realised how much he was trembling.

The masked intruder climbed through the hole and entered the room. His enormous, padded boots stomped over the rectangular piece of rubble, which had been ripped from the wall moments earlier.

As he got closer, Magnus noticed the intruder was carrying what looked like the hilt of a sword, which lay in its sheath and hung vertically down his back. He also had several other smaller weapons concealed in various compartments on his suit. Whoever these people were, it was clear they were not to be trifled with.

Magnus suddenly realised he had tears cascading down his cheeks. He gripped Andro tighter to him and buried his head in his arm as the intruder edged ever closer towards them. The masked man knelt in front of the teenager, who was still trembling in fear and placed the torch carefully on the floor. He then pushed a button on his mask, and it retracted back into his armour, revealing his face. He lifted his palms into the air in an unthreatening manner as he started to speak.

'Don't be afraid. I'm not here to hurt you,' he said in a calm voice.

Magnus hesitantly withdrew his face from his arm and peeked at the man in front of him. He was middle-aged, perhaps in his late thirties, with thick brown hair and piercing brown eyes. He noticed an emblem on the man's suit that was the shape of a shield with a sword down the middle and two snakes on either side of it.

Magnus remained silent as he waited for the man to speak again.

'Let me see your face.'

He brought his hand closer to Magnus' cheek. However, the teenager flinched like a frightened animal, and Andro leapt out of his arms to confront the intruder.

'Hey, back off!' the robot hissed whilst raising his arms in a fisticuffs motion.

'Whoa, whoa, it's okay, it's okay. No one's going to harm anyone,' the man exclaimed defensively, 'please, we don't have much time. I just want to see his face. You can trust me.'

He seemed to be straining to keep his calm composure as he tried to appease both the teenager and the aggressive robot hovering in front of his face. Andro wasn't backing down, however, and the tension in the room was at a knife's edge.

Magnus lifted his arm and placed it on Andro's head, gently moving him aside. He wasn't sure what made him do such a thing; in fact, part of him was screaming '*WHAT THE HELL ARE YOU DOING?*' inside his head. But despite the fact this person was carrying several deadly weapons and had just blown a hole in his bedroom, there was something about his calm demeanour that made Magnus believe they weren't in any danger.

Andro slowly lowered himself and was no longer blocking the man's view of Magnus' face. He reached for his torch and shone it in the teenager's eyes, blinding him once again. He observed the distinct mark around Magnus' eye and promptly lowered his torch.

Another suited person with a dark green visor on his helmet poked his head into the room.

'Captain, is it him?' he asked, sounding somewhat flustered.

'Yes, it's him,' the man replied as he sprung to his feet and turned to address the group standing outside the room.

'Clear the pathway back and make sure the drones don't get in our way,' he commanded with militaristic authority.

'YES, CAPTAIN!' The whole team shouted in unison as they each grabbed their weapons and swiftly moved out of sight.

Magnus found all of this baffling. There were so many questions running around in his head. He desperately wanted to ask the intruder what was going on, but when he opened his mouth to speak, no words came out. Thankfully Andro was on hand to speak on Magnus' behalf.

'W...what's going on? Who are you p...people?' the robot tried to sound as brave as he could, but his stuttering and hesitation revealed his unwavering consternation.

The man turned to face Magnus, completely blanking Andro in the process. He knelt on one knee, bowing his head and placed his right fist down on the floor.

'My name is Hunter Beckett,' he said as he raised his head to look Magnus in the eye. 'My team and I have been tasked with breaking you out of this place.'

Magnus shot him a look of confusion. This didn't make any sense to him. He glanced over at Andro, who looked equally dumbfounded.

'For what reason?' asked the robot.

'I've not got time to explain right now,' Hunter replied forcefully, still failing to address the robot directly. 'All I can tell you is that you're in danger. You need to come with us now, Magnus.'

Magnus' heart skipped a beat upon hearing the man utter his name. Andro's eyes widened, and he flew directly into Hunter's line of sight.

'How do you know that name?'

The robot sounded utterly confounded. Hunter simply pushed him aside.

'I know a lot about you, Magnus,' Hunter said as he reached his hand out in front of the teenager, 'If you come with me now, I will explain everything to you.'

'Don't do it, Magnus. I don't trust this guy,' Andro said, feeling rather scorned at being blanked so many times.

Magnus looked at the outstretched hand in front of him and paused.

He had no idea what to do at this moment. Five minutes ago, he'd been securely locked inside his seemingly safe, impenetrable stronghold with his friendly robot companion, and now his world had been completely flipped upside down. The first human being that Magnus had ever come into contact with who, moments ago, blew a giant hole in the only place he'd ever called home was now requesting he follow him into the unknown world. Was this real? Was it some sort of illusion? Could he trust this total stranger? It didn't seem like he had a choice.

Gun blasts could be heard from outside the room, and it sounded as if it was getting closer with each passing second.

'Please, Magnus,' Hunter said, sounding slightly more desperate than before.

Against his initial judgement, Magnus stretched out his arm and grabbed the hand in front of him. Almost instantly, Hunter hoisted Magnus up on his feet, nearly pulling his scrawny arm out of its socket. He grabbed his torch and reached into a compartment on the back of his suit. He pulled out a black helmet, similar to his own but with a bright red visor.

'Put this on, Magnus,' Hunter instructed as he handed the mask to the teenager, 'you're going to need it to breathe once we step outside.'

Magnus shot him a look of panic. Having done many history lessons with Andro and watched hours upon hours of news footage from the past fifty years, Magnus was well-versed in the dangers of breathing the natural air outside and its effects on the body. He wanted to ask what possible reason they had for going outside, but once again, he was too frightened to open his mouth. He promptly pulled the helmet over his head, and it locked into place, creating an airtight seal around his neck.

Hunter once again pressed a button on his suit, and his mask closed over his face. He looked over at Magnus, who was fiddling about with wires, trying to unplug Andro's docking station from the other side of the room.

'You won't need that, Magnus. We've got plenty of them at our base,' Hunter said with a hint of impatience.

Magnus was relieved by this, as the docking station was probably far too heavy for his skinny arms to carry.

'I need you to jump on my back,' the captain said whilst facing away and crouching down, 'put your arms around me.'

Magnus swung his arms around Hunter's neck, and he quickly jumped to his feet. Andro flew up to join Magnus at head height.

'Are you sure about this, Magnus? This doesn't seem like a good idea to me,' the little robot said fearfully.

'Everything will be okay, Andro. I promise,' Magnus replied in a whisper, though he wasn't entirely certain whether what he was saying was true or not.

'You best keep up, little robot,' Hunter remarked, 'and watch out for incoming laser fire.'

'WHAT?' Andro cried incredulously as Hunter suddenly took off through the hole in the wall, carrying Magnus on his back.

'Oh dear,' said the robot with resignation as he reluctantly followed them into the unknown.

Upon exiting the room, Magnus took one last glance back at the place he'd spent fifteen years of his life before finally facing forward to greet the new world ahead.

Magnus had always wondered what the building looked like outside his room. He knew it had to be a big facility, given how many voices he heard bellowing through the walls over the years. However, at this present time, his vision was clouded by smoke and rapid, flashing laser fire as the mercenaries did battle with an army of drones defending the prison.

Through the smoke and flying laser blasts, Magnus could make out floor upon floor of grey steel doors as far as the eye could see.

As they ran past each cell, Magnus could hear sounds of banging and yelling from inside. He could only imagine the sort of people they kept locked up in this place.

Suddenly, Magnus felt a laser blast fly straight past his face. Even through his mask, he could feel the heat emanating from the blast. A drone appeared from the floor below, relentlessly shooting at the captain to try and stop him in his tracks. Hunter pulled out a metal staff from his pocket. He pushed a button on the staff, and a blue energy shield formed, which deflected the laser blasts and sent them bouncing off in all directions. He then pulled a spherical metallic object from his pocket, which he threw straight in the direction of the drone. The metal ball stuck to the drone's face and activated a heat ray hot enough to melt thick steel. Within seconds the drone had completely disintegrated.

'These guys are certainly well equipped!' Andro commented whilst hovering at Magnus' side. Magnus simply nodded in agreement, still too frightened to reply with words.

As they carried on running, Magnus observed the ease with which Hunter and his band of mercenaries were dealing with these ruthless, flying robots. The technology and combat expertise on display was incredibly impressive. They were using weapons far beyond what Magnus had ever seen in Andro's outdated news footage, and the drones seemed ill-equipped to compete with them.

They reached the end of the prison floor, and Hunter grabbed onto the rail in front of them. Magnus felt a jolt as Hunter swung his legs over as if he was about to jump off and plummet fifty feet to the floor below.

'Hold on tight, Magnus,' said Hunter.

'What are you doing?' Andro cried as Hunter leapt off the edge without hesitation. Magnus gripped onto his body with all his might and clenched his eyes closed. Suddenly, he felt a strange sensation. They weren't actually falling. He opened his eyes to see that they were, in fact, hovering listlessly in mid-air.

Hunter's suit had various pockets, which blasted out pressurised air and kept them afloat. The strange sensation made Magnus feel a mixture of exhilaration and nausea.

Hunter activated the boosters on his feet, and he and Magnus began flying northwards towards the roof of the building. The other mercenaries joined them in the air and continued to fend off the drones, which were still relentless in their pursuit.

As they passed each floor, Magnus was astonished at the sheer height of the building. It had to have been at least five hundred feet tall with over two thousand individual cells. He turned his head to comment to Andro but realised his robot was no longer flying at his side. He looked down to see that he was in a tussle with a drone that was attempting to knock him out of the air. Andro shot out a red laser from his side and split the drone in half. Magnus observed this in utter shock, having had absolutely no idea Andro possessed this sort of destructive weaponry in his arsenal.

They finally reached the top floor, and Hunter immediately continued running the second his feet touched the ground.

He lunged at a door at the end of the corridor, which instantly came off its hinges, and ploughed straight into a large derelict office.

Four of his crew members followed him in, and the other two stood guard at the doorway. Hunter grabbed hold of a large, round, rusty latch attached to the ceiling and began applying all his strength to try and turn it. After a brief struggle, the latch finally gave way, and the door to the roof sprung open forcefully. Magnus suddenly felt a biting chill run down his back as the wind from outside blew cold air straight into the room.

More drones suddenly appeared from outside and began shooting in their direction as Hunter hoisted himself and Magnus through the open door. He raised his shield to deflect the laser blasts whilst grabbing a large, disk-shaped object lodged in the back of his armour. He threw the disk straight up in the air, and it started spinning and shooting out hundreds of tiny steel ball bearings. The balls attached themselves to the drones and proceeded to explode with great ferocity, blasting them all into a million pieces.

Once every drone in the immediate vicinity had been officially terminated, Hunter ran with all his might towards an aircraft parked in the centre of the roof.

Magnus looked behind him to check that Andro was nearby and saw the remaining mercenaries following them onto the roof. Andro stuck his head out of the hatch and looked around cautiously. Magnus breathed a sigh of relief upon seeing his friend had made it out of there in one piece.

'ANDRO!' shouted Magnus whilst waving his arm.

Andro noticed him through the group of mercenaries and immediately flew towards his friend.

Magnus felt a shudder down his spine as his body adjusted to the cold, windy weather on the prison rooftop. He'd never experienced 'natural' weather such as this, and so far, he wasn't finding it very pleasant. However, the cold wasn't the only sensation he was currently experiencing. He could also feel the weight of something approaching from his left-hand side as if he was holding it in his hands. He looked over to his left and noticed a drone heading towards them at an almighty speed, which Hunter didn't seem to have noticed.

Without thinking, Magnus stretched out his left hand, and the drone froze in the air, unable to move. Magnus clenched his fist, and the drone crumpled into a ball and dropped to the ground. Andro and the other mercenaries stopped in their tracks, unable to comprehend what they had just witnessed.

Magnus felt strange. It was an entirely new sensation he had never experienced before. He felt an overwhelming force take over his body as if the whole world was weighing down on top of him.

However, before he had time to question what he'd just experienced, the door to the aircraft opened, and Hunter sprinted inside without hesitation. There seemed to be hot air blowing as they ran through the gap, which made Magnus flinch on Hunter's back. Andro and the rest of the crew followed them in, and the door closed behind them. Two of the mercenaries jumped into the cockpit, and the rest took a seat in the main body of the plane.

'Strap yourself in, Magnus. This is going to be a bumpy ride,' Hunter said matter-of-factly.

Magnus looked at the mercenaries opposite him and observed their technique of fastening their seatbelt. He grabbed the belt attached to his chair and clicked it into place. Andro plonked himself in the chair next to his friend and proceeded to strap himself in too.

The plane suddenly began to move, and Magnus gripped the arms of his seat very tightly and clenched his eyes shut. The feeling of nausea returned as the plane began shaking turbulently due to a barrage of laser blasts from the outside. Luckily the plane had weaponry of its own, and the pilots were well adept at retaliating.

The plane continued to rise until it finally levelled out and suddenly shot forward like a bullet leaving its shell. Magnus' head jerked back against his headrest as the plane hurtled forward at an incredible speed.

The teenage boy was terrified. He'd flown planes in his video games and always wondered what it would be like to be in a real one, but this experience was enough to put him off ever doing it again.

As the plane flew, the attacking force of the drones began to peter out, unable to keep up with its tremendous speed.

With the team no longer under imminent threat, the atmosphere on the plane became much calmer and more tranquil.

Hunter retracted his mask back into his suit, and the rest of his team did the same.

Magnus, however, was unable to remove his mask because his hands were seemingly glued to the arms of his seat. One of the mercenaries, with purple lights on their suit, unhooked their seat belt, took off their mask and walked over to sit next to Magnus. It was a female in her early thirties with long brown hair tied in a bun and beautiful, fair skin. This was the first female Magnus had ever encountered in the flesh, and he was mesmerised by her ocean-blue eyes and heart-melting smile. She put her arm on his shoulder.

'It's okay, Magnus. We're safe now. You can let go.'

She spoke in a very calm, soothing voice, which reassured Magnus greatly. As if by magic, he found himself able to loosen his grip on the chair and relax his hands.

'How about we take this off?' she said, removing the mask from his head. She immediately noticed the fire-bolt shaped mark on his face.

'There. That's better, isn't it?'

Hunter smiled warmly.

'Well, I suppose this would be a good opportunity for us to introduce ourselves properly,' he said in a welcoming tone, 'Magnus, meet Max.'

Hunter gestured to the first soldier on the right, who had dark green lights on his suit and was sharpening the blades of his chosen weapon - a massive battle-axe.

He had short, spiky brown hair and was somewhat gruff in appearance, but nevertheless had a friendly face. He was built like an elephant, and Magnus was amazed by the sheer size of his bulging, vascular biceps.

Max nodded his head in the teenager's direction and stuck his thumb up as a gesture of respect.

'Next, we have Toro. My second in command.'

Toro was a big, burly man in his forties, not quite the size of Max but definitely well built. He had slick, greying hair and the thickest, bushiest moustache you could possibly imagine. His armour had dark blue lights, and his weapon of choice was some sort of gigantic firearm, which looked bigger and heavier than Magnus himself.

'Hey, kid,' he said in a deep, husky voice.

'Next to him, we have the twins Taylor and Carter.'

Hunter pointed to a man and a woman in their mid-twenties sitting side by side. They both had matching bleached blonde hair, which would certainly help them stand out in a crowded room. However, if not for their hair, no one would have guessed they were really twins, as their facial features looked nothing alike.

Taylor was taller than your average lady at six foot one; however, this made her a formidable opponent to fight in combat. Her armour had orange lights, and her weapon of choice was a long metal spear.

Her brother, Carter, on the other hand, was a bit shorter at five foot nine, something he got considerable stick for from his peers. However, it didn't bother him much as he, too, was rather proficient on the battlefield, wielding his multitude of knives with unmatched dexterity and precision. The lights on his armour were turquoise green.

'Hey, Magnus,' the twins both said in sync. They seemed to be smiling cheekily at each other as if they had some kind of secret joke going on that no one else was privy to.

'At the end, over there, is our youngest member of the group, Billy Parker,' said Hunter in a slightly disgruntled tone.

Magnus looked over to the young man with lime green lights on his suit that had his head down, sharpening one of his swords. He had jet-black hair and rodent-like facial features. Magnus guessed him to be in his late teens, and he certainly showed no interest in looking up from what he was doing.

'Billy, say hello to Magnus,' said Hunter in a reprimanding voice.

Billy rolled his eyes and glanced up to make eye contact with the nervous teenager.

'Hey,' he said blankly and immediately got back to sharpening his weapon.

Hunter shook his head disapprovingly and swiftly continued with the introductions.

'And sitting next to you, we have the best fighter of the group. My beautiful wife,' Hunter said with a proud smile as he gestured to the lady sitting next to Magnus. She shook her head in embarrassment.

'I'm Kayla,' she said as she reached for Magnus' hand and started shaking it vigorously, 'it's a pleasure to meet you, Magnus.'

She had a huge smile on her face as she looked over at Magnus' robot companion.

'It's a pleasure to meet you as well, Andro.'

The robot looked away sheepishly. Kayla glanced back at Magnus with a smile.

'I wish my robot was as cute as yours,' she whispered in his ear.

Hunter rose to his feet as if making a grand announcement.

'We...' he said, pausing for effect, '... are the Shadow Squad. We fight against the government's corrupt regime and provide shelter and supplies for those who need it most. We've waited a long time to meet you, Magnus. Having you on our team could be a great benefit to our cause,' said Hunter as he sat back down in his seat.

Kayla shot him a disparaging look as Magnus and Andro glanced at each other with the same quizzical expression.

'What did he mean by that?' The teenager wondered to himself.

- CHAPTER 4 -
ONSLAUGHT

After nearly an hour of flying, a male voice could be heard through the plane's speakers, 'Captain, we are beginning our descent.'

This prompted Hunter to tighten his seat belt strap.

'Max, Billy, you're on the guns,' he said sternly, 'everyone else, buckle up.'

Max and Billy hastily unstrapped themselves from their chairs and entered into two compartments hidden at the bottom end of the jet.

Taylor and Carter both smiled at each other.

'This is going to be fun!' Taylor said with giddy excitement.

Magnus was apprehensive; he wasn't sure he could handle much more 'fun' today. Kayla leant over and tightened his seat belt for him.

'Don't worry, Magnus, there's just going to be a bit of turbulence, that's all,' she said reassuringly.

Magnus clutched the arms of his seat once again in nervous anticipation. He wasn't sure what to expect, but he knew, whatever was about to happen, he probably wasn't going to enjoy it. He looked over at Andro, who was shaking vigorously, clearly equally perturbed.

As the plane began its descent below the clouds, it collided with an army of hundreds of battle drones that seemed to have anticipated their arrival. They instantly opened fire, and Max and Billy, who were now strapped into their gun turrets, began shooting back at the flying machines, knocking several of them out of the sky with unprecedented skill and accuracy.

The plane was jerking violently under the barrage of laser fire, and Magnus clasped down on the arms of his seat with all his might. He looked over at the twins opposite, who were both laughing hysterically and jeering as if they were on some kind of epic roller coaster ride.

Toro, on the other hand, was having far less fun and seemed to be in quite a lot of distress as the plane jerked violently from side to side. Every muscle on his face seemed tensed up as if he was sucking on something sour, and it was becoming abundantly clear he was enjoying this plane journey about as much as Magnus was.

Suddenly the jet was hit with a huge blast, which knocked the crew off balance for several seconds. Toro rolled his eyes in disdain.

'OH, COME ON!' He shouted with extreme frustration.

'Sorry, everyone,' said Max through the plane's speakers.

'Looks like someone could do with a few more years of target practice,' quipped Carter whilst chuckling to himself.

'It won't help,' replied Taylor with a wry smirk.

'Hey, if anyone thinks they can do a better job, I'm happy to trade places,' Max retorted, feeling slightly offended by the sudden onslaught of criticisms.

'Just keep firing and try not to get us killed!' Toro commanded, breathing heavily.

'You're the boss!' Max replied cockily.

'How are you doing, Billy?' Kayla yelled.

'I'd be better if you guys shut up,' said the moody teenager trying his best to focus on the job at hand.

Magnus and Andro exchanged glances. They couldn't believe how jubilant everyone was during this potentially fatal encounter.

The plane got closer to its landing platform, and the turbulence began to gradually subside as several hundreds of drones fell out of the sky in quick succession.

'Masks on,' said Hunter whilst applying his own face covering from inside his suit. All the crew members followed his instruction, including Kayla, who was helping Magnus put his mask on at the same time.

They came to a bumpy landing, and the jet finally stopped shaking. The squad unfastened their seatbelts in unison and instantly jumped to attention.

Hunter turned to Kayla, who was helping Magnus out of his seat.

'We'll fend them off while you get him inside.'

Kayla nodded at Hunter as the aircraft door opened, and the squad ran headfirst into the firing line. She hoisted Magnus up onto her back.

'In a minute, we're going to run like hell, okay, Magnus?'

The teenager nodded his head as the last members of the squad left the plane. Kayla turned to look at the still shivering robot hovering close by.

'Watch out for laser fire, Andro, and stay close to me.'

'Right behind you,' said the robot, trying his best not to reveal his anguish.

Kayla turned back to the doorway.

'Let's go,' she cried, immediately propelling herself forward and through the open door.

The sky was lit up with laser fire as the Shadow Squad did battle with the incessant battle drones. The jet was parked on top of an old multi-story car park, which was now surrounded from top to bottom. Without hesitation, Kayla sprinted straight through a door leading to a large winding staircase.

'Hold on tight to me, Magnus,' she said as she jumped over the handrail, and they began falling down the gap between the staircases. Magnus doubled the tightness of his grip around Kayla's body as they plummeted one hundred feet towards the ground. Andro did his best but was struggling to keep up with the speed with which they were falling.

Suddenly, a burning hot laser blasted through a glass window from outside, narrowly missing Magnus' helmet. A drone had spotted them from outside and was descending at the exact same speed. Kayla retrieved a gun from her inside pocket and fired at the drone, hitting it square in the face. However, as the drone fell out of view, two more drones arrived to take its place.

Kayla attempted to shoot at them, but her accuracy was off due to the intensity of the speed they were falling. She looked down and noticed the ground floor getting rapidly closer with each second that passed. She pushed a button on her suit that activated the boosters on her shoes, which halted them mere inches from the ground. However, the speed at which they had suddenly stopped in the air forced Magnus to lose his grip and slide off Kayla's back, landing heavily on the hard stone floor.

Kayla fired her gun at the drones outside, instantly turning them into spare parts.

'Magnus!' Andro cried out to his friend, who was writhing around on the floor. The fall had knocked most of the oxygen out of his lungs, and he was seriously struggling to breathe. Magnus started to become very frightened. The harder he tried to suck air into his lungs, the more tensed up his muscles became.

Kayla lowered herself to the ground and noticed Magnus hyperventilating on the floor.

'Help him. He can't breathe,' yelled Andro anxiously.

She crouched down and lifted his body in an upright position.

'Magnus, it's okay. You've just been winded by the fall. Listen to my voice. Try to calm your body,' said Kayla in a composed tone.

Magnus started to relax his muscles, and he felt he was suddenly able to catch his breath.

'I'm okay,' he said unconvincingly.

'Come on; we've got to keep moving. We're almost there.'

Kayla lifted Magnus onto her back once again and forcefully kicked through the fire escape leading to the open street.

Drones were falling out of the sky at an incredible rate. They were clearly no match for the Shadow Squad, who used every weapon and combat tactic in their arsenal to fend them off.

Kayla had summoned every ounce of her strength and speed to get them out of harm's way; however, it was becoming clear she was starting to tire as the level of sprinting began to drop and her breathing became heavier.

Suddenly, a hundred yards in front of them, an underground hatch opened in the middle of the street, and five more squad members jumped out armed with various new items of weaponry. They ran straight past Kayla, Magnus and Andro into the firing line of the drones. One of the squad members pressed a button on a large metal box, which sent a shock wave fifty feet into the air and knocked out ten drones at once.

Magnus looked at the streets around them and saw thousands of destroyed drones piled up against the walls of the buildings surrounding them. This clearly wasn't the first encounter between the drones and the Shadow Squad.

As they got closer towards the hatch, Kayla seemed to find a second wave of strength and began to pick up more speed.

They were mere seconds away from safety when a drone from behind them locked on to Magnus' position and fired directly at him. One of the laser blasts hit him on his lower back, sending a burning sensation and a wave of pain up his spine. Magnus cried out in terror as his body immediately started to go numb.

'MAGNUS!' Andro exclaimed.

Without halting, Kayla jumped straight into the hole in the ground and landed on a grated, metal floor. Andro followed her inside, and the door hatch immediately closed behind them. A light flickered on, and Kayla lifted Magnus off her back and laid him gently on the metallic floor. The teenager's entire body had gone completely limp.

'Magnus? Magnus, are you okay?' Andro said in a panicked voice. However, the boy couldn't reply. His muscles weren't responding to his commands, and his vision was becoming blurry.

'Was he hit? What's happening to him?' the robot asked in desperation.

'His body's going into shock,' Kayla said as she gripped his head in her hands, 'Magnus, can you hear me? Stay with me.'

She began to shake him vigorously, trying to keep him awake, but it was no use. His eyes rolled back inside their sockets, and everything turned to darkness.

- CHAPTER 5 -

THE ELITE

A fire raged in the fireplace of the Campbell family mansion as Tobias and his wife Rosa returned home from a luxurious night out in the city of Arcadia. Tobias had decided to treat his beautiful wife to a trip to the opera, followed by a six-course meal at her favourite fine dining restaurant to celebrate the milestone of her fiftieth birthday. Nights out were a rare occasion for the Campbell's, given the importance of Tobias' position as Commander-in-Chief of the Arcadian Government. They were determined to enjoy every second of this particular evening.

Upon their arrival back to their extravagant family home, Tobias bent down to type in his security code to unlock the door. However, after three failed attempts to key in the combination, he let his wife take over.

'Dear Lord, you really do have the worst memory in the world, don't you?' Rosa mocked playfully.

'Oh really? It has nothing to do with the fact we've drunk four bottles of red wine between us tonight,' Tobias replied, mildly hurt by his wife's jibe.

'I've drunk the same amount as you,' Rosa said with a smug smile as the door opened in front of them.

A female voice could be heard from the house speakers.

'Welcome home, Commander. I trust you two had a pleasant evening?'

It was Electra, their artificially intelligent house security system.

'We did. Thank you, Electra,' Tobias replied, slightly slurring his words.

'Shall I inform Jeffrey that you have returned home safely?'

'You might as well,' Tobias said with a shrug, 'that's if he hasn't bored himself to sleep by now.'

Jeffrey was their eighty-two-year-old butler; he had worked for the Campbell household for nearly sixty years. He was usually assigned the role of babysitter when the two parents fancied a night away from the children.

Tobias and Rosa both stumbled into the house and tried to take off their shoes as quietly as they could. Their attempts to keep the noise down were thwarted, however, by the fact they could barely keep their balance and were giggling like naughty teenagers. Rosa pressed her index finger to Tobias' lips.

'Shhh! You'll wake the children,' she said, trying to fight her own temptation to laugh.

'Oh, I wouldn't worry about them. I'm sure Jeffrey's monotonous voice has put them both in a coma by now,' Tobias joked.

Rosa hit him on the arm.

'Ow!' He exclaimed sarcastically.

'You should have more respect for that man!'

Rosa chastised her husband in a stern yet still playful tone.

'Oh, really!' said Tobias, leaning in and kissing his wife on the lips. 'Where's this newfound love for our decrepit old butler come from? You and he aren't having an affair, are you?'

Rosa tried to hide a brief look of repugnance.

'Don't be absurd! It comes from being a decent human being, not that you'd know anything about that, of course.'

'Ouch!'

'Plus the fact he continually agrees to watch our little monsters while you spoil me rotten.'

Rosa wrapped her arms around her husband's shoulders in a warm embrace.

'The perfect woman deserves the finest gifts on her birthday. Speaking of which, I have one more surprise for you,' Tobias said with excitement. He stepped behind his wife and placed his hands over her eyes.

'Oh, what have you done now?' she said with anxious anticipation.

'Just a small treat for the woman I love.'

He slowly walked her into their enormous kitchen.

'Oh, you are silly,' she said, trying to hide her obvious delight.

'Don't worry; you're going to like it.'

They stopped just short of the large island work surface in the centre of the room.

'Are you ready?' said Tobias, intentionally dragging out the suspense.

'Oh, for heaven's sake!' Rosa scoffed and pulled his hands away from her face. In front of them on the work surface was a large bottle of champagne lying dormant in a metal ice bucket and two half-full champagne flutes standing either side of it. She raised her eyebrows in an expression of mild disenchantment.

'Brilliant, more booze!' she said contemptuously.

'How about this?'

Tobias revealed a diamond necklace from his pocket and placed it around his wife's neck. It sparkled under the dimly lit kitchen lamps.

'Oh wow!' Rosa exclaimed. 'Yep, this'll do.'

She turned around and kissed her husband passionately on the lips.

'How did I get so lucky?'

'It's me who is the lucky one.'

Tobias grabbed the two champagne flutes and passed one of them to his wife. They both raised their glasses to each other.

'To the perfect marriage, the perfect family, and the perfect life.'

They clinked their glasses together and took a sip. In that moment, an old, weathered voice could be heard coming from the kitchen doorway.

'Not interrupting anything, am I?'

The voice startled Rosa, and she nearly choked on a mouthful of bubbles. They both looked behind them to see a balding old man dressed in a brown suit putting on a large, black coat at the kitchen entrance. Rosa took a deep breath.

'Jeffrey, you startled me,' she said whilst rubbing her chest.

'My apologies, Madame,' he replied, bowing his head. 'How was your evening?'

'It was fine, thank you, Jeffrey,' Tobias answered quickly with slight irritation.

'How were the kids?'

'Oh, you know, their usual delightful selves,' Jeffrey replied with a not so subtle hint of sarcasm, 'though I did manage to get them to bed without having to bribe them this time.'

'You'll have to tell us your secret,' Tobias joked.

'We really appreciate you looking after them for us, Jeffrey, thank you,' Rosa said with sincerity.

'You're most welcome, Madame. Is there anything else I can do for you before I leave?' Jeffrey asked flatly as he put his brown trilby hat on.

'No, thank you, Jeffrey; in fact, why don't you take the week off? You look like you could do with it,' Tobias said with a wry smile as the old man turned to leave.

'Goodnight Jeffrey,' Rosa called as the old man half-heartedly waved and closed the door behind him. Rosa and Tobias both started laughing.

'Oh man, that guy needs to retire,' Tobias said, shaking his head, which caused Rosa to laugh even harder.

'Yeah, right, we wouldn't last a week without him. That man is irreplaceable,' she replied mockingly.

'No one is irreplaceable. Except you, of course,' Tobias said as he leant in and kissed his wife. They both picked up their glasses once again to take a sip when Electra came back on over the kitchen speakers.

'Commander, you have a collect call from Grant Boswell currently on hold.'

Rosa rolled her eyes and sighed.

'Tell him to bugger off, Electra,' she said as she put her glass back down, irritated.

'Hang on, it might be urgent,' Tobias said with a concerned look on his face. Grant Boswell was his second in command in the Arcadian cabinet, and he knows never to disturb his boss at this late hour, especially on special occasions such as this.

'Tobias, it's my birthday. I'm not letting your pathetic lap dog ruin our perfect evening together,' said Rosa. She shot her husband a stern look that would make the sun freeze over, and Tobias couldn't quite fathom why she had such contempt for his second in command.

'Let's just find out what he wants, and then I'll tell him where to go, okay?'

Rosa let out a huge sigh before finally nodding her head in agreement.

'Put him on screen, Electra,' said Tobias.

Their kitchen wall suddenly opened up to reveal a large television screen. It flickered on, and a man in his forties with smooth, blonde hair dressed in a black suit came into view.

'What is it, Grant?' Tobias said furiously.

'I'm sorry to disturb you at this hour, Commander, but we have a serious problem that needs your attention.'

Grant's voice sounded noticeably shaken.

'This footage was sent to us less than an hour ago from a prison in the Southern province.'

The screen cut to the security footage of the Shadow Squad breaking into the prison and destroying countless drones in their path. Tobias and Rosa's eyes widened as they watched in complete shock.

'What the hell?' Tobias exclaimed with incredulity.

'You'd better go,' Rosa said. She kissed her husband on the cheek and promptly left the kitchen.

Tobias' heart skipped a beat. He recognised this prison. He knew what was inside it, and he knew that if anyone were to get their hands on it, the consequences could be devastating.

'Call a council meeting. I'm on my way,' Tobias commanded.

'Yes, sir.'

Grant ended the call, and the screen disappeared from view.

Tobias closed his eyes and hung his head as his mind registered the severity of the situation. He grabbed his coat and left the house immediately.

Tobias was deep in thought as he stepped into his custom-built flying pod and keyed in the location of the government capitol building. As the pod took off towards its destination, the commander desperately racked his brains, trying to figure out what he had just seen. Never in his entire career had he heard of any group outside the Arcadian walls with as much firepower and combat training as the rebels that stormed that prison. Who were these people? What were they looking for?

After a short ten-minute flight, the pod finally pulled up outside the multi-storied capitol building. Tobias exited the pod and quickly ran up the steps towards the entrance. He scanned his security card, and the front door immediately opened. He rushed into the foyer, passing several government employees on the way that all seemed shocked that their commander was at work at this time of night. He frantically climbed up some steps and passed down a long, winding corridor until he reached a door with the words 'Conference Room' painted on. He stopped in front of the door, adjusted his suit to make himself look slightly less dishevelled. After taking a few seconds to compose himself, he finally opened the door.

Inside there were four men and five women dressed in freshly pressed suits who sat around a large circular table. Upon noticing Tobias had entered the room, they immediately stood to attention.

Tobias, swiftly but calmly, walked towards the only chair in the room that was unoccupied and sat down at it. This permitted the rest of the room to sit down also.

There was a brief moment of silence in the room as everyone waited with bated breath for the Commander to speak. However, he simply sat with his head down, looking at the table deep in thought.

Grant, who was sitting to the Commander's right and stroking his well-kept beard, eventually broke the silence. He nervously cleared his throat and began to speak.

'I can only apologise to you all for calling you to this meeting at this time of night, but something urgent has been brought to my attention that I believe we all need to see.'

Everyone around the table was fixated upon Tobias' second in command.

'Less than two hours ago, a maximum-security prison in the Southern province was raided by masked assailants.'

Grant pressed a button on his remote, which ignited a hologram in the centre of the table.

'This is security footage from the prison in question.'

There were gasps and murmurs from around the table as the footage began to play.

Dianne Lloyd, a fifty-year-old woman with short blonde hair who was the minister in charge of public safety, began speaking from the other end of the table.

'This is impossible. What sort of weapons are they using?'

'They're no military-grade weapons we've ever built,' said a stocky man in his late forties who was sat to Dianne's left. This was Colonel John Braxton, who was the head of Arcadia's weapons and combat training division.

Tobias sat quietly. He wasn't even listening to the conversation going on around him. He had only one question on his mind.

'What's the name of this prison?' He asked, his eyes now locked to the hologram in front of him.

Grant took a second before answering.

'Periculo Prison,' he said with resignation.

Tobias' heart sank upon hearing those words. Periculo Prison housed some of the most dangerous criminals in the country. However, it wasn't those particular inmates he was concerned about.

Suddenly the hologram disintegrated.

'Unfortunately, that's all the footage we have,' Grant said as he set the remote down in front of him.

Tobias took a sip of water and glanced around the room at his board members.

There was a brief pause while everyone digested the footage they'd just seen.

'How is this possible?' asked Dianne with deep concern. 'No one outside of Arcadia's walls has ever been capable of producing that much fire power in our entire history!'

'Clearly, someone has found a way of building their own weapons,' Grant replied.

Ted Ratby, a large bald man in his sixties responsible for engineering and tracking deliveries in and out of the country, chimed into the conversation.

'Impossible! They don't have access to those sorts of supplies, or I would know about it.'

'It doesn't matter how they got their weapons!' Tobias interjected, sounding rather irritated. 'We need to find these people and stop them before they do any more damage.'

'It's only one prison, Tobias. They'll never be able to breach the walls of this city,' Braxton said with authoritative confidence.

'If eight rebels can breach the walls of a maximum-security prison and take out all its drones, then imagine what a hundred of them are capable of,' Tobias retorted angrily. 'We've absolutely no idea how many of these people exist out there. For all we know, they may have the destructive power of a small army. If they manage to break through the walls of this city, they could have the potential to completely dismantle our entire society.'

Each individual around the table exchanged worried glances.

Tobias looked at Grant with extreme intensity.

'I want to see all the security footage surrounding the Southern province in the last two hours. I want to find out who these people are and where they're hiding. This rebellion stops now.'

'Yes, Commander,' Grant replied as he got up from his seat and started making phone calls.

Tobias turned back to the table.

'Braxton, I need all security guards and military personnel surrounding this city armed and on high alert until we know what we're dealing with.'

'Yes, sir!'

Braxton nodded as he too got up from his seat and immediately exited the boardroom.

'Everyone else needs to stay vigilant and wait for my call. These criminals need to be stopped by any means necessary. Understood?'

'Yes, Commander,' the group said in unison.

'Meeting adjourned.'

The remaining men and women stood up and disbanded from the table. Tobias walked hastily over to Grant, who was speaking with urgency down the phone.

'...I need all that footage sent to my office as soon as possible, understood? Good!'

Grant hung up the phone. Tobias looked around to see if anyone else was in earshot, then he leaned in closer to Grant's face.

'Tell me they didn't steal the asset,' Tobias whispered.

Grant paused for a second, then reluctantly responded with a nod.

'Damn it!' Tobias exclaimed louder than he expected, prompting several people to look awkwardly in his direction.

'Our drones searched the building and found no trace of the boy. His room was blown to pieces,' Grant explained.

Tobias' heart was pounding in his chest as his greatest fears were confirmed.

'We need to find him, Grant! What that boy is capable of could end us all. We cannot afford to let him slip into the wrong hands,' Tobias said with extreme urgency.

'I assure you, Tobias, we will find him,' Grant replied in a convincing tone whilst keeping firm eye contact with his boss. 'Do you want me to inform The Master?'

'No!' Tobias replied a little too quickly. Grant shot him a look of confusion.

'No, we can handle this ourselves. There's no need to bother him with matters like this,' Tobias said, trying to keep his composure.

'He's going to find out eventually.'

Grant seemed indignant.

'Not if we deal with it first. He's too weak to handle a situation like this. Now go get me that footage and send it to my office computer,' Tobias said dismissively.

'Yes, sir.'

Grant nodded his head, though Tobias detected a hint of resistance in his expression as he left the room.

The Commander took a deep breath and realised his heart was beating furiously inside his chest. This was certainly not how he hoped he'd be spending the remainder of his wife's fiftieth birthday.

CHAPTER 6

MAGNUS WAKES

Drip... Drip... Drip... Drip... Drip... Drip.

A crescendo of water droplets broke Magnus out of what seemed like an eternal sleep. A blurred, bright light slowly came into vision as he attempted to open his tired, heavy eyelids. He could just about make out a greyish-black, round object floating directly above his head. Gradually his normal consciousness returned, and his blurred vision became sharper and more focused. Suddenly, it dawned on him what the object hovering over his head actually was. It was a battle drone identical in appearance to those that had attacked him and the Shadow Squad upon escaping his prison cell.

Magnus forced his head back into the pillow, trying to get as far away from the drone as possible. However, the robot didn't move an inch. It simply stayed floating above him like some kind of wild bird toying with its prey.

Suddenly a red light shone out of the drone's face, which scanned over Magnus' body. The teenager flinched and shut his eyes tightly, gripped by the fear of another attack. He couldn't bear to open his eyes, believing that the slightest movement would inevitably set the drone off. However, several seconds passed without the slightest hint of any aggressive behaviour. Magnus heard a door open at the other end of the room and promptly close seconds later. He cautiously opened his left eye to survey the room, and then finally his right. The drone had left him alone.

'*That was odd,*' Magnus thought to himself. He tried to lift his head but was overwhelmed by a feeling of dehydration and nausea. He slumped back in his unexpectedly cushiony pillow and alleviated the pressure from his aching muscles. His eyes surveyed the ceiling up above him. It was covered in patches of damp, and he noticed a leak to the right of his bed, which was dripping into a bucket on the floor. He looked over to his bedside table and saw a glass of water perched on top of it. Magnus' mouth was as dry as an ashtray, and he knew that one sip of water would be enough to rejuvenate his lifeless body. It took all his strength to reach over to the table and pick up the glass.

Suddenly the door opened once again and in came another flying robot. However, this time it was a robot that Magnus was pleased to see.

'ANDRO!' he yelled with glee as his robotic friend flew into his arms. 'Am I glad to see you!'

'I was so worried about you, Magnus. I thought you'd never wake up,' said Andro, relieved to see his friend was finally awake.

'Why? How long was I out for?' Magnus asked. It suddenly dawned on him that he had no concept of how much time had passed since the attack.

'You've been asleep for two days.'

Kayla's voice could be heard from across the room. She was standing in the doorway next to a petit girl in her mid-teens who had brown curly hair and striking blue eyes. She was wearing a bright, rainbow-striped jumper with a yellow smiley face on the front that was several sizes too big. She stared at Magnus rather intensely as if she was in some kind of hypnotic trance. This made him feel deeply uncomfortable, and he became extremely reluctant to make any further eye contact with her. Kayla bent down to address the girl, snapping her out of her daze.

'I'll stay with him, Amelia. You go and tell Hunter he's woken up,' she said in a whisper.

'Sure thing Kayla,' the girl replied with unexpected enthusiasm as she ran off out of sight.

Kayla turned to face the room again.

'Sorry about that,' she said with a chuckle, 'Amelia's stares can be rather intense sometimes, but she really has got a heart of gold.'

She walked over and sat on a chair to the left of Magnus' bed. Andro hovered the other side of him so that Magnus and Kayla could talk.

'So, how are you feeling? You gave us quite a scare two nights ago.'

'I gave them a scare?' Magnus thought incredulously as he sat himself up and gathered all the strength he could muster in order to speak.

'What happened?' he asked in a dry, raspy voice.

'One of the battle drones hit you in your lower back with its laser. Lucky for you, drones these days are only programmed to stun their victims, temporarily paralysing them. Thirty years ago, you wouldn't have been so lucky,' Kayla explained.

Magnus took a large gulp of water and placed the glass back on the table.

'Are you feeling alright?' she asked, gently putting her hand on his shoulder.

'A little bit sick,' he replied, trying his best not to sound too pathetic.

'That's normal, trust me. You wouldn't believe the amount of times I've gotten stunned by those infernal things, and it's never a pleasant experience. Hunter's bringing some food down with him any second, so that should make you feel a bit better,' Kayla said in a much more jovial tone. Magnus was relieved to hear this as his stomach felt like an empty abyss.

'Where are we?' he asked as he glanced around the room.

'You're in Ground Zero, Shadow Squad headquarters,' she said with a smile. 'It was originally built as a military base of operations before the virus wiped out most of the population. Hunter and his father repurposed it to be a shelter and training facility for resistance fighters. I'm sorry we couldn't provide a better room for you to rest in. We're pretty low on space at the moment. Hopefully, it won't be for much longer.'

Magnus looked around the room and couldn't help feeling a bit hard done by. Compared to his old room, which, it had to be said, he kept in pristine condition; this was nothing more than a cold, leaking cesspit. The prospect of having to stay in here was not a thrilling one, to say the least, but it seemed he had no other option but to put up with it for the time being.

Before he could dwell longer on his current affliction, however, the door to his room suddenly swung open, and Hunter stepped in holding a tray with a bowl of piping hot soup and some warm bread on a plate.

'Good morning Magnus, how are you feeling?'

He sounded far chirpier than the last time Magnus had seen him, though he still felt slightly intimidated by the man's authoritative presence.

'He's doing okay,' Kayla replied. 'Feeling a little bit sick, aren't you?'

Magnus nodded as Kayla stood up from her chair. Hunter walked further into the room and took his wife's place at Magnus' side.

'I'm not surprised. You took a nasty blow to the back. Horrible things, those battle drones! I'm truly sorry you had to go through that,' Hunter said genuinely. Magnus could detect a sense of guilt in his voice.

'In fact, I think I owe you several apologies for what we put you through two nights ago. It won't happen again, I promise you.'

This relieved Magnus greatly. He certainly never wanted to go through another night like that again.

'Here, I bet you're starving.'

Hunter placed the tray on Magnus' lap.

'This'll make you feel much better, believe me.'

Magnus had to admit, the soup looked and smelled delicious. Stewed meat and chunky vegetables in a creamy broth with some soft, doughy bread was just what the doctor ordered. Magnus had many questions for the man sitting to his left, the number one being why he wanted to break him out of prison in the first place. However, there were more pressing matters at hand, like the delectable prospect of filling the gigantic chasm that was his stomach. He dove straight in, dipping the bread in the soup and taking a huge bite.

'Careful, it's quite hot,' Hunter warned him; however, this didn't seem to faze the hungry teenager at all. He was eating like a starved beast at a buffet.

Kayla smiled and bent down to kiss her husband on the cheek.

'Well, I better go set up things for training. I'll leave you guys to it.'

'Okay, sweetheart,' said Hunter.

'Good to see you awake, Magnus,' Kayla said as she closed the door behind her.

Hunter sat back in his chair and smiled as he watched the famished boy devour his food like it was his last meal on this Earth.

'How is it, Magnus?' Andro asked, having never seen the teenager so eager to get food in his mouth. Magnus simply nodded and continued scoffing his face. He was in heaven. He enjoyed the cuisine at the prison, but it was never as flavoursome as the soup he was currently eating. Any questions he might have had for Hunter regarding his recent predicament and his subsequent future were completely gone from the forefront of his mind. Magnus hoped the soup would last forever.

However, being so preoccupied with eating his delicious meal, he failed to notice Hunter looking pensive in the chair to his left.

'How much do you know about the world, Magnus?' Hunter asked slowly and methodically.

Magnus thought for a second, swallowed the slice of soup-soaked bread he'd been swilling around in his mouth, and then he answered.

'Only what I've seen in old news footage from Andro's hard drive,' Magnus replied. He looked towards Hunter, who seemed to be waiting for him to continue. '…. I know that there was a virus which killed a lot of people.'

Magnus wasn't sure how much detail he was expected to go into at this point. He hoped that would be enough of a reply, so he could carry on eating.

'Do you know why?' Hunter asked with an inquisitive expression. Magnus simply shook his head. He looked over at Andro for help, but the robot just shrugged its shoulders.

'Half a century ago, a terrorist organisation known as the Purgo clan released a biological weapon in an airport in the middle-east which wiped out most of its population within a month. In a short space of time, the virus spread to other countries like wildfire and eventually made its way over here. No one knows the exact number of lives this virus has claimed, but I would estimate it's in the billions at this stage. It's given the highest powers of this country free reign to enslave what's left of its dwindling population and control its every move. Now machines patrol the streets every hour of every day, immobilising anyone who attempts to leave their home for any reason, regardless of how desperate they may be.'

Anger began building in Hunter's voice as he continued to explain.

'My father was among the very first to recognise how deeply disturbing the circumstances in our country had become. He's the one who created this resistance.'

Magnus had now stopped eating. He was totally captivated by Hunter's words; however, he was still unsure how any of this related to him.

'For fifteen years, we've been in hiding, training our bodies and our minds. I now believe we are finally ready to fight back and reclaim the land that belongs to us.'

Hunter's words struck a chord with Magnus. Having seen him and his team in action, he totally believed they were capable of fighting any army of any size. However, there was something that was still vexing him.

'Where do I fit into all this?' Magnus asked timidly. In some ways, he wasn't sure he wanted to know the answer.

Hunter took a deep breath before responding.

'You are a very special young man Magnus, more special than you could possibly imagine. I believe if you choose to help fight our cause with us, you could very well be the most important person on the planet right now.'

Hunter paused to let his words sink in.

Magnus had no idea what to make of any of this. As far as he was concerned, he was the least likely person on the planet worthy of this much praise. Why him? He was just a kid and had neither the courage nor the fighting prowess of any of the members of the Shadow Squad. What could he offer to this cause that had any value whatsoever?

His heart rate started to increase rapidly, along with his frustration at having yet more unanswered questions thrust upon him. Suddenly the glass of water to his right began to wobble and fall off the bedside table, seemingly of its own accord. Magnus was startled by the loud noise the glass made as it shattered against the floor. He glanced over at Andro, who looked just as surprised as him.

'That wasn't me,' the robot said with his arms raised. Magnus looked over in shock at Hunter, who had a suspicious smirk on his face.

'What just happened?' Magnus asked with deep confusion.

'I wasn't lying when I said you were special, Magnus. Deep inside of you, there is power beyond your comprehension.'

Hunter leaned forward.

'Do you remember two nights ago when you crushed that drone that was about to attack us, just by thinking it?'

Magnus thought for a second before nodding cautiously.

'That wasn't your imagination playing tricks on you. That was a force that has laid dormant within you your entire life, just waiting to be set free. If you concentrate hard enough, you have the power to move and control any and all objects with your mind.'

Magnus couldn't believe what he was being told. He's never been able to move anything without touching it before in his life. Surely it was all nonsense. It had to be a trick of some kind.

'I don't....'

Magnus turned away from Hunter, unable to finish his sentence.

'I know it's hard to believe. But I swear to you it's the truth. Many years before you were born, the government funded tests on various people in an attempt to find a vaccine for the virus. One vaccine in particular mutated the cells of its host and gave them telekinetic powers the likes of which no one had ever seen before. They were known as The Assets, and they were treated like lab rats. The government reached the conclusion that people with this sort of power would be impossible to control, and they were right. One such lab rat called Calvin Mortifer murdered the other Assets and proceeded to overthrow everyone in power. Now he resides behind his impenetrable fortress living a life of bliss while the rest of the country falls to pieces. For a long time, we believed he was the last individual with powers such as this until we discovered you.'

Hunter leaned in closer to Magnus' bed.

'You have this power, Magnus.'

Magnus' heart was pounding viciously inside his chest. He was unable to comprehend anything Hunter was saying. Suddenly, the lights above them began to flicker vigorously, and the spoon in his soup started bouncing violently against the corners of the bowl, making a loud clanging sound. Magnus looked down at the spoon, and it stopped moving. He glanced at Hunter, who nodded his head knowingly.

'Could this actually be true?' Magnus asked himself. He looked back at the spoon and concentrated hard. He wanted to prove Hunter wrong. There was no way he was making this metallic piece of cutlery move on its own!

Suddenly the spoon flew out of his bowl and began darting frantically around the room, hitting every wall in sight. Andro ducked for cover beneath the bed after the spoon flew past his head, almost hitting him several times. Magnus watched the spoon with utter shock and disbelief. He looked over at Hunter, who had a gigantic grin plastered over his face as the spoon finally fell to the floor.

'Amazing!' Hunter said with giddy excitement.

Magnus began shaking his head with his mouth agape. Had he really just made that spoon fly around the room merely by thinking it? Why didn't he know he could do this before? A rush of adrenaline spread through his body. This was the first moment of pure exhilaration Magnus had experienced in years. The feeling was incredible.

'I suspect you're going to have a lot of fun with this,' Hunter said as he rose to his feet. Andro tentatively poked his head out from underneath the bed.

'Finish your food, and I'll show you round the base. Would you like that?' asked Hunter.

Magnus nodded vigorously as he stuffed more soup soaked bread into his mouth. He was surprised by his own excitement and enthusiasm, as normally, his anxiety would have convinced him to decline the offer to leave the safe confines of his room. But after what just happened with that spoon, he felt completely invincible and couldn't wait to see what Hunter had in store for him at Ground Zero.

- CHAPTER 7 -

GROUND ZERO

The corridor outside Magnus' room was long and cramped. The lights were dim, and the walls were dark and grimy. Magnus felt as if he was inside some kind of abandoned sewer as opposed to a high tech military base. The place was in definite need of a refurbishment.

They passed several people who were making their way towards the elevator at the end of the corridor. Many of them were staring at Magnus with a mixture of shock and confusion. The exhilaration the teenager had experienced minutes ago completely washed away and was replaced by severe self-conscious anxiety. He hid behind Hunter's back, trying his hardest to avoid making eye contact with anyone. Hunter began explaining the layout of the base, clearly unaware of the teenager's anguish.

'There are many different floors to Ground Zero. We're on the first floor right now, and as you might have guessed, this is our sleeping quarters. You're likely to see many people coming and going on this floor, especially in the mornings.'

Magnus made a mental note not to come out of his room during morning times in order to avoid the large crowds.

'I'll take you around a couple of the floors today to give you a feel for the place, but feel free to explore at your own leisure and make yourself familiar with....'

Hunter's words trailed off as he momentarily stopped in his tracks. He'd noticed a young boy with dark brown hair sitting cross-legged against the wall and staring at the ground with a despondent expression on his face. Hunter knelt down to the boys level.

'Hey, Sam. What are you doing down here, buddy?' he asked in a soft, gentle voice. The boy just shrugged his shoulders.

'Did Billy kick you out again?'

Sam paused for a second and then nodded his head. Hunter rolled his eyes in frustration.

'For heaven's sake.'

'Please don't be angry; it was my fault,' Sam exclaimed, 'I was being annoying.'

'I'm not angry, Sam, but your brother really needs to change the way he treats people, especially his own brother. I'll have a word with him later. Why don't you run along and play in the Sanctum.'

'Okay,' said Sam as his sombre mood instantly morphed into jubilation. He jumped to his feet and ran energetically towards the elevator. Hunter turned to Magnus, who was still hiding behind his back.

'That was Billy's brother, Sam. Do you remember Billy from two nights ago?'

Magnus nodded. He remembered him all right! Billy was the moody teenager who refused to look him directly in the eye.

'Billy was ten years old when we found him, and Sam was just a toddler. Their scumbag parents abandoned them and left them to fend for themselves. Lord knows what would have happened to them if we hadn't have brought them here.'

Magnus looked stunned. He could barely comprehend the notion that someone could be so heartless to abandon their own flesh and blood, let alone two parents. He wondered if his own mother and father had done the same thing to him when he was a baby.

'Why did their parents leave them?' He asked inquisitively.

'I suspect they did it to save their own skin. But nobody really knows. The boys have never spoken about it, and I've never wished to pry into their business.'

Magnus looked down in disappointment. He wanted to find out more about this story, but he didn't want to appear nosey.

'Well... how did you find them?' he asked, trying to keep the conversation going.

'Our motion sensors picked up their trail while they were attempting to break into an abandoned bunker in search of food,' Hunter replied, 'we keep a close eye on the streets the same way the Arcadian drones do, although they cover much more ground than us. Anyone within a ten-mile radius brave enough to leave their homes in search of help will activate our motion sensors and send us a signal of their location. Once that happens, it's a race against the clock to get them to safety before the drones find them.'

As if on cue, a drone, similar to the one that woke Magnus up earlier, flew straight down the corridor in their direction. Magnus and Andro both hit the deck, fearing they were about to be ambushed again. However, the drone simply flew over their heads and carried on with its business. Hunter looked back to see Magnus and Andro cowering on the floor like frightened critters. A silent chuckle escaped his lips.

'You needn't worry about any of the drones in here, boys. They've all been reprogrammed to follow our orders.'

Magnus breathed a sigh of relief, although he was a little embarrassed by his overly dramatic reaction in front of all the people passing by. Hunter extended his hand to Magnus and pulled him to his feet. Andro returned up to head height, looking slightly annoyed.

'You could have reprogrammed them to be a bit friendlier,' the robot said, still sounding a little shaken.

'There's not much we can do on that front, I'm afraid. We don't have the resources to input personality into those things; we just work with what we have. They follow our commands, and that's all we can ask for,' said Hunter matter-of-factly.

'Commands?' said Andro, in a somewhat outraged tone. He shot Hunter a scathing look, which made the captain instantly realise the insensitive nature of the words he just spoke. He paused for a few seconds and then carried on walking.

'Come on; I'll show you guys something fun.'

Hunter beckoned the boy and his robot to follow him into the elevator. Magnus and Andro both looked at each other apprehensively as the doors closed behind them.

'You see that control panel in front of you with all the buttons?' asked Hunter, pointing straight ahead of them.

Magnus could see several buttons labelled one up to five, and underneath them was a sixth button labelled with the letter U.

'Pressing a button on this panel will take you to a certain floor. As I said before, we're currently on floor one. Floor two leads to the toilets and showers. Floors three and four I'm going show to you in just a moment, and finally, floor five is our decontamination chamber, which leads straight to the streets above. That's off-limits to everyone but the Shadow Squad.'

'Where does this button lead to?' Magnus asked, pointing to the button labelled 'U'.

'That leads to the bottom floor, which we call the Underworld, but that's off-limits to everyone. No one's allowed down there without my permission,' replied Hunter, rather sternly.

'Ooh, what's down there?' asked Andro, rather nosily.

'Nothing that you two need concern yourselves about, now Magnus, press the button for the fourth floor, please,' he said, swiftly changing the subject.

Magnus didn't know why, but he was suddenly curious about Hunter's obvious secrecy surrounding the 'Underworld', as he called it. But he wasn't going to dwell on it much further. Obviously, Hunter had no desire to divulge any more information about what was down there other than what he had already.

He pressed the button, and the elevator instantly started moving. The sudden, jerky motion knocked

Magnus to the ground as if the gravity inside had just been turned up to maximum.

'Careful Magnus,' said Hunter lifting him back up to his feet, 'I should have mentioned the elevators can be somewhat jarring at times.'

Magnus dusted himself off but still struggled to keep his balance. This was clearly something else he was going to have to get used to at Ground Zero. He looked up in the corner of the elevator and noticed a camera pointed straight at his face.

'What's that up there?' he asked, a little disconcerted.

Hunter looked up to where Magnus was pointing.

'That's one of our many security cameras. There's one in each elevator, as well as all the corridors on every floor. It's a good way for us to keep an eye on things, but don't worry, they're not in any of the bedrooms,' he said, trying his best to sound comforting.

Magnus was glad to hear it. Having a camera in his room filming his every move would likely do little to ease his anxiety.

Suddenly the elevator came to a crashing stop on the fourth floor, causing Magnus to fall back down to the ground. Hunter couldn't help but chuckle as he once again helped the teenager back to his feet.

'Here we are. This is where the real fun lies,' Hunter said enthusiastically, building the suspense.

The doors opened, and Magnus flinched as flashing laser fire bounced around the room of a large stadium full of soldiers wearing battle armour. They were doing training drills and seemed to have been split into separate groups.

One group could be seen leaping around various obstacle courses and dodging the laser fire of flying robots in pursuit.

Another group were fighting each other using various weapons made of rubber.

The rest were practising hand to hand combat and gravity-defying acrobatics. Magnus was mesmerised by what he was seeing. He felt like one of his video games had come to life right in front of his eyes.

'This is our training facility,' Hunter announced proudly whilst leaning on the handrail overlooking the arena, 'it's perhaps the most important room in the whole of Ground Zero. Here we practice various fighting styles such as martial arts, boxing and weapons handling, as well as learning defensive strategies to deal with those pesky combat drones.'

The twins Taylor and Carter were among the team in the assault course section of the room. Carter looked up to see Hunter giving Magnus and Andro the tour.

'Hey, it's Magnus!' he shouted excitedly and started waving in their direction. Suddenly he got a sharp hit to the chest by a laser blast, which knocked him straight to the floor. Magnus grasped the handrail in shock. Taylor began laughing at her brother, who seemed to have gotten the wind knocked out of him, as he tried to get back on his feet. Toro, on the other hand, looked far less amused.

'That's what you get for taking your eye off the job in hand,' he said scornfully, 'get up, you idiot.'

He walked over to Carter and gave him a hard kick on the arm.

'Sorry, Boss,' Carter responded, slightly out of breath. Magnus breathed a sigh of relief that the man wasn't seriously injured.

'As you can see, we've decreased the drone's energy source, so the laser blasts aren't as powerful,' Hunter explained, 'now they're more of a dull pinch as opposed to a sharp stab that knocks you out for two days.'

Magnus began nodding his head in comprehension. It was all starting to make sense to him how Hunter and his team were so adept at taking care of the many hundreds of battle drones with such efficiency the other night. Training like this on a daily basis would give you all the skills and knowledge necessary to predict their every pre-programmed move and react accordingly.

Magnus noticed Kayla and Max engaged in hand-to-hand combat at the far end of the room. It didn't seem like a fair fight at first, given Max's sheer size and strength advantages; however, Kayla was more than holding her own due to her superior speed and agility. She ducked from an incoming roundhouse kick and swept Max's muscular legs causing him to lose his balance and fall to the floor in a heap. She glanced over towards the elevator and noticed Magnus watching them in absolute awe. She gave him a friendly wave, which he returned with relish.

'So, what do you think of our training floor?' Hunter asked eagerly.

'Brilliant!' Magnus replied with giddy excitement. Andro looked at his friend in astonishment. After the other night, he thought this would be the last thing Magnus would be impressed by.

'It all looks pretty dangerous,' the robot said tentatively, 'you don't expect Magnus to do any of that back-flipping nonsense, do you?'

Magnus shot Andro an aggravated look and bumped him with his elbow.

'Shut up, Andro,' he said through gritted teeth.

'Don't worry. Magnus is a long way off any training of this kind,' said Hunter, trying to conceal a laugh. Magnus felt a wave of disappointment wash over him after hearing that.

'No, I've got something quite different in mind for your training, Magnus,' Hunter grinned as if withholding a deep, dark secret.

Magnus shot him an anxious look.

'What could he possibly have in store for me?' he wondered.

'Come, there's still plenty to see,' said Hunter, leading the boy and his robot back into the elevator. He pressed the number three button, and they began to descend.

'What's on floor three?' asked Magnus curiously.

'You'll see,' said Hunter.

Magnus glanced at him with slight irritation. He didn't believe that the building of tension was entirely necessary for every single floor. He took a deep breath as the elevator came to a stop once again, and the doors flew open. Magnus could see a giant hall full of people going about their day. Some were sitting at tables eating and chatting, others were standing in line for the buffet, and the rest were walking around mingling.

Magnus could feel his anxiety returning. He wasn't sure he was going to be able to cope with this many people all at once.

'This is our Great Hall. It's where everyone comes to eat and to socialise. I suppose you could call it our down-time space.'

Many heads turned in their direction as Hunter stepped inside. He looked back around to see Magnus still lingering in the elevator, reluctant to enter the hall.

'Come on in, Magnus,' he said, beckoning him, 'it's okay. Nothing bad is going to happen.'

Magnus gulped and realised his mouth was completely dry again. He inched forward and slowly stepped into the room. As he did so, he became increasingly aware that more and more people were staring at him and whispering under their breath. One old man in particular, who had a long, pointy nose, a thick, grey beard and a large pot belly, seemed to be staring at him in utter revulsion for some strange reason. This made the teenager feel ever more self-conscious; his eyes were glued to the ground as they made their way through the crowd.

He didn't like this one bit. Why were so many people staring at him? He was nothing special, yet everyone was looking at him as if he was some kind of criminal heretic.

He wanted to dash back to his room as soon as possible and lock the door behind him.

You'll have to forgive the stares, Magnus,' Hunter said as they walked towards the buffet line. 'Most of these people haven't had anything interesting to look at in years. Take it as a compliment.'

'Fat chance of that!' thought Magnus as he shot him a look of pure bafflement. What did they think he was going to do, some kind of magic trick?

As he was looking around, he recognised the young girl from earlier with the colourful jumper and intense stare. She was sitting, eating her lunch at a dining table next to an older gentleman wearing a thick, black coat and trilby hat. She smiled at him and waved. Magnus nervously waved back and then immediately broke eye contact.

'Not her again,' he thought to himself as he hurried to catch up to Hunter.

'We run a very tight ship here in Ground Zero,' said Hunter. 'As captain of this base, it's my responsibility to make sure the needs of everyone here are suitably catered for. As such, the Shadow Squad must leave the base at various intervals throughout the week to gather food and supplies and keep things running smoothly.'

'Where do you get the food from?' asked Magnus.

'Usually from abandoned bunkers located around the Southern province. Luckily for us, the food delivery pods are on autopilot, which means they still deliver to old bunkers that are uninhabited. We simply take what we need and bring it back here,' explained Hunter.

Magnus nodded in comprehension but was suddenly caught off guard when a deafening high-pitched alarm went off, which echoed across the Great Hall. He looked up at Hunter, who, all of a sudden, had a very serious expression on his face.

'I'm sorry, but I have to go. Wait here, Magnus,' he said with a stern tone as he suddenly turned around to leave.

'What's happening?' Magnus cried in a panicked voice, but Hunter was already pacing away from him.

'Just wait here,' Hunter repeated as his mask folded over his face, and he hastily ran towards the elevator. Magnus glanced at Andro, who seemed equally confounded.

'I wonder what all that was about,' Andro said as Magnus shrugged his shoulders in bewilderment. They both turned their attention back to the room full of people. Magnus expected there to be a bit more concern about the strange alarm that just went off, but there seemed to be little reaction at all, as if this was some sort of daily occurrence. All of a sudden, Magnus became fully aware that all eyes were once again zoned in on him.

The intimidating-looking bearded man who was openly glaring at Magnus from the moment he stepped in the room got up off his chair and began trudging over towards him. Magnus and Andro cautiously backed away but didn't get very far before the man started yelling.

'You shouldn't be here,' he said in an intimidating voice. 'They should have kept you locked up.'

Magnus noticed a repugnant odour getting progressively stronger as the old man drew closer. It was enough to bring a tear to his eye.

'Hey, Gerald,' said a rather burly looking ginger-haired woman sitting at a nearby table. 'You leave him alone! He ain't done nothin' to you.'

'Well, someone has to speak out,' the old man said, turning to address the crowd. 'I'm old enough to remember the damage that *his* kind is capable of. Mark my words, this boy will be the death of us all if we don't do something about it.'

'It won't be the boy that'll be the death of you if you carry on like this. It'll be me,' said the burly woman. Her comment sparked a huge laugh from the crowd, and Magnus breathed a short sigh of relief that someone was standing up for him.

'You keep your nose out of it, you meddling cow!' the old man yelled in a threatening manner.

'I wish I could leave my nose out of it, you smelly old dog.'

'Bugger off!'

'Are you going to make me?'

The woman suddenly leapt up from her table, and a huge row began to break out in the Great Hall.

Magnus felt a sudden urge to turn and run, but he was stopped in his tracks when he felt someone grab his right hand from behind him. He turned around and saw that it was the girl with the colourful jumper.

'Follow me,' she said, forcefully yanking on his arm. Magnus didn't really have a choice in the matter. The girl was pulling him with such strength that any resistance was futile.

Andro rolled his eyes.

'Now, where are we going?' he asked in frustration.

He followed the two teens as they made their way through the crowd to the left side of the Great Hall. The girl seemed to be leading Magnus towards a rather inconspicuous looking door. She pulled on a latch, and the door opened swiftly. She yanked him through, and Magnus fell to the floor on the other side. Andro flew in shortly afterwards, and the girl slammed the door securely shut behind them.

The room was pitch black, apart from the glowing green lights emanating from Andro's eyes. Magnus scrambled to his feet, slightly discombobulated. The only sound he could hear was the girl's voice echoing in the darkness.

'Where is that bloody light switch?' she said in a flustered tone, 'I know it's around here somewhere. Ah, there it is.'

Suddenly, a switch was flicked, and the lights blinked on to reveal another long, empty corridor. Magnus turned to look at the girl who was standing behind him.

'Sorry about that,' she said, slightly out of breath, 'I don't know why but I always struggle finding that switch.'

She started laughing for seemingly no reason.

'You'd think after ten months of living here, I'd be able to find my way around, but nope, I still constantly get lost, forget where light switches are located, cause all kinds of havoc. My family has a long history of people with memory problems, so I guess it was inevitable I'd end up this way.'

She was talking at an incredible speed, and her eyes didn't seem to be blinking one bit. Magnus and Andro looked at each other with mutual consternation, unable to comprehend what she was talking about and why she was still speaking at all.

'My dad says I'll probably not make it to the age of twenty at the rate I'm going, but I'm determined to prove him wrong on that front.'

She finally paused to take a breath. Magnus was starting to feel incredibly uncomfortable in this girl's presence. He didn't know where to look. He didn't know what to say. He simply nodded his head awkwardly with his mouth open as a tense silence filled the air.

'Sorry, I talk too much, don't I?' she continued.

Andro nodded his head as if to say, *'That's a huge understatement.'*

'That's another reason my dad says I won't make it past twenty. I'm always getting myself into trouble for talking too much. But I can't help it; sometimes, I just need to let it all out. Do you know what I mean?'

She didn't even pause to let Magnus answer before continuing.

'It's just a nervous thing, I think. If I feel uncomfortable in any situation, I just start rambling and rambling.'

'Stop, please,' said Magnus, cutting her off mid-sentence. He tried to sound as polite as he could, but he wasn't sure how much more of this waffling he could handle. His frustration was making his heart rate increase, and the lights started to flicker as a result. The girl looked around with her jaws agape.

'Whoa. Did you do that?' she asked in utter amazement. Magnus looked away in self-conscious embarrassment.

'That is so mega. I'd heard stories about your superpowers, but I never thought they were true. What else can you do?'

Sensing Magnus' increasing discomfort, Andro flew between the two teenagers.

'Will you please be quiet for one second little Miss?' said the robot in a no-nonsense tone, 'it's time for you to answer some of our questions if you don't mind.'

The girl fell silent with a distinctly shocked expression plastered on her face. She'd never seen a robot talk back with such audacious authority before. She was surprisingly impressed.

'Who are you? Where are we? What was that alarm all about? Why did Hunter leave in such a hurry? Why did that grumpy old man try to attack Magnus?'

He seemed to be getting progressively louder with each question he was asking.

'JUST WHAT THE HELL IS GOING ON IN THIS PLACE?'

Andro's tirade of questions finally came to an end, and silence momentarily filled the space. Magnus glanced at Andro in admiration. He felt incredibly grateful in that moment to have his robot sidekick there for support. They both waited anxiously for the young girl's response.

'Wow. That was a lot of questions,' she said as she looked down at the ground deep in thought. She seemed to be racking her brain, trying to remember what Andro had asked her first.

'Well, my name is Amelia Hart; I'm fourteen years old and, as we've already established, I talk way too much. We are standing in the corridor that connects the Great Hall to the kids' Sanctum, no adults allowed,' she said with a cheeky smile, 'the alarm that went off signals to the Shadow Squad that there are people above ground who need rescuing, which means they have a limited window to go do their thing.'

She mimicked punching the air as she said that. She looked up to the ceiling, desperately trying to remember what other questions she'd been asked.

'Oh yeah. The man who yelled at you is called Gerald. He's a miserable, smelly old fart who believes that you're extremely dangerous and will likely bring about the destruction of the human race. Other than that, he's a nice chap.'

To his surprise, that last sentence made Magnus laugh.

'For the record, I don't think you're dangerous at all,' she said, winking at him. Once again, Magnus had no idea how to respond.

'Thanks,' he replied rather sheepishly. Andro shot both teenagers a look of confusion.

'Come on; I'll show you where the real cool kids hang out,' she said as she grabbed Magnus' hand again and yanked him down the corridor against his will. Andro rolled his eyes once again.

'Doesn't anyone stay still in this place?' he asked in frustration, following the two teens down the long, winding corridor.

- CHAPTER 8 -

THE SANCTUM

Amelia led Magnus down the seemingly endless passageway, her grip on his arm growing increasingly tighter. Not only was she incredibly strong for her size, but she was fast as well, and Magnus found it rather difficult to keep up with her pace. Suddenly, they came to an abrupt halt in front of a large steel door. She looked at Magnus, and a cheeky smile materialised on her face.

'Are you ready to see something really cool?' she asked, barely able to contain her excitement. Magnus nodded apprehensively, feeling somewhat nervous about what he was about to see.

She knocked several times on the metal door, though it wasn't any random knock. It had a specific and calculated rhythm as if she was communicating some sort of code to whoever was on the other side. The door promptly opened the second she stopped knocking, and Magnus and Andro looked on in amazement at what they could see inside.

There were children everywhere of all different ages, shapes and sizes. They were playing ball games, running around, laughing euphorically and generally having a fantastic time. Magnus felt an overwhelming sense of jubilation emanating from this room, a sensation he had never experienced anywhere else before. Just watching the kids playing and enjoying themselves without a care in the world gave him a warm, comforting feeling inside and instantly put a smile on his face.

'What is this place?' Asked Magnus in unmistakable wonderment.

'It's called The Sanctum,' Amelia explained. 'It's the one room in Ground Zero that's just for us kids. That's why the door is programmed with a combination knock. I'll teach it to you later. Only kids under the age of eighteen are allowed to know it. Once someone passes that age, the combination is automatically changed, and they're no longer allowed inside. Strict rules in this place.'

'Do the rules apply to robots?' asked Andro.

Amelia let out a surprised laugh but then realised the robot was serious.

'That's a good question. Erm… We've never had a robot interested in joining before. Well, I guess, since you don't actually age, the rules don't apply to you,' she said encouragingly.

'Huzzah!' Andro declared, lifting his arms in the air ecstatically.

'I bet a bunch of the kids in here would enjoy playing some of the games on your hard drive as well,' said Magnus, tapping Andro on the head. Amelia's eyes grew wide in amazement.

'You've got built-in games?' she asked, utterly amazed by this revelation. Andro nodded vigorously.

'Two hundred and twenty-five games, to be precise,' said the robot, boastfully.

'Wow!' she exclaimed whilst turning to look at Magnus. 'Your robot is mega cool! May I play with him?'

'Be my guest,' said Magnus.

Without hesitation, Andro perched himself on Amelia's head, and two joysticks came out of his sides.

'Right Miss Hart, here's the selection of games. Use the right joystick to pick which one you'd like to play and press it down to begin,' the robot instructed.

'Ooh, Sheep Tossing, that looks like a fun one,' said Amelia eagerly.

Magnus rolled his eyes and laughed.

'Typical,' he thought to himself.

It was a strange feeling seeing someone else playing games with his robot. But he was nevertheless happy to share him, if only for a moment's peace and quiet. However, that peace didn't last very long, as Magnus heard a loud, screeching whistle sound coming from the centre of the room. He looked over and saw a group of older kids playing some kind of ball game he wasn't familiar with.

The game seemed to consist of two teams, one dressed in red shirts and the other dressed in blue shirts. Each player had their fists bound together with black spongy gloves and was bouncing a rubber ball from one end of the court to the other. At each end was a player holding a wooden bat. Their purpose seemed to be to defend the large square basket sitting behind them. Magnus recognised one of the bat-wielding defenders wearing a red shirt. It was Billy, and even in this jovial atmosphere, he still had the same gloomy expression plastered on his face as he did the other night. He towered over the other players with his tall stature and muscular build, and he seemed to relish throwing his weight around where possible and bossing the other kids about.

Magnus decided he was going to try and avoid him at all costs if he could. Luckily, Billy hadn't yet spotted him.

'No, no, no. Throw it. THROW IT! OH, DAMNATION!'

Magnus looked back at Amelia, who seemed to be struggling with the game she was playing. She removed Andro from on top of her head.

'Wow, that game is hard,' she said with surprised frustration.

Magnus chuckled.

'It's easy once you get the hang of it. The trick is to keep throwing the sheep in all directions whilst continually running in a straight line. If you stop at any point, even for a moment, then the wolves will just eat you.'

'I guess I need to keep practising. I also feel sorry for the poor sheep. It's not their fault the farmer got lost in the woods.'

'True,' Magnus said, nodding in agreement.

A group of younger kids began congregating around Andro. They seemed utterly fascinated by him. One of the kids was the little boy, Sam, who Magnus had seen earlier sitting in the corridor outside his room.

'What's your robot called?' asked Sam. Magnus wanted to reply, but he was too nervous to find the words.

'It's Andro,' said Amelia, noticing Magnus' hesitation, 'adorable isn't he?'

'He's so awesome! I wish I had my own robot,' said the small boy, completely consumed with envy, 'can I have a go with him?'

Magnus looked over at Andro, who was clearly relishing the attention he was currently receiving. The teenager nodded apprehensively, and Andro proceeded to plonk himself on the small boy's head. Amelia smiled in Magnus' direction.

'He is going to be so popular in here,' she said with ardent warmth.

Magnus was relieved that the majority of the children's attention was on his robot and not on himself.

'Well, well, well, the wanderer returns.'

A voice came from behind Amelia. It was an older boy with brown, curly hair and a skinny but well-toned body. He was wearing a blue shirt and holding a wooden bat in his hand.

'You missed practice today,' he said, looking scornfully at Amelia.

'I've been busy,' she replied defensively.

'Busy being incredibly annoying, you mean?' he said, grinning cheekily at Magnus, who wasn't quite sure if he should agree or not.

'Shut up!' said Amelia, rolling her eyes. 'Magnus, this is my lame older brother Tom.'

'Always a pleasure to meet new recruits, Magnus,' said Tom, confidently extending his arm towards him, 'I've heard a lot about you through the grapevine.'

Magnus noticed the resemblance between Tom and Amelia instantly. There couldn't have been more than a few years between them. He reached out to return the handshake, and Tom clasped down hard on his hand. Magnus winced slightly as Tom's grip grew even tighter around his fragile fingers. It felt like he'd got them caught in a metal vice. After several seconds, Tom finally released Magnus' hand, which immediately went limp due to low blood circulation. Magnus placed his hand in his pocket to conceal his affliction.

'You'll have to forgive my brother,' said Amelia in a mocking tone, 'he's desperate to prove how manly he is so that Hunter will one day pick him for Shadow Squad training.'

'It's only a matter of time,' said Tom, trying his best not to sound bothered by his sister's condescension. 'If *someone* showed up for Battleball practice, I might stand a better chance.'

'Alright, I'm sorry, okay? I'll be there next time,' she said with a flippant inflexion.

Magnus looked at both of them with slight confusion.

'What's Battleball?' he asked timidly.

'Oh, it's only the greatest sport ever invented by mankind,' replied Tom with no hint of sarcasm. 'It requires speed, accuracy, coordination and agility, all of which I have in droves. I play in keeper position.'

He started swinging his bat as if hitting an invisible ball.

'We've got a big tournament coming up soon where we actually get the opportunity to play for the Shadow Squad. It's going to be unbelievably epic!'

'HEY, TOM!' a voice shouted from the court behind them.

Tom turned his head and saw Billy pacing back and forth like a caged lion.

'ARE WE FINISHING THIS GAME OR NOT?'

'Alright, alright, keep your knickers on,' replied Tom as he turned back to the group, 'someone's grumpy today.'

'Are you winning by any chance?' asked Amelia, already knowing the answer.

'Yes, but only by two points. Anyone would think we were ten nil up or something.'

'Well, it's not as if he needs a reason to be a miserable sod,' joked Amelia under her breath.

'What's taking so long?' asked Billy, appearing suddenly behind Tom. Magnus nearly jumped out of his skin.

'Ah, if it isn't the little boy wonder. So you're the one that's holding up my game,' said Billy, looking down at Magnus antagonistically.

'What happened to your face, Maggie?' he asked with a noticeable grimace as he glared at the mark around Magnus' eye.

'Did you lose a fight with a blow torch or something?'

He was clearly finding himself very amusing. However, the others weren't laughing.

Magnus looked down at the ground anxiously. He was once again starting to miss the safe confines of his old prison cell.

'Shut up, Billy,' Amelia snapped, jumping to her new friend's defence. 'Why don't you go back to playing your stupid game and leave Magnus alone.'

Billy simply smirked and nudged Magnus with his elbow.

'Your girlfriend can't seem to take a joke, Maggie,' he said obnoxiously. Amelia shot him an exasperated stare.

Tom put his hand on Billy's shoulder.

'Come on, Billy. Let's get back on the court,' he said, trying to calm things down. However, Billy swatted his hand away.

'I'll get back on the court when I'm ready,' he replied aggressively. Tom shook his head in disapproval as he turned around and assumed his position on the court. Billy glanced over to his brother, who was still playing games with Andro.

'Hey, Squirt! Get that stupid thing off your head right now!' he commanded maliciously whilst assuming his position back on the court. Sam let out a huge sigh as he reluctantly stopped playing and pulled Andro off his head.

Amelia turned to Magnus, who looked noticeably upset.

'Pay no attention to him, Magnus. There's absolutely nothing wrong with your face. He's just an idiot who thinks he's God's gift to comedy,' she said, trying her best to make him feel better. 'I don't even know why he bothers hanging out with us down here. It's obvious nobody likes him, though I guess we're the only ones he can get away with bossing around. He'll be eighteen soon anyway, and then we'll finally be rid of him.'

This relieved Magnus greatly. He had to admit, he didn't like Billy one bit, and the thought of just having to stand in the same room with him made his heart sink.

'Come on, let's watch my brother kick his backside into submission,' said Amelia, grabbing Magnus' arm and pulling him towards the side-line of the Battleball court. He really wished she'd find a less belligerent technique to get him to follow her.

Magnus looked out over the court to see if he could get to grips with how this game was played. He counted ten players in total and one referee. Four of the players on each team were wearing the black gloves, and only one was batting. The referee blew their whistle and the game resumed.

It seemed pretty intense. The players wearing the gloves were knocking the ball around with impressive dexterity and precision. It was obvious to Magnus that these kids had to practice very hard to play this game as well as they did. Though he had to admit, he didn't really understand what was happening.

Observing his expression of bewilderment, Amelia pulled Magnus closer to her so she could explain how it all worked.

'Okay, here's what you need to know. The ones wearing the gloves are called Strikers. They can hit the ball with any part of their body in any direction, but they're not allowed to let it bounce more than once. Their aim is to get the ball into the other team's basket by any means necessary. The ones holding bats at either end are the Keepers. Their purpose is to defend their team's basket using their bat and any other part of their body. If they leave their area at any point, then possession goes to the opposing team. The team with the most balls in their opponents' basket at the end of the game wins,' she explained meticulously.

Magnus noticed the Keepers were standing behind a white line in the shape of a semicircle. So, this must be the 'area' Amelia was referring to.

'What are the gloves for?' asked Magnus. It had been bugging him since he laid eyes on them.

'They prevent the players from picking up the ball and throwing it. That would be cheating. Only the Keepers or the ref are allowed to pick up the ball.'

Magnus nodded, comprehending. Things were starting to make a lot more sense to him, and he found he was able to follow things more effectively. He'd noticed a few times that Billy was batting the ball towards a hoop dangling from the ceiling with a netted mesh inside.

'What's that up there?' he asked, pointing towards the hoop.

'Oh yes, I forgot to mention,' said Amelia, 'at any point in the game, the Keeper can attempt to knock the ball through that hoop. Doing so automatically wins you the match.'

Magnus looked at her, amazed.

'Wow! So, essentially you could win the match within the first five seconds?'

'Technically, yes. But that never happens, or at least I've never seen it happen since I started playing. In my opinion, the Keeper should be aiming the ball towards his teammates in order to gain the advantage, not wasting their time trying to knock it through a hoop that's only slightly bigger than the ball itself.'

Magnus' attention was suddenly drawn back to the game as the red team fired the ball towards Tom's basket. His heart skipped a beat at the thought that the red team might score a goal against the blues. However, Tom's fast reactions enabled him to successfully bat it out of harm's way. There were several more ferocious attempts by the red team to knock the ball past him, but he was just too fast for them. Magnus was incredibly impressed with Tom's defensive skills during the seemingly never-ending onslaught.

Eventually, Tom managed to knock the ball towards his teammate, who punched it to the other end of the court. A blue Striker stood in prime position for an attack on the red team's basket; however, Billy was ready and waiting. The Striker headed the ball towards the red's basket, and Billy knocked it back at him. Suddenly a red player came out of nowhere and ran straight into the blue striker, knocking him to the floor. The referee blew her whistle, and the game came to a halt.

'Foul. Blue's free hit,' said the ref.

Billy threw his bat to the ground in extreme anger.

'OH, COME ON!' Billy shouted. 'THAT WASN'T A FOUL; HE TRIPPED OVER HIMSELF.'

However, the referee didn't respond. In fact, no one seemed to be paying all that much attention to his protests, not even his own teammates. There was clearly an unspoken acknowledgement that it was, in fact, an illegal manoeuvre.

'What happens now?' asked Magnus.

'The Keeper gets a free hit towards the hoop. If he misses, then the game continues as normal,' answered Amelia.

The ball was passed over to Tom, and all the Strikers went and stood on the side-line of the court. Billy stood in his area at the other end with his arms crossed and aggressively shaking his head in disbelief.

The crowd waited with bated breath as Tom held the ball out in front of him and raised his bat in anticipation for the whistle. The referee blew her whistle, and Tom threw the ball into the air. He took an almighty swing of his bat and whacked the ball with tremendous force straight towards the hanging hoop.

Time seemed to stop for Magnus as he watched the ball hurtle towards the hoop at an incredible speed. To everyone's astonishment, the ball slipped through the hoop and landed in the mesh. He'd scored the winning goal. A great cheer erupted from the crowd, and Amelia and Magnus both jumped to their feet and began applauding with utter delight.

'*What a fantastic game,*' Magnus thought to himself as he witnessed the players of the blue team lifting Tom up onto their shoulders. He couldn't wait to try Battleball out for himself.

Suddenly, he was knocked off-balance by Amelia wrapping her arms around his waist. He'd never been touched in this manner by another human being before, and he wasn't quite prepared for how he was supposed to respond. His body went stiff as a board, and he looked over to Andro for assistance. However, the robot simply shrugged his arms in confusion.

After what felt like an eternity, Amelia finally broke the hug and stepped away from Magnus.

'Sorry about that,' she said, looking a little embarrassed.

'It's okay,' he replied nervously.

There was a distinct and obvious tension in the air between the two teens, both refusing to look the other in the eye. The tension was soon broken, however, by Billy shouting over the cheering crowd.

'MAGNUS CHEATED!' he yelled at the top of his lungs, and the cheering instantly subsided.

'What did he say?' asked Amelia, thankful for a change of subject.

'THIS GAME IS NOT OVER BECAUSE MAGNUS CHEATED!' Billy repeated.

'Oh, what are you going on about now?' asked Tom in frustration, still perched on three people's shoulders.

'No one has hit a ball through that hoop in years. The second the bald weirdo with telekinetic powers shows up, all of a sudden, you're the perfect shot? It's obvious there's cheating going on between you two,' Billy yelled and pointed his finger at the nervous teenager accusingly.

All eyes were suddenly on Magnus, who felt deeply hurt by the accusation that he'd helped Tom cheat in some way.

'You're talking rubbish, Billy!' said Amelia, jumping to Magnus' aid once again.

'Yeah, stop being a sore loser. We won fair and square, right guys?' said Tom, as a huge cheer returned from the teenagers beneath him, and the celebrations started up again.

Billy looked around with disbelief that no one was paying any notice to his claims.

Amelia glanced at Magnus, who had turned his attention back to the floor.

'Just ignore him, Magnus. He's always accusing someone of cheating whenever he loses at this game. It's quite pathetic, really,' she said, reassuringly, 'come on, let's join the fun.'

Magnus' smile returned when he realised the other players weren't buying into Billy's accusation and had continued their celebrations. He tried to cast aside the insulting comments and join in with the fun.

'HEY, MAGGIE!' Billy shouted whilst holding a ball in one hand and a bat in the other. Magnus looked at him, confused.

'CATCH!'

Billy threw the ball into the air and hit it with the bat sending it hurtling towards Magnus' face at top speed. Magnus looked away, and without thinking, held out his hand, causing the ball to stop in mid-air. The crowd of children looked on in bemusement as the ball hovered aimlessly above their heads. Magnus' heart was beating ferociously in his chest, and the hovering ball was beginning to expand. The sound of stretched rubber began to crescendo as the ball grew in size until finally there was a loud bang, and it exploded into a hundred pieces.

Cries of shock and whispered gasps could be heard from the bewildered adolescent crowd. Magnus opened his eyes and turned to face them. He looked at all the concerned expressions in front of him as many children began to back away in fear. Billy shot him another disgusted look.

'Freak!' he hissed with utter contempt.

Magnus' emotions were at their maximum threshold, and the lights began to strobe. He needed to get out of there. Within an instant, he turned around and bolted towards the exit.

'MAGNUS!' Amelia cried as she rushed after him, closely followed by Andro. Tom turned his head in Billy's direction.

'Nice going, mate!' he said disdainfully.

Magnus had tears in his eyes as he dashed down the long, winding passageway towards the Great Hall. He ran as fast as his legs could carry him, desperate to make it back to his room away from all of these awful people.

He burst through the concealed door of the Great Hall and paused for a second as hundreds of prying eyes turned and glared at him. Magnus took a few seconds to analyse the quickest route through the crowd and finally made a run for it. He found he was able to navigate his way through the room quite comfortably due to his small stature and nimble physique. He reached the elevator at the other end of the hall and vigorously pressed the button for the doors to open. He looked back to see Andro and Amelia struggling to pass through the crowd without being obstructed.

'MAGNUS, WAIT!' Amelia cried out as the doors of the elevator opened, and Magnus leapt inside. He quickly pressed the button for the first floor, and the doors closed mere seconds before Amelia and Andro had caught up.

'Come on,' said Amelia, 'there's another lift this way.'

She ran through another side door leading away from the Great Hall, and Andro followed her closely.

As the lift descended, Magnus could feel his heart thudding in his chest. The lights in the elevator were shimmering spasmodically, and the power was starting to fail. He finally reached the first floor, but the doors didn't open for him due to the faltering electronics.

Magnus felt trapped. He thought if he could just get back to his room and lock the door behind him, everything would be okay again. He stuck out his arm, stretched his fingers wide, and the door began to shake violently. It suddenly wrenched from its hinges and shot back twenty metres into the corridor in front, nearly hitting several people on the way.

Magnus felt a mixture of shock, anger and embarrassment rush through his body all at the same time. It was becoming too much for him to handle.

'Everything will be alright once you get back to your room,' he told himself. He leapt through the now open doorway and ran down the corridor, bumping into the grumpy old man from earlier.

'You again! Come here, you little menace. You should be locked up like a dog,' said Gerald belligerently. But Magnus didn't respond. He ran straight past him and refused to let his legs stop running until he was safe.

'Just get back to your room. Just get back to your room,' he repeated as a mantra in his head to try and calm himself down.

As he turned the corner towards his bedroom, he noticed a door open up at the other end of the corridor, and Amelia and Andro came bounding out of it. Magnus' speed increased as he finally reached the door to his room and swung it open. He slammed it shut behind him with a great deal of force, mere seconds before Andro had caught up to him. He pulled the latch tightly, which immediately locked him inside.

'Magnus. Magnus, it's me. Open up,' Andro called through the door whilst knocking heavily. However, Magnus didn't respond to him. He felt so humiliated by what had just taken place he just wanted the ground to swallow him whole. He lay down on his bed, curled up in a ball and closed his eyes. He never wanted to leave his room ever again.

- CHAPTER 9 -

TRAITOR

'You need to come home, Tobias. The kids are driving me up the bloody wall. I don't know how much more of this I can handle,' Rosa moaned during a video call to Tobias, who was sitting behind the desk in his office. She was sitting upright on a couch in their enormous living room, sipping on a large glass of red wine whilst their two young children, Lucas and Molly, ran around her screaming hysterically.

'Where's Jeffrey?' Tobias asked with frustration.

'You gave him the week off, remember?' Rosa replied through gritted teeth.

'Damn it! I'll ring him and tell him it's an emergency.'

Tobias sighed as he reached for the phone.

'I don't need Jeffrey here, Tobias. I need my husband. You've been working flat out for nearly three days straight. Now's the time to come home and be with your family,' Rosa said desperately.

'I wish I could, my love,' Tobias responded with resignation, 'but we're still no closer to finding these rebels, and I need to be on hand in case any news comes through.'

'And what use are you going to be if you don't get any rest? If you carry on like this, you're going to burn out. I'm already burnt out looking after the kids.'

'Yes, I can see that.'

'I need you to come home,' Rosa repeated with tears forming in her eyes.

'Look, as soon as this is over, I'll treat you to a week away at your favourite spa, just you and me. No kids, no stress, no worries. How does that sound?'

Rosa smiled.

'Oh Tobias, that sounds... LUCAS, STOP PUNCHING YOUR SISTER THIS SECOND!'

Her smile disappeared within an instant as she bellowed at her son off-screen. Her sudden aggressive tone made Tobias jump out of his skin. He'd been on the receiving end of it several times throughout their marriage, and it always sent a cold shiver up his spine. Rosa turned back to face the camera, and her demeanour suddenly morphed from hostile to sombre.

'Please come home soon,' she pleaded.

'It won't be for much longer, Rosa, I promise. Just hang in there.'

Tobias tried to console his wife, who seemed on the verge of a mental breakdown.

'I love you,' he said sincerely.

'I love you,' she repeated back to him, though he could tell by her blank expression that she was definitely going to make him suffer when he returned home.

The screen went black, and the room became silent.

Tobias breathed a huge sigh and slumped back in his chair. This was the first moment of peace he'd had in days, and he was determined to savour it. He put his hands to his head and began gently massaging his temples. The feeling momentarily soothed him as every muscle in his body started to relax.

Suddenly the screen flickered back on again, and Tobias jumped in his seat. It was the Master in his usual hooded attire sitting in his dark, ominous chamber. Tobias' heart skipped in terror. This was a call he definitely wasn't expecting to have to take.

'Hello, Tobias,' said the Master in a booming voice that echoed around the office. Tobias adjusted himself in an attempt to look slightly less unkempt.

'Master... you're awake,' the Commander said nervously. His eyes were darting around the room as his mind began frantically racing to try and figure out how his previously sedated boss could have woken up to make this call.

'Indeed,' the Master replied with a slight wince in his voice as if every breath was a struggle.

There was an uncomfortable pause between them as Tobias tried to think of how best to respond.

'It's... good to see you,' he said, filling the awkward silence.

'I'm not here to exchange pleasantries with you, Tobias!' the Master said sternly.

'Of course not,' Tobias hung his head submissively.

'I've just been informed of some rather disturbing news regarding a rebellion in the Southern province. Apparently, they have a certain Asset in their possession,' said the Master in a composed voice.

Tobias' eye twitched, and his heart sank.

'Damn!' he said under his breath.

'You told me all the Assets were destroyed. You've been hiding this one from me all this time.'

The Master's voice was growing in malevolence with every word he spoke.

'No, Master. I was simply saving him for the opportune moment.'

Tobias was starting to fumble his words. He had no idea how the Master found out about any of this or, indeed, how he was going explain it to him.

'And when were you going to inform me about it, Tobias?' the Master asked with accusing hostility.

'As soon as it became relevant, my Lord. This is a simple matter that I am taking care of. I didn't feel I needed to concern you with it,' Tobias answered defensively.

'It's been fifty-two hours, Tobias!' the Master boomed. 'You still haven't got the faintest idea where these people are hiding.'

'The situation is under control, my Lord. We are working with the best technology in the world to locate these rebels and bring them to justice. It's only a matter of time.'

Tobias' speech seemed to be accelerating with every second that passed as he fought to defend his actions.

'Your technology is no match for these rebels. Every hour you waste is time they will spend corrupting the Asset's mind.'

'What would you have me do, Master?'

'Send out every surveillance drone we have in our possession. I want to see one on every street corner within a fifty-mile radius of the Southern province. Also, you are to turn off the stun function on their laser cannons.'

Tobias looked at him in disbelief.

'But my Lord, innocent people could get killed,' he said in protest.

'This is war, Tobias. It's thinking like that, which makes you look weak to our enemies. The rebels made the first move; now, we need to strike back with the full force of our arsenal. The very second you discover their location, you will report straight to me. You are not to leave this building until the Asset has been found. Do I make myself clear?' said the Master with intense malice in his voice.

'Crystal,' Tobias replied begrudgingly.

'Do not disappoint me again, Commander. This is your final warning.'

Suddenly the screen went blank, and silence returned to the room.

Tobias closed his eyes and collapsed back into his chair. He suddenly realised his heart was racing at a million miles a second, and he was sweating profusely. He pulled the plug on all the screens in his office. He didn't think he could handle any more unsolicited phone calls today.

'How did the Master find out about this?' he asked himself. Tobias had been sedating the old man for years due to his worsening health, and all of a sudden, he knew everything there was to know about the Asset and rebellion. There could only be one explanation for this. There had to be a traitor in the Arcadian government, and Tobias had a pretty good idea of who it might be. He leapt to his feet and burst through his office door like a madman. He stomped down the corridor of the Capitol building towards the office of his second in command, ignoring several colleagues as he passed by. He opened the door to Grant Boswell's office but found it was empty.

'Is everything alright, Tobias?' a female's voice said from behind him.

Tobias turned back round suddenly, like a child who'd just been caught stealing sweets from a candy store. Standing a little closer than he expected was Dianne Lloyd looking slightly bemused.

'Oh, it's you, Dianne,' he said, catching his breath, 'have you seen Grant anywhere?'

He continued scanning the hallway for any sign of him.

'I believe he went up to the weapons division. He didn't say why.'

Before she could say another word, Tobias bolted down the hall towards the elevator, leaving the public safety minister feeling somewhat baffled. He pushed the button for the tenth floor, and the elevator began to rise. As he waited patiently to arrive on the correct floor, he began having an internal battle inside his head.

'Could Grant really be the traitor?' he asked himself. They've been friends for many decades, and he's never shown any signs of insubordination before. But Grant was the only person Tobias ever trusted with the knowledge of the Asset's existence.

'It couldn't be anyone else, could it?'

124

The elevator finally stopped on the tenth floor, and the doors opened to reveal a massive training centre full of soldiers performing combat drills. It had been many years since Tobias had any reason to come up to this particular floor, and he'd forgotten how efficient the Arcadian army was at fighting.

He hastily made his way around the training arena, trying his best not to draw unnecessary attention to himself. He noticed Grant talking with Colonel Braxton on the other side of the hall. Grant was idly sipping his mid-afternoon coffee, and Braxton seemed to be explaining some sort of schematic diagram to him. Grant looked up and noticed Tobias marching with incredible pace in his direction. He broke off his conversation with Braxton and started walking casually towards his boss, looking noticeably satisfied with himself.

'Ah Tobias, I was just about to come and see you,' he said with great enthusiasm. However, he suddenly noticed that the Commander wasn't slowing down his approach, and he had a distinctly furious expression painted on his face.

Without halting, Tobias pushed Grant through a side door and promptly slammed it behind him. Braxton looked up from his schematics, appearing somewhat confused.

Grant's piping hot coffee spilt over the chest of his clean white shirt, and the searing heat made him cry out in agony. Tobias picked him up off the floor and shoved him very hard against the wall, restraining his hands. He put his arm against Grant's throat and pressed into it with all his body weight.

'What the hell are you doing?' Grant cried out in shock.

'I've just had a lovely little video chat with the Master,' Tobias said aggressively. 'He tells me he knows all about the Asset, the rebellion, and of course, the fact that it's been nearly three days, and our incompetent team is no closer to discovering their location.'

He leaned in, applying more pressure to Grant's larynx.

'What? How?' Grant wheezed, desperately gasping for air.

'Well, I was hoping you'd be able to fill me in on that one, Grant, considering up until now we were the only two people in this government with any knowledge of the Asset's existence, and I sure as hell wasn't the one who told him.'

Tobias was spitting out every word ferociously and looked as though he was about to pop a blood vessel in his temple.

'Tobias, I promise you, I had nothing to do with it. I would never wake the Master without your permission, and I certainly wouldn't have told him about the Asset,' Grant said with absolute conviction.

'Why should I believe you?' Tobias asked dismissively.

'Because I understand the consequences if the Master gets his hands on the boy. Do you really think I want that to happen?' Grant replied convincingly as he glared into the Commander's eyes.

Tobias was desperately trying to get a read on him. He was sure he'd caught the perpetrator, but every word and gesture Grant uttered seemed to solidify his innocence.

There was a sudden knock on the door, which broke the ever-escalating tension in the room. It opened, and Braxton stepped in carrying a large box. He looked over at the two men as Tobias swiftly loosened his grip on his colleague and stepped away. Grant leant on the wall for support as he fought hard to catch his breath.

'Am I interrupting something?' Asked Braxton, unsure of how to react.

Tobias cleared his throat.

'Not at all John, what can we do for you?' he replied, trying his hardest to look like a dignified leader.

'I have just received the final model of the probe you requested. It's ready to go once it's had your seal of approval.'

Braxton laid the box down on the table in front of him.

'Probe? What probe?' Tobias asked, looking somewhat confused. He turned to look at Grant, whose breathing was gradually returning to normal.

'I requested the production of a new people scanner capable of covering vast distances in very short time frames,' Grant explained, 'Braxton and his team have been working around the clock to get it built as soon as humanly possible.'

Braxton opened the box, and a small, metallic ball with one big red eye flew out and started whizzing around the room like a giant flea in search of blood.

'It has extremely powerful sensors capable of detecting human life with a range of up to fifty miles. It should be suitable to cover the Southern province. If the rebels set one foot outside, this probe will know about it,' said Braxton, sounding rather pleased with himself.

'I've also programmed it to detect specific faces based on the security footage you supplied me with. They won't remain hidden for much longer; I can assure you.'

Tobias felt a gigantic grin growing on his face. This might actually be the solution to this problem.

'John, I could kiss you,' he declared with absolute glee.

'That won't be necessary, Sir,' replied Braxton, taking a rather large step back from his boss. He pushed a button inside the box, and the probe flew back inside.

'How did you make it so quickly?' asked Tobias in astonishment.

'We simply tweaked a few parts of an old prototype our previous engineer designed. Everything was in place; we just had to add the scanners.'

'That's excellent work, Braxton. Send it out as soon as possible,' Grant said with authority.

'Yes, Sir.'

Braxton bowed his head, picked up the box and promptly left the room.

Tobias turned his head back to Grant but was reluctant to make eye contact with him.

'Problem solved,' said Grant, still looking incredibly angry with his boss. Tobias glanced away sheepishly as Grant picked up his now empty coffee mug and stormed out of the room, slamming the door as he left.

The commander felt a sting of embarrassment. He'd just attacked his second in command and accused him of being a traitor with no empirical proof of any kind. The conviction in Grant's pleas of innocence was as convincing as it's possible to be.

Had he gotten this all wrong? If so, whom else in his government could he not trust? He realised he was going to have to tread very carefully from now on in order to uncover the truth behind all this.

- CHAPTER 10 -
COUNSELLING MAGNUS

It had been several hours since Magnus fled the Sanctum after his humiliating Battleball encounter, but Andro and Amelia continued to wait patiently outside his bedroom door. Amelia started throwing a rubber ball at the wall as a way to pass the time, and Andro had gone into power-down mode to conserve his energy.

All of a sudden, Amelia heard footsteps emanating from around the corner and glanced up to see who was coming. It was Kayla. She had just returned from the rescue mission on the streets above and was still wearing her combat suit. Amelia instantly perked up the moment she saw her idol.

'Hey, Kayla,' she said as she jumped to her feet.

'Hi, Amelia,' Kayla replied, looking slightly perplexed, 'any idea what happened to the elevator? The door's been ripped off.'

Amelia shook her head and looked away rather awkwardly.

'We heard the alarm earlier. Have we got some new recruits?' she asked, quickly changing the subject.

Kayla looked down at the ground with a sombre expression on her face. She didn't want to be the one to kill Amelia's upbeat mood, but she didn't want to have lie to her either.

'Unfortunately not,' Kayla uttered despondently, 'we didn't make it to them in time.'

Amelia's smile instantly disappeared, and she hung her head in sorrow.

'We're holding a minutes silence in their honour tomorrow morning,' said Kayla.

Amelia nodded her head. She never enjoyed these minute silences for two reasons; firstly, she enjoyed talking way too much, and secondly, it brought back memories of all those who had passed on. But never the less, she understood the importance of paying respect to those who had lost their lives.

'How's Magnus doing?' asked Kayla, hoping to lighten the mood a bit. However, Amelia seemed reluctant to answer.

'Well...' she replied tentatively. She wasn't quite sure where to start. 'There was a bit of an incident in the Sanctum earlier today.'

'What sort of incident?' asked Kayla, looking concerned. But before Amelia could answer, Andro suddenly sprang to life and jumped into the conversation.

'A young brute accused Magnus of cheating while they were playing their stupid game and decided to hit a ball right at his face,' the robot yelled out angrily.

Kayla rolled her eyes and looked knowingly at Amelia. 'Let me guess, Billy?'

'Yep,' replied Amelia without a moment's hesitation.

Kayla sighed.

'For crying out loud!' she exclaimed in an aggravated tone as Andro continued his rant.

'Magnus has locked himself in his room for hours now and refuses to come out or let anyone else in. This is the longest we've ever been separated!'

The robot started to sound deeply worried for his friend.

'I knew this would happen. I told Hunter it was too soon to introduce him to the public,' Kayla said, shaking her head. She turned to look at Amelia. 'Have you been waiting out here all this time?'

Amelia nodded.

'I wanted to make sure he was alright.'

'You must be starving. Go, get some dinner. I'm sure your father will be wondering where you've gotten to.'

'Are you sure?' asked Amelia, reluctant to leave her post. However, she had to admit; her stomach was starting to make some hungry sounding noises.

'Go on. I'll let you know if Magnus comes out of his room.'

'Thanks, Kayla,' said Amelia as she turned and ran off down the corridor. Kayla looked back at Andro, who still had the same irate expression on his face.

'Don't worry, Andro, we'll make this right again, I promise,' she said as she walked past him and knocked on the door softly.

'Magnus? It's Kayla. Amelia told me what happened today. I'm coming in if that's alright?'

She didn't wait for a reply. She fished a key out of her pocket and unlocked the door. The second it swung open, Kayla was taken aback when she noticed a chair and a food tray floating around the room in mid-air, seemingly of their own accord. She looked over to the bed and saw Magnus curled up in the foetal position facing away from her. She began walking closer towards him, grabbing the floating chair and placing it down next to his bed.

'Magnus?' she said softly.

'Please go away,' he replied in a hoarse voice. It was evident he'd been crying for a good long time. Kayla sat down next to the bed.

'If you want me to leave, then I will. But before I do, I just wanted to say how sorry I am about what you went through today. Billy has a lot of problems that he's dealing with in his own way, but he should never have treated you in that manner. It was out of order, and that's not how we conduct ourselves here. He will be suitably punished once Hunter finds out about it, believe me.'

Kayla hoped her words would provide some small semblance of comfort for him, but she could tell Magnus was still very upset by his lack of response. Andro hovered at the end of the bed, and the floating tray hit him in the back. Kayla stood up from her chair.

'I'll leave you in peace,' she said, walking towards the door.

'Why am I the way I am?' asked Magnus, almost in a whisper. Kayla stopped in her tracks and turned back around.

'What do you mean?' She replied with a perplexed expression. Magnus rolled over to face her.

'Why am I a freak?'

Kayla paused for a moment, trying to decide how best to reply.

'Now you listen to me, Magnus,' she said, moving back to his bedside, 'you are not a freak. Do you hear me? Don't let anyone make you believe that about yourself. You're just different, that's all, and sometimes people find those who are different to be hard to understand. But that doesn't mean there's anything wrong with you; in fact, it makes you even more special. Give the people here time to get to know you, and they'll soon realise how amazing you really are.'

'I don't want them to get to know me. I'm never leaving this room ever again. I hate it here,' Magnus said angrily, as he turned his body away from her once again, 'I was perfectly happy when it was just me and Andro locked away from the world.'

Kayla looked towards Andro at the end of the bed, whose eyes looked down in sorrow. She turned back to face Magnus again.

'I understand how overwhelming everything has been the past few days for you, and I'm absolutely furious with Hunter for rushing things. It wasn't fair. He's just so eager to start your training; he didn't think about the impact it might have on you.'

As she said that, there was a brief glint in Magnus' eyes. Watching the Shadow Squad doing their combat drills this morning was one of the only aspects of the day he actually enjoyed. He had to admit, the prospect of training under Hunter's wing was an incredibly exciting one.

'If you want to stay in here with Andro, that's fine. I'll arrange with Hunter that no one disturbs you from now on. But I think you should give this place a second chance. There are some truly wonderful people here, and once Hunter's taught you everything he knows, no one's going to be brave enough to mess with you,' she said with a warm smile. 'I'll leave it with you. Would you like me to bring you some supper?'

Magnus simply shook his head.

'Okay then. Well, if you decide you need anything, tell Andro to come and find me. He knows where my room is,' she said as she stood up from her chair. 'Good night, Magnus.'

Kayla leant forward and kissed Magnus on the side of his head. He was surprised by the sudden contact but didn't find it to be unpleasant.

'Good night, Andro,' she said, opening the door to leave.

'Good night,' the robot replied with a smile as Kayla closed the door behind her.

Magnus rolled over onto his back and looked at his robot friend.

'I'm sorry I locked you out, Andro,' he said genuinely.

Andro flew over to Magnus' side.

'It's okay, Magnus. I understand. Although I do think you overreacted a bit.'

'Oh, really. I suppose you know what it feels like to be called a freak, do you?'

Magnus felt somewhat irritated by his robot's condescending remark.

'No, I don't. But I know what being made to feel small and insignificant is like. When we first arrived here, I was treated like another mindless drone whose only purpose was to carry out people's commands. Like you, I just wanted to hide away from the world. But Kayla was right. As soon as people realised there was more to me than meets the eye, they started treating me differently. They treated me with respect.'

Magnus looked away, shaking his head.

'You don't really want to be cooped up in here with me forever, do you?' asked Andro.

'Why not? We've been locked up together for years.'

Magnus was shocked his friend was trying to talk him out of this.

Andro shone a light in the centre of the room and played a clip he'd recorded a few days earlier:

'I don't want to do anything I've done a thousand times before, okay, Andro? I want something different.'

The clip ended, and Andro's light went off.

'I've already apologised about that,' said Magnus.

'You used to yearn to see what life was like outside the walls of your bedroom, remember? You've been given that chance, and you want to go back to being locked up again?'

'I never thought it would be like this. I never thought I'd be so scared all the time,' Magnus uttered, feeling increasingly more vulnerable with each word he spoke.

'If you focus only on the negative aspects of life, then you'll always be too scared to do anything. You'll never grow as a person. There are a lot of genuinely good

136

people here who seem to want to get to know you. Maybe you should give them a chance,' the robot said as he flew over to his docking station. Magnus paused to let Andro's words sink in. He thought about all the people he'd met today and all those who had been kind to him and stuck up for him while he was being picked on.

'We can discuss it more in the morning when you're feeling better,' said the robot as he shut his eyes and powered down.

'Good night, Andro,' said Magnus.

He had to admit that his robot was making a lot of sense. Maybe he had overreacted a tiny bit.

He went to get up to switch the light off but instantly stopped himself. There was something he wanted to try. He looked over at the switch near the door and slowly lifted his hand. He concentrated hard on the switch, and in an instant, the light went out, and the room was consumed by darkness. Magnus smiled to himself.

'Tomorrow, things are going to be different,' he thought determinedly.

- CHAPTER 11 -

A NEW DAY

The next morning, Magnus woke up bright and early and was beaming with energy. Throughout the night, he'd been imagining the prospect of learning how to fight with the intensity of the Shadow Squad, how to play Battleball with the skill and accuracy of Amelia's brother Tom, and how to finally take control of his newly acquired powers. The thought of accomplishing even one of these skills filled him with immense excitement, and this time he was determined not to let his fear hold him back.

However, if he was going to accomplish anything today, he was going to need some energy fuel inside him. He suddenly realised that he hadn't eaten anything since yesterday morning and his stomach was growling like a wild beast. But that wasn't the only unusual sound Magnus could hear this morning. There were also some strange noises emanating from the floor below him.

Magnus' curiosity was too strong for him to ignore. He slowly stepped out of his bed, crouched down and gently put his ear to the floor. He could hear the sounds of clanging metal and heavy machinery vibrating through the floorboards. He also could have sworn he heard a man's voice singing, but it was too faint for him to make out a particular tune or any words.

Magnus found this very peculiar indeed. Yesterday, Hunter had told him that the bottom floor was off-limits to everyone except him, but he could definitely hear someone singing down there. Who could it be?

However, before Magnus could think about it any further, his stomach gave an almighty rumble, signalling that his curiosity would have to wait. He desperately needed to get out and find some food.

He tiptoed past Andro, who was still sleeping soundly and slowly opened his creaking door. As he stepped through the gap, he looked back at the robot, and a sting of guilt rushed through his body. He felt bad that he was willingly leaving his best friend behind, but he knew that if he'd woken him up, then Andro would have wanted to follow him, and Magnus had a burning desire and determination to prove to himself that he was brave enough to venture out alone.

He carefully closed the door behind him and wandered down the corridor towards the elevator, whose door was still ripped from its hinges. He was surprised to see the corridor so empty, considering how crowded it had been yesterday. Everyone must have still been asleep. He stepped into the elevator and pressed the button for the third floor. He was relieved to see that it was still working properly despite the electrical issues and lack of door. It jerked back to life and began to rise; this time, however, Magnus managed to stay on his feet the whole time.

The elevator stopped at the third floor, and Magnus stepped out into the Great Hall. The room was very quiet, with only a few people sitting down eating breakfast. Magnus was shocked by how big it actually was. He hadn't gotten a proper look at it yesterday, but it appeared to have doubled in size overnight with so few people taking up the space.

Magnus looked around the room and noticed Amelia and Tom sitting at one of the dining tables eating their breakfast. Next to them was the same older gentleman Magnus had seen with Amelia yesterday. He was reading a book and casually sipping a hot drink from his mug.

Magnus waved at Amelia, and she instantly jumped out of her seat and sprinted towards him. Tom began to chuckle as he continued wolfing down his breakfast. She stopped abruptly in front of Magnus, almost bumping into him.

'Hey Magnus,' she said excitedly.

'Hi,' he replied with an awkward smile.

'I'm sorry about what happened yesterday. Billy was out of order. Nothing like that will ever happen again, I promise,' she said at breakneck speed.

'It's okay, Amelia,' Magnus replied, holding his hands up, 'it's forgotten about.'

'You must be hungry,' she said, noticing the obvious gurgle sounds coming from his stomach. Magnus nodded his head vigorously.

'Come on, let's get you some porridge.'

She grabbed his hand and guided him towards the food station. Magnus had never heard of porridge before, but he was intrigued and excited to try something new. However, that excitement quickly turned to repugnance once he'd seen what was on offer. In front of them were five large metal containers full of some sort of bubbling, white sludge. Amelia handed Magnus a bowl, which he reluctantly accepted.

'What is this, Amelia?' he asked with trepidation.

'It's porridge,' she replied matter-of-factly. She noticed the look of repulsion on his face. 'Haven't you ever had porridge before?' she asked, sounding rather shocked.

Magnus shook his head.

'Well, it's nicer than it looks, trust me,' she said, trying to sound as reassuring as possible.

'It would have to be,' Magnus thought to himself as he grabbed the ladle sticking out of the giant vat of white goo and poured a big dollop into his bowl.

The two teenagers walked back over to the table where Tom and the old man were sitting.

'Hey Magnus,' Tom greeted with a smile, 'we weren't sure if we'd see you today.'

'Magnus...' said Amelia, cutting her brother off. '...this is my father, George. He's the only qualified doctor in Ground Zero. You ever have any health issues; he's the man to go to.'

George glanced up from his book and smiled at the teenager.

'So this is the great Magnus I've heard so much about,' he said as he shook the young boy's hand.

'Yeah, Amelia hasn't shut up about you all morning,' Tom sniggered. Amelia's cheeks began to flush as she glared at her brother scornfully.

'Well, people like Magnus don't come around very often, do they?' she said, looking slightly embarrassed.

Both teenagers sat down next to each other at the table. Magnus was still looking at the porridge as if it was going to poison him.

'What's up, lad?' asked George, 'it's just a bit of porridge. It's not going to kill you. A growing boy like you needs to keep up his strength.'

Magnus looked at Tom, who was greedily gobbling his bowl of porridge like it was his last meal. He closed his eyes, took a deep breath, filled his spoon with the white gloop and plunged it deep into his mouth. The first sensation he felt was pain. The porridge was unexpectedly hot, and steam started blowing from his mouth. Amelia tried her best to stifle a laugh that was aching to break free from her lips.

'You're supposed to blow on it before you put it in your mouth, Magnus,' Amelia explained, 'just swirl it around until it cools down.'

Magnus did as he was instructed, but the damage was done. His tongue felt like it was on fire. This was his first experience with piping hot food, and so far, he wasn't enjoying it all that much. However, once the burning sensation subsided and he was able to swallow comfortably, Magnus was surprised how much he was enjoying the flavour of the porridge despite its revolting appearance. His second mouthful was much more satisfying now that he knew to blow on it first.

'So what are you doing up at this time, Magnus?' asked George. 'There are not usually many people other than us three in here this early in the morning.'

Magnus thought for a second and then replied.

'I just couldn't sleep,' he said casually.

'I know what you mean,' said Amelia, 'we don't sleep much either. I think it's a genetic thing because my Mom barely used to sleep at all. She'd always say three hours max was enough, but most people believe they need at least seven.'

'Shut up, Amelia,' said Tom rolling his eyes, 'Magnus doesn't care about any of this.'

'Sorry I spoke,' she replied in a petty tone.

Magnus carried on eating as an awkward silence fell upon the hall. That silence was broken, however, by a group of people getting off the elevator. Magnus turned to look at them and noticed that all their eyes were suddenly fixed on him. He lowered his head and continued eating. George leered at the prying eyes.

'Something the matter?' he asked aggressively as the group suddenly averted their eyes. 'Can't a boy eat his breakfast in peace anymore? Absolutely ridiculous.'

George shook his head and leaned in closer to Magnus.

'Don't worry, boy, anyone tries to give you grief; they'll have to deal with me.'

'And me!' Amelia chimed in to join the back end of her father's comment.

'No one's going touch you while we're around, mate,' said Tom as he scraped the last remnants of porridge oats from the bottom of his bowl.

Magnus smiled. He felt a lot safer knowing his friends were there to stick up for him.

One of the side doors opened, and Kayla walked into the Great Hall. She glanced around the room and was shocked to see Magnus out of his bedroom and socialising with people so soon after their conversation last night. She wandered over to their table with a puzzled smile on her face.

'Hey, Kayla,' said Amelia, waving enthusiastically.

'Good morning, everyone. Magnus, I thought you decided to stay in your room.'

Magnus swallowed his mouth full of porridge before turning to look up at Kayla.

'I changed my mind. Andro convinced me; I've been locked away for long enough, and it's about time I made some friends,' Magnus said whilst glancing at Amelia.

'Well, I'm glad to hear it. You're hanging out with the coolest kids in town over here, so making friends won't be an issue for you,' said Kayla, which gave Amelia the biggest smile ever.

'She's not wrong,' said Tom boastfully as he stood up from the table, 'Amelia, are you coming?'

Amelia looked at her brother with a clueless expression. Then she suddenly remembered what he was talking about.

'Oh, yeah. Tom asked me to help him practice for the Battleball tournament. Would you like to come with us, Magnus? We can teach you how to play.'

'Sure. That sounds great,' he said with an enthusiastic nod. He turned to look back at Kayla. 'Would you be able to tell Hunter I'd like to start my training soon if it's alright with him?'

Kayla looked at him in utter shock.

'No, of course, that's... that's excellent Magnus. I'll let him know right away,' she said, trying to contain her blatant excitement. 'I'll see all of you later.'

'Bye, Kayla.'

Amelia started waving frantically again as Kayla turned and left the room the way she came in.

Tom picked up his empty bowl from the table.

'I'm going to get everything set up. You guys coming or not?'

'Give the boy a chance to digest his breakfast,' said George.

'We'll follow you in a minute,' Amelia replied. Tom dumped his bowl in a bucket of water and briskly made his way towards the Sanctum.

Magnus was fast approaching the bottom of his bowl also. Having never tasted porridge before, he was pleasantly surprised at how much he'd enjoyed it. He also noticed how sprightly he suddenly felt, as if someone had just turned his power gauge up to maximum. No food at the prison had ever made him feel this much vitality before, and once he had scooped every last dollop of porridge from the bottom of his bowl, he wiped his mouth and sprung to his feet. Amelia and George both looked up in bewilderment.

'Race you to the Sanctum,' he said with a cheeky grin on his face. Without giving Amelia time to process the challenge, Magnus took off like a rocket.

'Hey, wait up,' Amelia cried as she too leapt out of her chair and ran after him.

George looked at the empty bowls that had been discarded on the table.

'I'll wash up then, shall I?' he yelled across the hall, but both teenagers had already disappeared from sight. 'Oh, that boy's going to have so much indigestion.'

George chuckled to himself as he returned his attention back to his book.

Down the corridor, the two teens were racing like a couple of wild animals, desperately scrambling to be the first to arrive at the Sanctum. Magnus had a good lead, but Amelia was gaining on him. He was seconds from reaching the door when Amelia suddenly grabbed hold of his arm and yanked him backwards, knocking him to the floor. She slammed her hand on the door and cheered in victory.

'I win,' she said, completely out of breath. Magnus leapt to his feet.

'Hey, that's not fair. You cheated,' he replied, holding his chest. His heart was beating like an atomic particle ready to explode, and he was starting to get a stitch in his abdomen.

'Sorry. I get overly competitive when people challenge me.'

'I noticed,' he said, taking a deep breath, 'do you have to be so rough, though? I think if you yank my arm one more time, you're going to rip it straight off.'

'Okay, I promise to stop yanking your arm,' said Amelia. 'How about I make it up to you by showing you how to do the secret knock.'

Magnus nodded his head.

'It goes like this.'

She started clapping the same unique rhythm she showed Magnus yesterday, though he wasn't convinced he'd be able to replicate it.

'Ok, now you try it on the door.'

Magnus stepped forward and started knocking, trying his best to repeat the same rhythm he'd just heard. Surprisingly, he managed to get it spot on, and the door opened a second later.

'Wow. You're a quick learner,' Amelia applauded, 'it usually takes kids ages before they get it right.'

Magnus felt rather pleased with himself as they stepped inside the Sanctum. Tom had already set up the Battleball court and had gotten straight to work on his target practice routine.

Amelia opened a box and fished out a couple of pairs of black gloves.

'Here,' she said, throwing a pair to Magnus, 'I'll teach you how to be a Striker.'

Magnus put the gloves on and followed Amelia onto the court. Tom hit a ball towards his sister, and she began bouncing it on top of her gloves.

Magnus was very impressed by the amount of control she had over the ball and felt a rush of ambition to become equally accomplished at it.

'Right, Magnus, I'm going to bounce the ball towards you, and I want you to bounce it straight back to me,' said Amelia.

Magnus nodded apprehensively. She hit the ball into the air; however, Magnus wasn't quite ready. He hit the ball topside, and it bounced on the ground and spun back to Amelia's gloves.

'Well done! One bounce is okay in this game, but it's better to hit it back to me without a bounce. It's less likely to get intercepted that way,' Amelia explained patiently. 'Let's try again.'

Magnus nodded as she once again volleyed the ball in his direction. Magnus had a clear view of it this time and struck it dead centre. The ball came flying back at Amelia, and she knocked it towards Tom. Tom swung his bat and hit the ball with great force, sending it flying towards the centre hoop. It bounced off the left edge and fell to the floor.

'Unlucky,' Amelia called over to her brother in a mocking tone.

'I'm going to get it through that hoop today; you just watch.' Tom said determinedly.

'I've heard that before,' Amelia retorted, shaking her head.

'Hey, I did it yesterday, didn't I?'

'That was a fluke, and you know it,' Amelia scoffed.

'Careful, you're starting to sound like Billy.'

Tom shook his head and went back to hit more balls at the hoop. Amelia turned back to continue her lesson with Magnus.

'That was a good hit, Magnus. Well controlled and a good amount of power,' she said encouragingly.

Magnus smiled, delighted that he was starting to get the hang of it.

'Now we're going to try passing it to each other whilst moving.'

Amelia once again hit the ball to Magnus. He went to hit it back to her but noticed she'd quickly changed position. Magnus adjusted his line of sight and hit the ball, sending it in the appropriate direction.

'Excellent!' Amelia yelled. 'Now you move.'

Magnus followed her instruction and changed his position as the ball once again was launched in his direction.

The two teens kept bouncing it back and forth whilst continuously changing their position on the court. Magnus was really starting to get into this. He was enjoying himself so much that the fear and anxiety he felt yesterday had become little more than a distant memory. In fact, this was the most fun he could remember ever having in his life.

'Fantastic Magnus! You're a natural,' Amelia complimented him once again. 'Now try and get it past Tom.'

Amelia punched the ball to Magnus, who aimed it at Tom's basket. The ball went flying but was easily intercepted by Tom's bat. Magnus felt a sting of disappointment that he'd missed his chance to score a goal. The ball bounced back to him, and he aimed it at the basket again. Tom's reactions were still too quick for him, and he easily knocked the ball out of harm's way once more.

Magnus was starting to get annoyed with himself. He wanted more than anything to get that ball in the basket but kept repeatedly being thwarted by his superior opponent.

His focus was suddenly broken when the Sanctum doors opened, and Billy stepped into the room. Magnus' heart sank upon seeing the towering teenager wearing the same miserable expression he always had on his face. Amelia stepped in front of Magnus as she shot Billy a contemptuous look. However, Billy just held his hands in the air.

'Before you get your knickers in a twist, I'm not here to cause trouble,' he said unexpectedly. Amelia and Magnus both looked at each other, confused.

'I was told to come down here and let you know that Hunter will be beginning Magnus' training this afternoon. He wants you to meet him on the fourth floor at one o'clock. He also said I should apologise for my behaviour yesterday, so here's my apology, I guess,' he said, predictably disingenuous. His body language and frequent eye rolls made it evident that Billy was doing this against his will, but that didn't bother Magnus. Seeing the intimidating brute that humiliated him yesterday with his tail between his legs filled him with immense satisfaction, and his fear of him was beginning to dwindle dramatically. Billy looked over at Tom, who was trying to conceal a smirk. The angry teen shot him a look of pure loathing before turning around and retreating through the Sanctum doors.

'Well, that was a surprise,' said Amelia, utterly confounded. 'He's never apologised to anyone before, at least not with any witnesses.'

'Hunter must have given him a good bollocking,' said Tom whilst picking up another ball.

'You hear that, Magnus?' said Amelia. 'Hunter's going to start your Shadow Squad training today.'

'Lucky, little sod!' said Tom with an envious snigger.

Magnus was beyond excited. He wondered what his first lesson would be like. Would Hunter have him doing backflips off obstacles? Would he be learning how to dodge laser attacks? Or would he be teaching him how to fight in combat?

The prospect of any of these scenarios was making Magnus salivate, and he was thoroughly enjoying getting lost in each scenario. However, he was suddenly knocked back to reality when a ball bounced against his head.

'Ouch,' he said with surprise.

'Come on,' said Amelia, reaching for another ball, 'let's focus on the job in hand, shall we?'

CHAPTER 12

TRAINING BEGINS

After several hours of playing Battleball with Amelia and Tom, Magnus had to stop due to a burning sensation in his stomach. This was his first time experiencing indigestion, and Tom suggested that next time, he wait at least an hour after eating before doing any strenuous exercise. Tom continued his batting practice in the Sanctum, and Amelia and Magnus spent the rest of the morning in the Great Hall, chatting and getting to know one another.

'So you were locked away when you were a baby, and you don't even know the reason?' asked Amelia, utterly confounded.

Magnus shrugged his shoulders.

'I suppose whoever is responsible felt I didn't belong in society,' he replied apathetically.

'It must have been so lonely for you.'

'Not really; I had Andro for company. Besides, the loneliness I can handle. It's people staring at me and talking behind my back that I have trouble dealing with.'

Magnus looked around the hall and noticed Gerald stealing glances at him whilst playing some kind of card game with a group of older gentlemen.

'Oh, just ignore them. People who talk about others only do so because their lives aren't interesting enough to begin with. Consider yourself lucky you're not as boring as those sad old gits.'

Magnus laughed. He admired Amelia's resilience and carefree attitude.

'Did you never want to use your powers to try and escape?' She asked inquisitively.

Magnus shook his head.

'I didn't even know I had these powers until I came here.'

'Whoa, really? That's insane! So this has been an interesting few days for you then.'

'You could say that,' Magnus replied with a chuckle.

All of a sudden, an alarm started ringing in the Great Hall. This alarm was different to the one that went off yesterday. It was much lower pitched and not as deafening. Magnus turned to Amelia, who had her head down, looking at the ground.

'What's this alarm for then?'

'Shhh!' said Amelia putting her finger to her lips.

Magnus suddenly realised the whole room had gone completely silent as if someone had just pressed the mute button on the entire base. He gazed around and saw Gerald was still glaring in his direction. He quickly turned his attention back to Amelia and noticed she had tears welling up in her eyes.

After a minute of complete silence, the alarm went off once again, and the crowd noise returned to normal.

'Are you okay, Amelia?' asked Magnus cautiously.

'I'm fine,' she replied, wiping away her tears.

'What was that about then?'

'Every so often, they do a minutes silence to honour those who have passed on. It always makes me feel a bit emotional.'

Magnus was relieved the tears had stopped. He didn't enjoy seeing his friend upset in this way. He looked down at Amelia's multi-coloured jumper with the big yellow face smiling up at him. There was something bugging him about it.

'Can I ask you a question?' he asked coyly.

'Of course, fire away.'

'Why do you wear a jumper that's several sizes too big for you?'

Amelia looked down and smiled as if recalling a happy memory.

'It was my mother's,' she responded. 'She used to wear it when I was a baby, and apparently, it always used to make me smile. It's the only thing I have left to remind me of her, so I try to wear it as often as I can.'

'If you don't mind me asking, what happened to her?' asked Magnus curiously.

Amelia took a moment before answering.

'She was taken by Arcadian soldiers when I was ten. Every couple of years, the government creates a new vaccine to test on participants picked at random. My mother was one of the unlucky ones who got picked. She was taken from our home in the middle of the night by the soldiers, and we've never seen her again since,' said Amelia, pensively.

'Do you think she's still alive?' asked Magnus, deeply invested in her story.

'Sometimes I do. Some days I imagine that she escaped and is out there on the streets searching for us. I've always been pretty optimistic about this sort of thing, but I try not to mention anything like that in front of my dad or brother. They've pretty much given up hope they'll ever see her again.'

An awkward silence fell upon their table. This was clearly a very difficult topic for Amelia to talk about, and Magnus was struggling to find any words of comfort for her. However, the silence was broken by the sound of a bell coming from the buffet line. Amelia perked up all of a sudden.

'Ooh, lunchtime!' she said excitedly.

They both got up out of their chairs and joined the queue for lunch. Magnus was delighted when he got to the front and saw the same delicious soup on offer from yesterday. He filled his bowl to the brim, grabbed several breaded buns and promptly returned to the dining table, eager to fill his belly. He wasted no time before plunging straight into his delectable food. Amelia began laughing at the speed with which her friend was eating.

'Slow down; you'll give yourself indigestion again if you're not careful,'

Magnus begrudgingly decelerated the rate he was ingesting his food. He definitely didn't want to feel that burning sensation again.

He looked over at Amelia, who seemed to be staring at him, deep in thought. He removed the metal spoon from his soup-covered lips and placed it back in the bowl.

'What?' he asked bluntly.

'Oh nothing,' she replied hesitantly. 'There's just one thing I'm struggling to make sense of.'

'Just one thing?' Magnus joked. 'What's that then?'

'If you never knew who your parents were, where did the name Magnus Powell come from?'

Magnus shrugged his shoulders again.

'This is a question I've asked Andro a million times. Unfortunately, he can't recall. It was simply programmed into him to call me that name.'

'How strange. Your past is fascinating. It's so shrouded in mystery,' she said, looking at him with sheer enchantment, 'I don't think I'd be able to cope, not knowing the truth about myself. I think my head would probably explode.'

'It did use to bother me; I have to admit. I had so many questions about where I came from and the purpose of my existence, and it bugged me that Andro couldn't enlighten me with any of it. But over the years, I just taught myself to stop thinking about it. No point in worrying about something nobody can explain.'

Amelia nodded.

'Very true.'

'I tell you what has been bothering me since I arrived here, though....'

Magnus looked around to check no one was listening and leaned in closer to Amelia.

'What's happening on the bottom floor?' he asked in a whisper.

'What do you mean?' Amelia replied with a puzzled look.

'I heard some loud noises coming from down there this morning, and I think I definitely heard the sound of someone singing.'

This made Amelia laugh.

'Well, as far as I am aware, only Hunter has a key for that floor, and he doesn't strike me as the singing type. Are you sure you didn't hear someone next door to you? Maybe it was Gerald singing in his sleep,' she said with a chuckle.

Magnus shook his head.

'No, it was definitely coming from downstairs. I wonder what's down there,' he said, drifting off into his own thoughts.

'I wouldn't worry about it, Magnus,' said Amelia. 'If there was anything strange happening in the Underworld, I'm sure someone would know about it by now.'

Amelia looked up at the clock. It was three minutes to one.

'Magnus,' she said urgently, 'you'd better start making your way to the training arena. Hunter won't be best pleased if you're late for your first lesson.'

Magnus couldn't believe that was the time already. He and Amelia had been chatting for so long he'd forgotten all about his training lesson. He quickly wolfed down the last few bites of his lunch and got up from the table.

'Thanks, Amelia. I'll see you later,' he said, putting his bowl in the water bucket.

'Good luck,' Amelia replied, sticking her thumbs up as Magnus dashed towards the elevator.

As he pressed the button for the fourth floor, he suddenly felt very nervous. He had no idea what Hunter had in store for their first lesson together, but he knew it was probably going to be pretty tough. He took a deep inhalation of air and relaxed his body as the elevator ground to a halt on the fourth floor.

Magnus could see Hunter kneeling down with his eyes closed in the centre of the empty training room. He seemed to be in some sort of meditative trance. Magnus stepped into the room, and Hunter's eyes suddenly sprung open.

'Magnus. Thank you for being on time. I've been very much looking forward to this,' Hunter said, jumping to his feet.

'Me too,' Magnus replied, gazing around the empty room. 'Where are the others?' he asked, expecting to see the rest of the Shadow Squad.

'It's just going to be us two for the time being,' Hunter replied.

Magnus felt somewhat disheartened. He was hoping he'd get a chance to see Kayla, Max and the rest of the gang in action once again.

'Like I said yesterday, your training is going to be different to anything you've seen before in this place. In fact, it's new territory for me as well. Your powers will require special attention if you're going to learn how to control them properly. This is what we'll be focusing on for the foreseeable future,' said Hunter as straightforwardly as he could. 'Let's get started.'

Hunter opened a large blue sack and pulled out several balls of varying sizes. He carefully placed each ball on the ground in front of him and discarded the empty sack.

'Your powers are incredibly volatile at this stage, Magnus, and you need to learn how to vary your application of telekinetic force. The reason everything keeps exploding around you is that you're applying too much pressure to items that can't handle the strain. The more you practice lifting objects of different sizes and weights, the more your concentration and control should improve, hopefully resulting in fewer explosions.'

Magnus nodded in comprehension. He definitely wanted the unexpected combusting to stop, but he wasn't sure this method was going to work, considering it was completely new territory. Did Hunter really know what he was doing?

'First things first, as members of the Shadow Squad, we pride ourselves in showing each and every human being the utmost respect and humility. We show this by taking a knee and bowing our heads to one another before each and every training session.'

Hunter demonstrated by bending down on one knee, bowing his head and placing his right fist down on the ground. Magnus remembered how Hunter had done this the first night they met in his prison cell. He repeated the gesture, and Hunter rose to his feet.

'Good. Now we can officially begin. Stand up straight.'

Magnus rose to his feet and faced his mentor, awaiting further direction.

'Right then, I want you to relax your body and close your eyes.'

Magnus promptly did as he was instructed.

'Try to feel the presence of these balls lined up in a row in front of you.'

Magnus wasn't quite sure how he was supposed to feel the presence of something with his eyes closed, but he tried his best to relax his mind and concentrate hard. Suddenly, he was beginning to see patches of light that looked like waves pulsating around the room. He saw the outline of Hunter's body in the centre of his vision, and he could also see the balls lined up in front of him.

'Can you feel them?' asked Hunter.

'Yes,' Magnus replied with surprise, 'yes, I can feel them.'

'Good. Now, I want you to try and lift the third ball from the left using only your mind. Concentrate hard.'

Magnus held out his hand and focused all his attention on the ball positioned third from the left. It instantly flew up into the air and hit Hunter square in the face. Magnus opened his eyes to see his mentor rubbing his forehead, looking slightly off-balance.

'Oops, sorry, Hunter,' said Magnus with a panicked expression on his face.

'It's fine, Magnus.' Hunter took a deep breath. 'Try again, this time, apply less pressure to the ball farthest right.'

Magnus closed his eyes and focused his attention on the far right ball. This was a much smaller ball than the others and seemed to be made of very thin plastic. He held out his hand, and the ball began to move. However, it didn't get far before it started to crumple up into a much smaller ball and fell to the floor. Magnus opened his eyes again and sighed with frustration.

'It's okay. This is what we're here for,' said Hunter trying to console the teenager, 'this time, I want you to focus on the ball furthest left.'

This ball was much bigger than the rest and seemed to be made from very thick, heavy plastic. Magnus closed his eyes, reached out his hand, and the ball began to rise from the ground. This one rose much more steadily than the other two and, to Hunter's delight, seemed to be maintaining its shape.

'Excellent, Magnus!' Hunter exclaimed.

Magnus opened his eyes to see the ball floating steadily in front of him. He laughed excitedly.

'Now keep it steady in that position. I want you to lift this ball at the same time and bring it up to eye level.'

Hunter pointed to a smaller rubber ball on the ground.

Magnus stuck out his other arm whilst still concentrating on the floating plastic ball, and the rubber ball began to lift also, joining the plastic one at head height.

'Fantastic. Well done.' Hunter applauded. However, Magnus was starting to lose control over the heavier plastic ball, and it began to drop rapidly. It hit the ground with a thud, and the shock made Magnus exert too much strength on the rubber ball, which resulted in another unexpected explosion.

Magnus fell to the floor out of breath. Hunter knelt down next to him.

'Easy now, you're okay. Let's have a short break,' Hunter said as he opened a bottle of water and passed it to Magnus.

The teenager suddenly realised how dry his throat felt. It was as if someone had put a vacuum in his mouth and sucked all the moisture out. Magnus thought this was very strange indeed, considering he hadn't felt thirsty a few minutes ago. He started to chug rapidly from the water bottle in order to rejuvenate his body.

'Using your powers requires a lot of physical and mental strength and will make you feel dehydrated a lot of the time. It helps to always have a bottle of water nearby in case you start to feel lightheaded,' Hunter explained.

Magnus pried the bottle from his lips and gave himself a second to get his breath back.

'I'm sorry about the balls I ruined,' said the teenager, feeling rather guilty about the damage he was doing to Hunter's property.

'There's no need to apologise about that, Magnus. You're doing brilliantly. In fact, you're already doing much better than I had anticipated,' Hunter said, sounding pleasantly surprised.

Magnus thought he couldn't have expected much from him if that was the case. He took one last swig of water and jumped back up to his feet.

'Are you sure you're ready to carry on?' asked Hunter.

'Absolutely!' Magnus replied with complete conviction.

'Okay then. This time, I'm going to throw the ball in the air, and you're going to stop it before it hits the ground. Ready?'

Magnus nodded. Hunter picked up the large plastic ball and threw it high into the air. Magnus held out his hand and stopped the ball as it dropped.

'Well done,' said Hunter as he picked up another ball, 'Now I'm going to throw this ball in the air, and I want you to catch it mid-air whilst lowering the other one to the ground.'

Magnus nodded. Hunter threw the ball into the air, and Magnus held out his hand to catch the ball whilst lowering the other. The plastic ball reached the ground much more gently than last time; however, Magnus was struggling to concentrate on two things at once. The ball, which was suspended in the air, crumpled under the excessive force and fell to the ground.

'Oh, it's useless. I can't do it!' Magnus exclaimed angrily. He was absolutely furious with himself.

'Magnus, it's okay,' said Hunter. 'Look, this is your first lesson. You're bound to make mistakes, and that's a good thing. It's the only way to progress.'

Magnus shook his head and took another swig of water.

'Can I ask you a question?' asked the teenager, breathing heavily.

'Of course.' Hunter replied.

'How do you know this is going to work? You said, yourself, this is new territory. What if I never get a grip of these powers?'

Hunter looked down at the ground as he gathered his thoughts.

'I'll tell you a story, Magnus. My father was once friends with a man who had similar powers to yours. Like you, this man was terrified of the sort of damage he could do with a single flick of his finger. My father worked with him for many years perfecting techniques that would help him learn how to focus and control his powers, and once he did, he was able to do some truly incredible things. But it took a lot of hard work and perseverance to get to that stage. We're only on the first lesson, but we have the benefit of my father's example to learn from. Which reminds me....'

Hunter turned and started walking over to a large closet.

Magnus stewed over what Hunter had just told him. The knowledge that there was someone with powers like him filled him with unmitigated intrigue.

'What happened to him?' asked Magnus, but Hunter didn't respond. He was too busy rifling through the cupboard, searching for something.

'Ah, hah. Here it is,' Hunter said as he pulled out what looked like another small plastic ball. Magnus looked at it, slightly underwhelmed.

'It's a ball,' said Magnus, shrugging his shoulders.

'You should never judge something by its appearance,' said Hunter as he pressed a button on the side of the ball, and it sprang to life. It started whizzing around the room like some sort of demented hummingbird.

'This is Flip. He's a little robot my father designed to help test reflexes. If you're able to catch him using your powers, then you'll be doing very well indeed.'

Magnus' eyes were darting all around the room, trying to keep track of this little robot that was travelling extremely fast. He threw out his hand to try and stop it in mid-air, but it moved out the way, and the force he had applied ended up knocking over a weapons stand. He tried again, but this time he flipped a table upside down. The robot was simply too quick for him, and Magnus was beginning to get extremely frustrated with it. Before he could do any more damage, however, Hunter put on an electrically charged glove and held his hand out. Within seconds Flip had returned to the glove and powered down.

'Pretty mega, isn't he?' said Hunter.

'He's pretty annoying!' Magnus replied, out of breath.

'Well, you'd better get used to him. He's going to be your homework assignment.'

Magnus looked confused.

'What do you mean?'

'I want you to take this back to your room and practice trying to capture him using your powers.'

Hunter threw Flip into the air, and Magnus caught him. The teenager didn't seem too thrilled with this idea.

'You want me to take this back to my room?' he said incredulously.

'Exactly. A small, enclosed space will make it much easier for you to focus on him properly. Also, there's less chance of you breaking anything in your room, except maybe Andro,' Hunter said with a chuckle. 'Come on, let's carry on with the ball exercises.'

Two hours went by before Hunter finally called time on their lesson. He was impressed that Magnus had started to show considerable progress with his ball control after only one lesson, though his powers started to wane as he became increasingly exhausted.

'We'll continue this tomorrow, Magnus. In the meantime, I suggest you go to your room and practice as much as you can with Flip. Make sure you take plenty of water with you,' said Hunter.

Magnus picked up Flip along with his electronic glove and made his way back to his room. As he was walking down the corridor on the first floor, he started to feel excited to tell Andro all about the progress he'd made today. The second he entered his room, he turned Andro on, and the robot vaulted off his docking station.

'Good morning, Magnus; I hope you had a good night's rest,' he said, outstretching his arms.

'Hey, buddy. Actually, it's the middle of the afternoon,' Magnus replied.

'What?'

Andro checked his built-in clock.

'You're right. What happened?'

'I wanted to see how I'd do by myself for a while,' said Magnus. 'I played Battleball with Amelia and Tom this morning, and I've just come back from my first training session with Hunter this afternoon.'

Magnus pulled out Flip from his pocket.

'Look what I can do.'

He let go of the tiny robot, but it stayed levitating in the air. Magnus began moving his hand around, and the small sphere hovered slowly around the room like a hot air balloon.

Andro looked on in awe of what his friend had achieved after only his first lesson, though he couldn't shake off a feeling of sadness that he hadn't been awake to see it.

'It's mega, isn't it?' said Magnus.

'Mega?' Andro repeated, sounding a tad confused. He'd never heard Magnus use that expression before.

'Yeah. I've heard people say that a few times in here. I think it means good?' said Magnus, slightly unsure of himself.

Flip flew back to his hand.

'Hunter says I've got to practice with it turned on.'

Andro looked at him, puzzled.

'What do you mean turned on?'

Magnus pushed the button on the side, and Flip immediately sprung to life and started darting around the room like an out of control firework.

'Hunter says this will help me focus the precision of my powers,' said Magnus.

Flip started spinning around Andro incredibly fast until he was nothing more than a blur. He was starting to make Andro feel extremely dizzy.

'I think it's more likely to induce a migraine,' said Andro, who seemed distinctly unimpressed.

Magnus put the electronic glove on, and Flip zipped back to his hand.

'I think I need to sit down,' said Andro, looking noticeably off balance. He perched himself on his docking station and observed Magnus playing with his new toy. The robot had to admit; he felt a twinge of jealousy.

CHAPTER 13

THE UNDERWORLD

After a couple of rather intense opening days at Ground Zero, Magnus slowly started to settle quite comfortably into his new home. Weeks passed into months in the underground base, and he was beginning to really find his feet, especially in the sports department. Having practised playing Battleball every morning with Amelia and Tom, Magnus was turning into quite the talented striker. He won his first official tournament after scoring five goals in a row against the red team. Billy predictably protested the win by once again accusing Magnus of cheating, but as usual, nobody paid him much attention.

As well as playing sports Magnus also had taken a liking to a card game that was popular with the adults of Ground Zero called 'Arcadian Deception'. The game involved two players or more, and each player is dealt seven cards each, with numerous Arcadian themed characters on the front. The aim of the game is to take bets on which player you think has the best hand based on questions asked by your opponents and trying to get a read of their reactions. Cards can be sacrificed and replaced with better cards from the pack, but this can reveal key information about your hand to your opponents. The winner is the one with all the tokens at the end of the match. Magnus enjoyed this game because he liked learning how to read people's microexpressions and how to conceal his own emotions in order to bluff. He felt that this would be a great advantage to win card games and help him take control of his powers in the future.

As time went on, Magnus had begun slowly distancing himself from Andro by allowing other children to play with him throughout the day. He had realised for some time now that he was probably getting too old to need his robot around all the time, and he was more than happy for other kids to make good use of Andro while he hung out with his friends.

For the first time in his life, Magnus felt like he belonged to a family, and he couldn't have been happier about it. He still experienced the occasional detestable stare from the likes of Gerald from time to time, but he learnt not to pay any attention to it. He had made enough friends that he could rely upon to stick up for him if anything got heated.

His training with Hunter was also starting to improve. He was now able to control multiple balls at once without crushing or breaking anything, and his concentration and focus had improved dramatically. However, he was still having issues with Flip. No matter how hard he tried, he simply couldn't keep up with that pesky little robot.

'Why doesn't this thing have a beginner's setting?' he asked Amelia one late evening in his bedroom. His increasing frustration at being thwarted by Flip was starting to amuse her.

'Maybe it's to prevent you from getting complacent,' she suggested, 'if it was easy, you probably wouldn't bother practising with it.'

'You'd think it would run out of energy at some point. But it doesn't; it just keeps going and going,' said Magnus belligerently.

He finally decided enough was enough. He put the electric glove on and apprehended the flying orb before it started to give him a headache.

'I'm sure you'll get the hang of it eventually,' she said, trying her best to sound encouraging.

Magnus had started inviting Amelia back to his room more regularly of late. He would do his practice with Flip while Amelia did her favourite activity in the whole world - talking. They would chat for hours into the evening about every topic under the sun; movies, music, history, Gerald's repugnant body odour, and Magnus had to admit that he was really starting to enjoy her company since she stopped being so intense with him.

'How are your lessons with Hunter going?' asked Amelia.

'Pretty good, although he didn't show up today for some reason. I waited for him for twenty minutes. It must have slipped his mind.'

'How odd,' replied Amelia, 'come to think of it, I've not seen him all day either. Sounds like he's gone AWOL.'

Magnus shrugged his shoulders. He'd been working flat out for the past few months and felt they both probably deserved a day off. Amelia looked over at Andro's empty docking station.

'Speaking of going AWOL, where's Andro tonight?' she asked, sounding slightly boggled.

'I lent him to Sam for the day. He should keep him occupied for quite a while,' Magnus replied with a wry smile.

'I might have known. Every time I see that boy, he's got Andro stuck to his head. He's obsessed.'

'Yeah, well, I'm just glad someone's making good use of him.'

Suddenly the door swung open dramatically, almost coming off its hinges. Andro flew inside and quickly shut the door behind him in a panic.

'Andro?' Amelia said in startled surprise. 'We were just talking about you. Is everything okay?'

'It's that boy, Sam. He won't leave me alone. He's absolutely addicted to that Sheep Tossing game, despite the fact he's completed it five times. I don't think I can take much more of him,' said the robot, shaking his head in desperation.

Magnus simply laughed. He found it amusing that his robot was finally getting a taste of his own medicine.

'I managed to distract him with a game of hide and seek, but that won't keep him at bay for very long. There are only so many places to hide in Ground Zero, and it's only a matter of time before he comes looking for me in here. You guys have to help me.'

'What do you want us to do about it?' asked Magnus, trying to hide a smirk.

'I don't know. Tell him he can't play with me any longer. Tell him I'm faulty or something. Anything! Amelia, he'll listen to you.'

'Don't get me involved in this.'

Amelia held her hands up evasively. The last thing she wanted was to get sucked into Andro's drama.

Suddenly there was a knock on the door, which made Andro jump out of his plastic skin.

'It's him!' He cried and automatically flew under the bed.

Magnus rolled his eyes and stood up to answer the door. He opened it halfway and saw Sam's innocent little face looking straight up at him.

'Hey, Sam,' said Magnus, trying to act surprised, 'how's it going?'

'Pretty good,' the boy replied casually, 'have you seen Andro?'

It was clear he was trying to get a better look inside the room, but Magnus stepped in the way of his view.

'No, I haven't seen him; I thought he was with you,' said Magnus, choosing to play dumb.

'We're playing a game of hide and seek. Can I come in and look for him?'

He stepped forward, but Magnus cut him off.

'Not at the moment, Sam, Amelia and I are hanging out in here right now.'

He opened the door to show Amelia sitting on the chair next to his bed. She waved at him jovially.

'Hi, Amelia,' said Sam waving back to her.

'Why don't you have a look for him in the kitchen? There's plenty of great hiding places down there; I'm sure he'll be in one of those,' said Magnus, hoping the ten-year-old boy would take the bait and leave them alone.

'I never even thought of looking there. Thanks, Magnus,' Sam replied with youthful excitement.

'No problem.'

Without hesitation, Sam took off down the corridor towards the elevator, and Magnus closed his door.

Realising the coast was clear, Andro finally crawled out from under the bed. Magnus and Amelia instantly burst out laughing.

'Thanks,' said Andro sarcastically, 'now he's never going to stop looking for me. You couldn't have just told him I was broken or something.'

'Look, if you're too scared to tell him to leave you alone, then that's your problem. Don't drag us down with you,' said Magnus in a reprimanding tone.

Amelia chuckled under her breath. She was surprisingly impressed by Magnus' confidence to stick up for himself when speaking to his robot. It was a side of him she didn't get to see too often, and it was clear that Andro was the only one he truly felt comfortable speaking his mind with.

Andro sighed and flew over to his docking station.

'I need to charge my battery. I've been running on reserved power for the past hour and a half,' said the robot as he plugged himself in, 'let me know if he comes back, won't you?'

'Sure thing,' Magnus replied as Andro closed his eyes and powered down.

Amelia smiled at the sleeping robot.

'He is too adorable.'

'If you say so.'

Magnus raised one of his eyebrows as he walked over and sat on his bed.

An awkward silence suddenly swallowed the room. Magnus looked at Amelia, and he could tell she wanted to say something to him but was hesitant to do so.

'Is everything okay?' he asked cautiously.

'Oh yeah... everything's fine,' she said flippantly. Though Magnus could tell, she seemed nervous about something as her left eye began to twitch.

'There was something I wanted to ask you, actually,' she said, avoiding looking at him directly.

'Okay,' Magnus replied, bracing himself for whatever was coming.

Within an instant, however, her expression changed from nervousness to utter bafflement.

'Can you hear that?' she asked, looking around the room.

'Hear what?'

'That rumbling sound.'

She got on her hands and knees and pressed her ear to the floor.

'It's coming from downstairs,' she said in a bewildered tone.

'Oh, that. I hear that pretty much every night,' said Magnus.

Amelia listened as hard as she could. Over the rumbling sound of heavy machinery, she could hear the distant cries of a man wailing in agony. Amelia sprung from the ground as if she'd just been shocked back to life.

'There's someone down there,' she said, distinctly perturbed.

'See, I told you so,' replied Magnus.

'I can't believe it. I thought you'd just imagined it, but there is definitely someone down there. They sound like they're in terrible distress.'

Magnus fought the temptation to roll his eyes. He'd told Amelia about these strange noises months ago, but she didn't pay him any attention at the time.

'We have to go down there,' said Amelia.

'What are you talking about?'

'Whoever is down there sounds like he's in desperate need of some help. Just listen to those cries.'

'Amelia, we're not allowed to go down there, remember? Hunter would go mental if he found out we were even thinking about it,' Magnus protested, but he could tell it was falling on deaf ears. Amelia got up from her seat and started searching around the room.

'What are you looking for?'

'I need something small and sharp, like a pin,' she said, rummaging under his bed.

'What for?'

'To pick a lock.'

Magnus looked at her in shocked bafflement.

'You know how to pick a lock?' he asked incredulously.

'Well, no, but how hard can it be?'

She suddenly stopped and looked over at Andro.

'Amelia, I really don't think this is a good idea,' said Magnus, but once again, she wasn't listening. She'd already started unhooking Andro from his docking station. Andro's eyes blinked on, and he seemed distinctly discombobulated.

'Is it morning already?' asked the robot, rather hazily.

Amelia picked him up and went to open the door.

'Amelia, stop!' said Magnus in a stern voice.

She turned to look at him.

'Someone needs our help, Magnus. Come on; you know you want to find out who's down there just as much as I do.'

She opened the door and walked through it, carrying Andro in her arms.

Magnus shook his head. He hated to admit it, but Amelia was right; he did want to find out who was down there causing all that noise. He'd wanted to find out for months, but he didn't want to do so against Hunter's wishes. The boy was terribly conflicted about what he was going to do. Eventually, his curiosity was too strong to ignore, and he reluctantly got up from his bed and followed his friends down the corridor.

'What's happening? Where are we going?' asked Andro, with increasing concern. 'You're not taking me to play with Sam again, are you?'

'No, nothing like that, Andro,' said Amelia as she pressed the button for the elevator. Magnus caught up to them as the newly repaired elevator doors opened in front of them. They both stepped in, and Amelia pressed the button with the letter U on it.

Andro threw her a puzzled look.

'Amelia, I think you pressed the wrong button,' he said as the elevator began its descent.

'We're heading to the ground floor, Andro,' she replied unflinchingly.

'What?' the robot exclaimed. 'But it's off-limits!'

The elevator ground to a halt, and the doors opened to reveal another steel door blocking their pathway.

'Is this the door that requires Hunter's key?' asked Magnus.

'It must be,' replied Amelia.

Magnus felt a rush of adrenaline pass through his body. The excitement of breaking the rules combined with the fear of getting caught made his heart flutter with palpable exhilaration. Amelia, on the other hand, seemed unusually calm and focused on the job at hand. She opened a compartment on Andro's left side and fished out his thin, metal arm.

'What are you doing now?' the robot asked, but he got no response.

She inserted two of Andro's fingers into the lock and began jerking them around inside.

'I'm quite sure this is not what I was designed for Amelia,' said Andro indignantly.

'Shush, Andro,' said Magnus, fearing the robot might alert someone above to their presence.

Suddenly they heard another agonising cry from the other side of the door. This one echoed through the walls and sent a cold shiver down Magnus' spine.

'Hurry up,' he said impatiently.

'That's not helping,' Amelia responded with obvious frustration.

Time was running out for the teens to open this door. Magnus knew that any second, someone could push the button for the elevator, and both teenagers would be forced to explain what they were doing in the Underworld. Magnus closed his eyes and scanned the door. He suddenly realised that he could sense a latch on the other side of it. He extended his hand out in front of him, and the latch instantly unhinged. The door slowly creaked open to reveal a long, dark tunnel. Amelia looked at Magnus and smiled.

'That's one way of breaking in, I guess. Come on.'

She immediately stepped through the door into the darkness. Magnus and Andro followed apprehensively. Their footsteps echoed all around them, and at the end of the tunnel, they could see a shimmering orange light emanating from the gap of a half-open door. Magnus' heart was pumping rapidly in his chest as they edged ever closer. They finally reached the open door and stuck their heads through the gap to have a look inside.

The shimmering light was sufficiently blinding, and Magnus had to put a hand over his eyes to prevent doing permanent damage to his retinas. He apprehensively stepped into the room, and a drone flew right over his head. It noticed Magnus immediately and activated a high pitched, screeching alarm. Andro jumped in terror and flew behind a large machine whilst Magnus and Amelia both froze in place.

Suddenly the shimmering light disappeared, and Magnus removed his hand from his eyes.

The room was larger than he expected, but it was filled to the brim with gigantic rumbling machinery spread across numerous workstations. The walls were covered in shelves full of a variety of different weapons, gadgets and gizmos, and several drones could be seen flying around, carrying out numerous workmanlike tasks.

In the centre of the room, Magnus could see a man with long, bushy grey hair; he was sitting on a stool and holding a blowtorch. He was facing away from them and wearing a large metal face visor and black safety gloves. Behind him were five monitors, each showing security footage from various floors in Ground Zero.

The old man turned in his chair and looked over at Magnus and Amelia, who were still standing at the entrance like ice sculptures. He took out a small remote from his pocket and aimed it at the screeching drone, which went silent within an instant.

'I wondered when I'd get a visit from you,' the man said in a raspy, weathered voice. 'My God, you look just like him.'

'*I look just like who?*' Magnus asked himself as he became overwhelmed with a feeling of unease.

The man stood up from his stool and took off his visor, revealing an old, wrinkled face and long, scraggly grey beard. He had a black patch over his right eye, and his left eye was red and puffy. It was clear the old man had been crying.

'Welcome to the Underworld,' he said, surprisingly joyful. 'I must admit I wasn't expecting to meet you this late at night. Who's your lady friend?'

'My name's Amelia,' she responded after a briefly hesitant pause.

'How did you two get in here? I don't believe Hunter will have given you the key.'

Neither teenager responded. They simply looked at each other rather guiltily.

'You must have used your powers. Did you, Magnus? I'll have to make my locks more secure in future,' the man said with a knowing smile.

'We heard someone crying,' said Amelia.

'Ah, sorry about that,' said the old man. 'Sometimes, I forget I'm not alone in this place. Today happens to be the fifteenth anniversary of my wife's passing. I'm feeling rather fragile.'

'I'm sorry to hear that,' replied Amelia, sympathetically, 'Magnus said he hears singing some nights too.'

'Yep, that's me as well,' he admitted with a look of mild self-consciousness, 'I wrote a song for my wife in the early days of our courtship. When I sing it, it reminds me of how beautiful she was.'

Amelia looked at him, completely mesmerised. That was the most romantic thing she'd ever heard in her life. She was a sucker for passionate displays of affection such as this.

'Excuse me, sir,' Magnus said in a faint whisper, 'who...who are you?'

'You're going to have to speak up, boy. I'm afraid my ears aren't what they used to be.'

'WHO ARE YOU?' Magnus repeated, this time far too loud.

'Alright, I didn't say I was deaf,' he said jokingly.

Magnus looked away in embarrassment.

'My name is Jethro. I'm the founder and engineer of this base,' he replied.

Magnus and Amelia's eyes grew wide.

'You founded Ground Zero?' said Amelia, incredulously.

'Indeed I did, Miss, back in the days when I was young and handsome!'

'Are you... Hunter's father?' asked Magnus.

'That's me. Though you'd never have guessed I even had a son the amount he comes to visit.'

Jethro suddenly noticed something poking its head out from behind a nearby machine.

'Is that Andro I see before me?' he exclaimed excitedly.

'Jethro?' the robot replied with immense surprise. He suddenly shot out from behind the machine and flew directly into the old man's arms. Jethro started laughing joyfully as the robot swung his metal arms around him in a warm embrace. Magnus and Amelia looked at each other, utterly dumbfounded. The old man and the robot were acting as if they were the best of friends.

'You've not changed a bit, little buddy,' said Jethro.

'I wish I could say the same thing about you. Where did all this hair come from?' Andro retorted, making Jethro laugh even harder.

Magnus cleared his throat rather audibly, and the hysterics promptly subsided.

'Sorry to interrupt, but what's going on here?' asked Magnus, entirely confused.

'Andro and I go way back. He is, hands down, the best robot I ever created,' Jethro said with exuberant conviction.

Magnus looked even more baffled.

'You created him?' he repeated in disbelief.

'Yes, and I've been trying to replicate him ever since. Unfortunately, these Arcadian drones are a far cry from the sorts of machines I used to make. These days they're fitted with low personality chips, which don't give you a lot to work with when it comes to reprogramming them. Nope, Andro is one of a kind.' Jethro said with a proud smile.

Magnus couldn't believe what he was hearing. How could this man have invented the robot who raised him for fifteen years? He was really struggling to put the pieces together in his head.

'What is this place?' asked Amelia as she glanced around the room in awe.

'This is my sanctuary. It's where I build all the equipment, weapons, body armour, machinery, anything the Shadow Squad requires to do their job. Honestly, the fun never ends in this place,' Jethro said in jest.

183

'So you just stay locked in here all day long, building things? Don't you ever see anybody?' asked Amelia in a pitying tone of voice.

'Well, I watch people on the monitors as they go about their business, and I make sure everything is running smoothly throughout the base. Plus, my son comes to visit occasionally when I've got a fresh batch of new weapons or equipment for him, but we barely speak anymore. I think deep down he still holds a lot of resentment towards me.'

'That must be hard to deal with,' Amelia said with a sympathetic nod.

'Perhaps I deserve it. I was never the greatest father to him. My life has always been my work,' Jethro said pensively. He sat back against his chair and started tinkering with something metallic on his desk.

'Sorry, I still don't quite understand,' said Magnus, failing to hide his growing impatience. 'If you invented Andro, how did he end up with me in my prison cell?'

Jethro didn't answer straight away, and a silence fell upon the room. The old man took a deep breath; he put down the object he was fiddling with and turned to face Magnus once again.

'Are you sure you want to know the truth, Magnus?' asked Jethro in a much more serious tone.

The boy nodded without hesitation.

'I was the one who locked you away all those years ago.'

- CHAPTER 14 -

ESCAPE

Magnus paused for a moment, unable to comprehend the unexpected bombshell Jethro had just dropped on him.

'What... what do you mean?' he stuttered, desperately trying to get his words out.

'I'm responsible for your confinement at Periculo Prison.'

Jethro took a moment to compose himself before continuing.

'Many years ago, before you were born, I was Arcadia's leading engineer, responsible for the manufacturing of weapons and training soldiers how to use them in combat. I was extremely proficient at my job and well respected among my peers. However, one day I was informed by my commander that a baby had been born with the power to move objects with his mind - a power he shared with Arcadia's omnipotent leader. We all knew that if the Master ever found out about your existence, he would exploit your skills to start another war in order to grow his dominance overseas. I wasn't prepared to let that happen. So, my Commander and I agreed it was best for everyone's safety to lock you away, somewhere no one would think to look for you; until the time was right for you to be free to live among us in peace.'

Jethro was explaining as if reading from a script. It was clear he'd spent a lot of time rehearsing this speech.

Magnus was zoned in on Jethro's story and completely ignorant that his heartbeat had started to race again uncontrollably.

'That was the plan anyway. Everything was set up perfectly. I left Arcadia in the dead of night fifteen years ago, delivered you to the prison and set up Andro to look after you. I installed an immobiliser in your cell, which would suppress your powers and prevent you from escaping. You remember that hexagonal shaped box with the blinking green light attached to the ceiling?'

Magnus nodded.

'I originally designed it to use on the Master, but upon my return... well, let's just say things didn't go quite as planned,' said Jethro trying to hide his interminable guilt. 'From that day on, I vowed to do all that was necessary to take back the city I helped build and avenge the death of my beautiful wife, Maria.'

Silence fell upon the room as the two teens stared at the old man in disbelief. Magnus was struggling to put together any of what he'd just been told. He'd waited his whole life for someone to explain to him the reason for his incarceration, but none of this made any sense to him.

'So... you kept me in prison all those years, for what? Until you finally found an appropriate use for me?' Magnus asked, outrage growing in his voice.

'Now calm down, Magnus. Hunter and I wanted to break you out sooner, believe me, but we didn't have the resources or the manpower to do so,' Jethro said defensively. He could see that Magnus was getting increasingly upset.

'I know this is hard to believe right now, Magnus, but every action I took was for your own good and the good of this country. There's no telling the damage that the Master could have inflicted on the world with you in his possession. It would have been carnage on a level we've never encountered before. I don't expect you to forgive me, but I also don't regret my actions,' Jethro stated with unwavering conviction.

Magnus shot the old man a hateful stare as tears began streaming from his eyes. The anger he felt in that moment was beyond anything he had ever experienced in his life, and he was struggling to keep himself together. The room suddenly began shaking violently, and random objects started flying chaotically around the room in all directions. Jethro braced himself as bits of machinery began hurtling towards him at an almighty speed.

'Magnus, stop!' cried Amelia as a power drill flew past her head. 'You have to calm down.'

But he couldn't. Magnus felt betrayed by the people who'd brought him here. Hunter knew about all this from the very beginning. He had ample opportunity to reveal the truth about Magnus' past, but instead, his mentor chose to conceal it in order to nurture a power he could one day exploit for his own means.

Magnus' breathing had become sharp and rapid. His eyes began to bulge in their sockets, and his hands were shaking beyond his control. He needed to get out of there as soon as possible before he did some serious damage. He turned and ran out the door and down the dark tunnel towards the elevator.

'MAGNUS, COME BACK!' Amelia cried hysterically as she turned and ran after him.

He sprinted down the passageway as fast as he could until he reached the elevator. He took a second to make up his mind about which button to press, but he couldn't decide. No matter where he went in Ground Zero, there was nowhere for him to hide. He needed to find a way to escape the base.

'Magnus, where are you going?' cried Amelia.

'I'm getting out of here,' he said whilst pressing the button for the fifth floor. The doors promptly shut before Amelia could catch up, and the elevator began its ascension. Magnus could hear the faint sounds of Amelia's voice shouting his name, but it was too late to turn back now.

Amelia raced back into Jethro's workstation.

'Is there any other way out of here?' she asked urgently, 'I've never seen Magnus this upset. I fear he's going to do something dangerous.'

'There's a secret passage back to the first floor through this door,' said Jethro as he pressed his hand to the wall, and a hidden doorway swung open. 'Hurry. I'll sound the alert.'

Amelia and Andro both shot through the door, and Jethro pressed a button on his desk, setting off a high-pitched alarm in every room in Ground Zero.

Magnus jolted as the deafening siren echoed through the elevator. He knew the alarm was because of him, and he knew it wouldn't be long before the Shadow Squad came after him. He was going to have to act quickly if he was going to make it to the surface.

Amelia and Andro raced to the first floor, and a crowd had started to congregate in the corridor. They seemed totally perplexed about what was happening, as this was clearly a siren they weren't too familiar with. Amelia saw Hunter and Kayla step out of their room with equally puzzled expressions on their faces.

'KAYLA!' Amelia cried out as she frantically pushed her way through the crowd.

'Amelia, what's going on?' Kayla replied with deep concern. She could see the growing fear in Amelia's eyes.

'Magnus and I... well, it's my fault really, but I would never have gone down there if I knew this was going to happen.'

Amelia was stumbling over her words as she tried to explain herself. Kayla grabbed her by the shoulders and held her firmly.

'Amelia, slow down and start from the top. What happened?'

'We heard screaming coming from the Underworld and went to see who was down there. We met Hunter's father, who revealed the truth about Magnus' past.'

Hunter closed his eyes in dismay.

'Where's Magnus now?' he asked urgently.

'He got in the elevator. I think he's going to try and leave the base!' Amelia cried.

'Oh no!' exclaimed Kayla. Hunter instantly turned to address the crowd behind him.

'Shadow Squad, suit up. We need to stop Magnus before he reaches the surface!'

Hunter ran back into his room, grabbed two suits and threw one of them to his wife.

'Wait here, Amelia,' Kayla said as she and Hunter sprinted towards the elevator on the opposite end of the corridor.

Amelia looked at Andro with desperate apprehension as the remaining Shadow Squad members rushed past them with tremendous haste.

Magnus finally reached the top floor of the base, and the doors opened to reveal a long metal bridge surrounded by thick stone walls. On the other side of the bridge was a ladder leading towards the doorway to the streets above. Magnus could see two Shadow Squad members standing guard in front of the ladder. They seemed to be embroiled in some kind of competitive thumb war, which told Magnus that this was most likely the twins Carter and Taylor messing about during their night shift. Carter looked up and noticed Magnus standing in the elevator.

'Magnus? What are you doing up here, little buddy?' he asked as he and his sister broke away from their thumb-wrestling match.

Magnus didn't have time to explain himself. He ran straight onto the bridge, and without warning, hot air instantly shot out from the walls on either side of him.

'Magnus, watch out!' yelled Taylor as the teenager cried out in pain. The burning sensation on his skin was almost unbearable as he tried his best to cover his face and hands. He sprinted as fast as he could to the other side of the bridge, and the air promptly stopped blowing.

'MAGNUS, STOP!' cried Carter as the teenager raised both his hands above his head and the twins lifted weightlessly off the ground. Magnus thrust his hands behind him, and the guards flew straight past him and landed with a thud on the other side of the bridge.

Magnus began climbing the ladder and pressed a button on the wall to his left. The doors on the roof slowly opened up, and air started rushing into the base. Magnus held his breath. He suddenly realised he'd forgotten to put on his mask. But there was no way he could go back for it now. He pulled his sleeve over his nose and mouth and hoisted himself up onto the street above. The door slammed instantly behind him, and Magnus looked out over the empty void in front of him.

The silence was deafening, but it comforted Magnus immensely. This was an ambience that definitely suited him more than the hustle and bustle of Ground Zero. His heart rate began to find a normal rhythm again, and he was finally able to think more rationally. It suddenly dawned on him the gravity of the situation, which in hindsight, he probably should have thought through more carefully. He was stood in the middle of nowhere with no food, shelter or supplies, and he would likely have the Shadow Squad on his tail at any moment. Magnus gave himself a quick second to contemplate his next plan of action. He couldn't turn back, but he wasn't going to get very far without a mask to help him breathe. What was he going to do?

Recognising that he couldn't just keep standing there forever, Magnus started moving forward down the empty street in the hope something would present itself that could assist him.

Suddenly, Magnus stopped in his tracks. A few yards in front of him, he could see a single hovering drone with a blinking red light patrolling the area. Luckily for the teenager, the drone hadn't spotted him yet, and Magnus began backing away slowly, trying his best to make as little noise as possible. He gently turned his body 180 degrees, and all of a sudden, his heart stopped, and his feet froze to the spot.

In front of him was a drone with strikingly similar features to the pesky robot he'd spent the past few weeks trying to pin down in his bedroom. But this one was different to Flip. It looked noticeably menacing with its blinking red light staring the teenager dead in his eye. Before Magnus had time to react, the drone scanned him from head to toe using a bright red laser and sounded a high-pitched alert that echoed through the baron streets surrounding them. Magnus outstretched his hand to apprehend the drone, but it shot up into the sky like a bullet and disappeared from view.

Magnus' heart began racing in his chest again. That siren was bound to have alerted others to his presence. He turned his head and noticed the drone he had tried to avoid earlier had now spotted him and was quickly heading in his direction, followed closely by ten other drones in hot pursuit.

Magnus turned back and started sprinting the opposite way as a huge swarm of flying robots began firing their lasers at him. Magnus thrust his hands out in all directions, causing several drones to explode instantly in the air, but there were too many. He ran as fast as his little legs could carry him, hoping he would be able to find cover of some kind and rob them of their advantage. He glanced behind him and noticed the doors of Ground Zero opening and several members of the Shadow Squad emerging from the underground base. The drones suddenly turned their attention towards the team and began a barrage of laser fire in their direction. They seemed to be holding their own against the attacking machines quite well, but Magnus noticed they were less efficient without the majority of their weapons and gadgets to assist them.

Magnus turned back to face the way he was running and suddenly ground his body to a halt. He looked up to see hundreds of glowing red lights staring at him from the sky above. An army of drones had filled every available space in the sky and instantly began to converge straight towards the frightened teenager. He was entirely surrounded.

With nowhere left to hide, Magnus tried a new manoeuvre. He started levitating the metallic parts of old broken down machines from the corners of the streets around him and fired them at the attacking drones. This knocked several robots out of the sky, but it had little to no effect on the swarm as a whole.

Suddenly a shield came down in front of his face, which deflected any laser fire heading his way. Magnus looked up and instantly recognised the purple lights on their Shadow Squad armour. It was Kayla.

'Magnus!' she cried. 'Put this mask on.'

Kayla handed him a mask she'd grabbed from the inside of her suit, and he immediately applied it to his face.

'You need to come back inside right now.'

Magnus shook his head vigorously.

'It's not safe for you out here. You'll get yourself killed.'

Suddenly Kayla yelped in pain and fell to the ground. A laser blast had hit her in her lower abdomen and burnt a hole in her suit.

'KAYLA!' Magnus cried as his friend began writhing in pain on the floor. He looked around for help, but the drones were increasingly overwhelming the Shadow Squad.

'What have I done?' Magnus thought to himself in utter turmoil.

Suddenly he noticed a Shadow Squad member he'd never seen before emerging from the underground base wearing a crisp white suit and holding a large metal box. They set the box down on the ground, pulled a lever up, and sparks started shooting out in all directions. Within a matter of seconds, every single drone in the near vicinity fell out of the sky as if someone had just pressed the OFF switch.

The team started to regroup and carry each other out of the way of the falling machines.

Hunter looked around and saw Magnus sitting over Kayla, who was holding her abdomen in agony.

'KAYLA?' he cried as he ran over towards them.

'Hunter. I'm... I'm sorry I... I didn't mean for this to happen,' Magnus pleaded with tears streaming down his face.

Hunter didn't respond. He bent down and lifted his wife into his arms and started carrying her back to the base as fast he could. Magnus began sobbing behind his mask. He looked up and noticed the man in the white armour heading towards him and kneeling down to his level.

'You'd better follow us back inside, Magnus, before more drones show up.'

Magnus recognised the voice immediately. It was Jethro, the man he'd met less than an hour ago, the reason he fled the base in the first place. He was definitely the last person Magnus wanted to see at this moment in time.

'I know you don't trust me right now, and I understand why. Please give me a chance to explain things more clearly to you.'

Magnus didn't react. He certainly didn't want to go back down with him, but he also didn't want to wait around for more drones to show up.

'There's nothing for you on these streets, Magnus; trust me, I've looked. If you stay out here, you will almost certainly die,' said Jethro bluntly.

It seemed he had no other option. Magnus reluctantly grabbed Jethro's hand and hoisted himself up to his feet. He had no idea how he was going to face all the people he'd just put in mortal peril. An intense feeling of guilt and regret spread across his body as he followed Jethro back through the doors to Ground Zero. He desperately hoped Kayla could forgive him for what he'd just done.

- CHAPTER 15 -
ASSET FOUND

Tobias had become incredibly despondent after spending the past few months sitting in his office apprehensively waiting for any news regarding the missing Asset. He had told his team not to disturb him under any circumstances until they had conclusive evidence of the boy's whereabouts. Still, so far, there wasn't even a whiff of a sighting despite the dramatic increase in surveillance drones under the Master's request. This relieved Tobias, however. He hated to admit it, but a part of him hoped that something unfortunate had happened to the boy that meant that he would never be found. Just thinking such a thing made the Commander feel sick to his stomach, but he reconciled with himself that the alternative outcome would be infinitely worse for everyone.

The phone calls from his wife Rosa had also increased to the point of absurdity. Every day she would call complaining about the kids and demanding he come home to ease her burden. He made sure Jeffery was on hand to help her whenever she needed it, but it simply wasn't enough. Eventually, Tobias had to resort to killing the electricity to his office. He knew this would eventually come around to bite him in the backside once he was finally able to return home, but he couldn't handle the constant nagging and complaining during this stressful time.

He frequently started to wonder how it had all gotten to this point. Not long ago, he lived the perfect lifestyle with a dream career, a happy family and not a care in the world. Now it had turned into an anxiety-driven nightmare as everything began to crumble around him.

To make matters worse, he was about as close to identifying the traitor in his cabinet as he was to finding the Asset. He'd resorted to treating everyone at the Capitol as a suspect and hoped someone would eventually slip up and reveal himself. But that didn't seem likely.

All he could do was sit in silence and wait for the news he hoped would never come.

There was a sudden and rather loud knock on Tobias' office door late into the evening, which startled him back to life.

'Who is it?' Tobias asked, catching his breath.

'It's Grant.'

Tobias gave a big sigh of relief upon hearing his colleague's voice. Despite his initial suspicions a few months back that he was the traitor, right now, it seemed Grant was the only man in his department Tobias knew he could trust. He straightened his tie and sat up at his desk, trying to look less dishevelled.

'Come in,' he said calmly.

The door opened, and Grant stepped inside rather briskly, holding Braxton's people-scanning drone in his hand. He looked around in surprise upon noticing that none of the lights were on in the office.

'What is it, Grant?' asked Tobias, looking uneasy.

'I tried to call you with the news, but the line was dead.'

'What news?'

'We've found the boy,' Grant replied, getting straight to the point.

Tobias' heart skipped a beat, and he jumped out of his chair. Grant pressed a button on the drone, and a hologram appeared, showing Magnus getting scanned on the London streets.

'This was taken just over an hour ago in the Southern province right outside an old underground military base.'

'Military base?' Tobias repeated, utterly perplexed.

'It was constructed before the war started to be a top-secret training facility for the army. I bet you anything that's where the rebels are hiding him,' said Grant with extreme confidence.

Tobias observed the hologram with a fearful expression.

'The boy's not wearing a mask,' the Commander said in confusion, 'his lungs will have collapsed by now surely.'

Grant could have sworn he detected a hint of wishful thinking in Tobias' tone, but he chose not to question it.

'Well, the drones have searched the streets and found no trace of his body. My guess is they're keeping him hidden underground. We need to send a squadron out to search that base as soon as possible.'

Tobias turned away from Grant to give himself time to think. After months of waiting, they'd finally found the boy's location. But this was not a moment of triumph. The commander's next move would likely result in the start of a new world war more devastating than any that have come before. The conflict inside his mind was becoming too excruciating to bear. It was an impossible decision, and Tobias would have given up everything he owned not to have to be the one to make it.

'Shall I send you the coordinates?' asked Grant, breaking the commander out of his anxiety-induced trance. He couldn't hide from this any longer. It was time to take action.

'Yes, and send them over to Braxton too. Tell him to get his soldiers ready to move within the hour,' Tobias said authoritatively, 'I'll inform the Master that the boy has been found.'

Grant bowed his head and turned to leave, but Tobias stopped him in his tracks.

'Oh, and Grant. Great work!' he said, extending his hand to his second in command. However, Grant didn't return the handshake. He simply gave his boss a nod and turned to leave the office. It was obvious he still hadn't forgiven Tobias for the way he'd treated him last time they spoke. He shut the door behind him, and the office plunged back into darkness.

Tobias took a deep breath as he confronted the idea of visiting the Master face to face. There was no turning back from this now. He tentatively made his way to the elevator and pressed the button for the bottom floor. Sweat started running down Tobias' brow as he began his descent into the Master's chamber. The elevator doors opened to reveal a dimly lit hallway filled with extravagant ornaments positioned all around the room.

Since his rise to power, the Master had been an avid collector of priceless artefacts for many years. If it was made of gold and shimmered under the light, he needed to possess it.

At the far end of the hallway, two Arcadian soldiers stood guard at a large door made of thick steel. Tobias made his way down the hall and nodded to one of them to let him past. The guard pressed a button on the wall, and the door began opening from the centre like the perilous jaws of a great white shark.

The Master's chamber was even darker than the hallway, with only a few dimly lit lamps scattered around the room. As Tobias stepped inside, he passed various glass cages big enough to fit an adult-sized human and little else. These small glass cubicles allowed the Master to carry out his favourite pastime – inflicting pain and torture upon his victims without the inconvenience of having to leave his chamber.

At the far end of the room was a bed that had been lifted vertically and placed against the wall. Tobias could see the Master sleeping upright in the bed with various tubes connecting his body to intricate machines standing on either side of him. His breathing was long and slow and sounded like that of a sleeping dragon guarding a mountain of gold. However, despite the fact he was asleep, he was still wearing his black robe and a mask covering his face.

Tobias cleared his throat, and the Master suddenly woke from his deep slumber. He lifted his head and noticed the commander knelt in front of him, bowing his head.

'Tobias?' he whispered in a slight daze.

'My apologies for waking you, my Lord,' said Tobias, as he slowly rose to his feet.

'Not at all. I'm disappointed you haven't come to visit me sooner.'

'The pursuit of the Asset took longer than expected, my Lord, for which I take full responsibility.'

'I'm not interested in your excuses Commander,' said the Master coldly, 'what news do you bring?'

'We have finally found the Asset's location. The rebels are hiding him in an underground base beneath the Southern province. Our soldiers are ready to be dispatched upon your command.'

'At last,' said the Master with twisted glee, 'go ahead and dispatch your men, and bring the boy back to me alive.'

'Yes, Master,' Tobias replied and immediately turned to leave.

'Not so fast, Commander.'

Tobias promptly stopped in his tracks but continued to face away from his leader.

'I want you to accompany your soldiers on this mission.'

Tobias turned around in shock.

'Me? You want me to leave the city?' He said in an outraged tone. 'Why?'

'Desperate times call for desperate measures, Tobias. I need to know that I can still trust you to lead this city under my rule. What better way could there be for you to prove your loyalty to me?' The Master replied with smug satisfaction.

'But Master, I'm not a soldier. I haven't had sufficient combat or weapons training. If anything, I'm likely to do more harm than good,' Tobias disputed with desperate conviction.

'Nonsense! You're being melodramatic.'

'What about my family? Who's going to guarantee their safety if something goes wrong?'

'No harm will come to your family Tobias; you needn't worry about that.'

Tobias started shaking his head vigorously. He had to find a way out of this situation somehow, and he was rapidly running out of excuses.

'My Lord, I really don't think this is a good idea....'

'ENOUGH!' The Master barked forcefully as the lights around the room began to shimmer and the walls started to shake. Tobias went silent and dropped his head like a frightened animal.

'You're not getting out of this, Commander, so stop trying. You're going to lead your men to that base, and you're going to ensure the boy is delivered back to me entirely unscathed. Do you understand?'

Tobias couldn't react. He was too gripped with fear.

'COMMANDER!' the Master shouted. 'DO YOU UNDERSTAND?

'Yes, my Lord,' Tobias finally replied, completely shaken to the bone.

'Good. Now leave me in peace.'

Tobias bowed his head and hastily backed out of the Master's chamber. He walked through the hallway and into the elevator as the doors closed behind him. Tobias fell to his knees and began hyperventilating on the floor. He couldn't comprehend what the Master was asking of him. It made no sense for the commander to leave the city to fight in a mission this dangerous. That was the job of a trained soldier, not a politician. He had no experience being out in the field. So what was he going to do?

He had to pull himself together and start thinking more clearly. All he had to do was lay low and let Colonel Braxton lead the charge against the rebels. He didn't even have to get involved.

Tobias stood up straight and made himself look more presentable as the elevator arrived on the tenth floor.

The doors opened, and the commander could see the Arcadian soldiers gathering their weapons and their armour in preparation for battle. Braxton immediately approached and handed him his newly made, custom-built body armour.

'This is for you, Sir,' he said.

Tobias shot him a look of surprise.

'How did he know I was coming on this mission?' he asked himself as he started to suit up.

'Grant has informed me of the coordinates to this military base, and our plane is ready to fly out as soon as you are Commander,' said Braxton.

'Very good, Colonel. The Master wants the Asset back immediately. Have your men ready to board the aircraft as soon as possible,' Tobias said with authority.

'Yes, sir,' Braxton nodded as he turned to address his team. 'Soldiers of Arcadia, listen to me. The Master has ordered the immediate capture of this boy.'

He pressed a button on his remote, and a hologram appeared in front of the soldiers of Magnus's face.

'He is being held captive by rebels in an underground base located in the Southern province. Our mission is to extract him by any means necessary and bring him back to this city unharmed. His safety is our number one priority. Understood?'

'YES, SIR!' the soldiers all shouted in unison.

'There's a plane waiting for us outside the city walls. We'll rendezvous there in fifteen minutes. Company MOVE OUT!' Braxton shouted, and his soldiers all began heading towards the Capitol building's hanger.

Tobias tried to remain composed as he boarded his private pod, but he was wrestling with his fear of having to leave the safe confines of his city.

As the pod made its way through the decontamination chamber and out onto the helipad, Tobias put his mask over his face. He wanted to construct a plan of action to sabotage this mission; however, time was very quickly running out. The pod finally stopped outside the city walls, and Braxton opened the door for the commander. Tobias stepped out onto the helipad and started making his way towards the plane.

Suddenly, two soldiers standing on either side of him seized Tobias by his arms.

'What the? What are you doing?' cried the commander in shock as he attempted to break loose of their grasp. However, their grip was far too strong for him. Tobias looked up to see Braxton strolling towards him, looking unusually calm and composed.

'Colonel, what's the meaning of this? Tell your men to let me go,' Tobias ordered.

'I'm sorry, Tobias, but I can't do that,' Braxton replied calmly.

'What are you talking about?'

'The Master no longer requires your services, Tobias. You are hereby permanently banished from the city of Arcadia.'

'What?' Tobias replied incredulously. He paused for a moment before shaking his head. A sudden realisation had manifested in his mind.

'You're the traitor!' he said with spiteful disdain. 'You've been feeding the Master information behind my back, haven't you!'

The anger Tobias felt at that moment was unconscionable.

'I'm not the one who betrayed his country, Tobias. Did you honestly believe you'd be able to take control of this mission without the Master's input? You can't even take control of your own family,' Braxton said with utter contempt. 'You're a disgrace to this city, and you're lucky your punishment isn't more severe. If I had my way, I would have had you strung up by your pathetic little neck for this insubordination.'

Tobias looked at him with deep hatred and fear. He tried to think of something, anything that would get him out of this situation. But it was becoming increasingly apparent that the jig was up.

'Now, if you'll excuse me, I have a mission to complete. Farewell, Commander.'

Braxton turned his back on Tobias and began making his way towards the plane.

Suddenly the soldiers holding Tobias' arms yanked him backwards, forcing him off his feet.

'No, WAIT!' Tobias cried. He fought with all his might to resist the force of his muscular soldiers, but he didn't have the strength to overpower them. They pulled him towards the end of the platform, and without hesitation, threw him off with great exertion.

Tobias screamed at the top of his lungs in sheer panic as he plunged through the clouds towards the ground ten thousand feet below. He was desperately pushing buttons on his suit, hoping one of them would activate the boosters and break his fall. However, given that this was a brand new suit, he had absolutely no idea where the right button was located. He was mere feet from the ground when his boosters finally kicked in, and his body stopped in mid-air. He breathed a huge sigh of relief as he slowly lowered himself to the ground, but his legs were like jelly, and they could barely hold his weight.

Tobias fell to his knees, breathing heavily. He'd never experienced terror of that magnitude in his entire life. A couple of seconds later and his body would have turned to mush inside his brand new high tech suit.

He cried out in despair. His mind suddenly went to his family, whom he loved more than anything in the world.

'What are they going to do now that I'm gone? Will the Master banish them as well?' Thoughts of the worst possible scenarios began rushing around his head.

Rosa, Molly and Lucas' faces flashed through his mind as a huge lump grew in his throat. He glanced up to the sky to see the Arcadian plane fly off in the direction of the Southern province.

Countless lives were in mortal danger, and there was nothing Tobias could do to prevent it.

- CHAPTER 16 -
MAGNUS' GUILT

Magnus sat patiently outside the sick bay, waiting for any news regarding Kayla's current condition. The guilt he felt for trying to escape and putting his friend's life in mortal danger made him feel sick to his stomach, and he hoped more than anything that she would find it in her heart to forgive him. To make matters worse, his skin felt like it was on fire, having walked through the decontamination chamber a second time on his way back into Ground Zero. He certainly wasn't going to go through there again without wearing some form of protective body armour. George had given him some ointment to put on the affected areas, but the painful burning sensation still persisted.

Amelia sat down on a chair next to Magnus and noticed him gently rubbing the red, swollen skin on the back of his hands.

'How are the burns?' she asked, looking deeply concerned for him.

'Still pretty sore,' Magnus replied rather monotonously. It was clear he wasn't really in the mood for small talk.

'Do you need some more ointment? I can go in and ask Dad for some more if you want.'

Magnus simply shook his head. He didn't believe applying more ointment to his body would ease the pain he was feeling both inside and out. Amelia slumped in her chair, feeling somewhat useless.

'It's not your fault, you know,' she said, gently putting a hand on his shoulder, 'those drones are only supposed to stun people. I've never seen them use their full energy blasters before.'

Magnus continued shaking his head.

'It is my fault. If I hadn't have run away, none of this would have ever happened,' he said, filled with insurmountable regret.

'No one can blame you, Magnus, not after what you've been through.'

'I blame myself, Amelia, and it's more than I can bear. Maybe Gerald was right - maybe it would have been better if I'd have stayed locked up in prison.'

'You can't go listening to what Gerald says. He's nothing more than a smelly demented old fool. You, on the other hand, are the most amazing human being I've ever met, and I've met some pretty amazing people,' she said, hoping a more jovial tone would lighten the mood. However, Magnus didn't seem to be listening.

Amelia looked down at the ground in resignation. She desperately wanted to find a way to comfort her friend, but it seemed there was nothing she could say or do that could help him feel any better. She finally reconciled that perhaps it was best she stopped talking for a while and simply wait with him for any news.

Inside the sick bay, George was finishing off tending to Kayla's wound while Hunter and Jethro sat on either side of her. Hunter had tears welling up in his eyes as he looked upon his wife sleeping peacefully in bed. He couldn't bear seeing her in this condition.

Jethro looked at his son anxiously as if wanting to say something, but before he could open his mouth Hunter suddenly broke the silence.

'When did you invent that EMP machine?' he asked curiously.

Jethro looked at him in surprise. After everything that had just happened, he definitely wasn't expecting a discussion about his new invention.

'Two days ago,' he responded. 'I was looking for an opportunity to test it out without disabling the electricity in here. I'm glad I could actually put it to some good use.'

'We could have really benefitted from that when we broke Magnus out of prison. You should have told me that's what you were building,' said Hunter sternly.

'Well, if I informed you about every little thing I was working on down there, you'd have been waiting forever to break him out.'

'Fair enough.' Hunter nodded in agreement. He greatly admired his father for the things he could create out of the scraps they found on the street, but he knew not to put any pressure on him. The finished product was always worth the wait.

Another awkward silence fell upon them as the two men watched George work his magic on Kayla's wound. Jethro once again opened his mouth to speak, but the words still wouldn't come to him.

'What is it, Dad?' asked Hunter rather impatiently.

Jethro took a deep breath before replying.

'I think we need to have a talk about the boy,' he said hesitantly.

'What about him?'

'Did you see how long he was able to breathe the air above ground without the use of a mask? I've never known of anyone who could do such a thing for that length of time. This could be the breakthrough we've been searching for all these years,' Jethro said, trying his best to contain his obvious excitement.

'Let's not talk about this now, Dad! It's neither the time nor the place,' Hunter replied in a tired voice. It was abundantly clear he didn't want to have this conversation.

'I know this isn't the best time, but I really think it's important that you let me look at him as soon as possible.'

'I said not now, Dad!' Hunter snapped. 'You've done quite enough damage already for one evening.'

Jethro looked at his son in outrage.

'What have I done, except tell the boy the truth? Something you seem incapable of doing.'

'Because I knew how he was going to react,' Hunter interjected forcefully, 'Magnus is a very sensitive young man. You might have recognised that if you'd have bothered to take the time to get to know him instead of hiding away in your underground cave. You can't just drop a bombshell on someone like that and expect him not to get upset.'

'Don't give me that nonsense. He's been here for months now, and you've had ample opportunity to tell him the truth about his past, but you chose not to. Don't try to make me feel guilty because of your own cowardice.'

'Oh, get out, Dad!' Hunter barked. 'I'm not having this conversation with you right now. Go back to your play den; I know that's where you really want to be.'

The atmosphere had gotten noticeably tense in the room, and George decided to carry on as if he wasn't listening. Jethro raised his hands in the air and promptly stood up from his seat.

'Fine. I know when I'm outstaying my welcome. If you need me for anything, you know where to find me. I'll be in my 'underground cave',' he replied coldly. Hunter ignored the remark as his father took his leave and shut the door behind him.

As Jethro stepped into the corridor outside the sickbay, Magnus and Amelia both perked their heads up to see what was happening. However, Jethro didn't make eye contact with either of them as he marched down the hall and out of sight. His conversation with Hunter had gotten him riled up, and he felt the best thing for him to do would be to return to the Underworld, where he could be of some use.

George finally stopped wiping the blood from Kayla's wound and threw the red-stained cloth into a nearby bin.

'Right, I've finished dressing her wound,' said George trying not to sound too uncomfortable about the conversation he'd just overheard, 'it should fully heal within a matter of weeks. We're lucky her armour absorbed most of the impact of the blast.'

George walked over to a washbasin and began scrubbing the blood from his hands.

'Thank you, George,' said Hunter, looking somewhat distracted by his thoughts, 'I'm sorry you had to hear that conversation. My father and I have a lot of unresolved issues.'

'It's none of my business Hunter,' replied George rather bluntly. 'Now, I recommend she hold off from any exercise and gets plenty of rest in the next few days to ensure a full recovery. Any sudden physical movements could re-open the wound and get it infected. Then she'll be in real trouble.'

'Understood,' said Hunter nodding in agreement.

'I'll leave you two in peace.'

George swiftly made his way out of the room, leaving Hunter alone with his wife.

Magnus and Amelia both jumped to their feet upon noticing George enter the hallway.

'How is she, Dad?' asked Amelia anxiously.

'She'll be fine. Luckily there was no internal bleeding, so I was able to stitch her up without any problems.'

Magnus breathed an enormous sigh of relief.

'Can I see her? I need to tell her how sorry I am,' Magnus pleaded.

'I don't think that's a good idea right now, Magnus. She needs to rest,' George replied with a stern look in his eye.

'It's okay, George. Let him in.'

Hunter's voice could be heard through the gap in the doorway. George sighed and stepped out of the way, allowing Magnus to pass him. Amelia wanted to follow her friend inside, but her father stepped in the way whilst shaking his head. Magnus walked into the room, and George quickly closed the door behind him.

The teenager looked at Kayla sleeping soundly in front of him. He hoped she'd be awake so that he could apologise to her properly, but it seemed he would have to wait. He knelt down in front of his mentor and bowed his head in shame. Hunter turned to face Magnus and placed his hand on the teenager's head.

'It's all right, Magnus. You don't have to bow,' he said in a calm voice.

'Yes, I do. I feel dreadful. I'm so sorry for all the trouble I've caused,' said Magnus, reluctant to lift his head and look directly into the eyes of his teacher.

'Don't apologise, Magnus. You're not to blame. This is my fault,' said Hunter remorsefully.

Magnus looked puzzled. *'How could this be his fault?'* he asked himself as he slowly stood up straight.

'My father was right; I should have told you the truth about your past sooner. I was waiting for the right time, but we were so busy with your training the past few months, the right time never came. I really am sorry, Magnus, for everything.'

Magnus looked down at the ground. He had to admit that a few hours ago, he was furious with Hunter for not telling him the truth, but right now, his own guilt substantially outweighed any blame he held over his mentor.

'I understand if you wish to stop your training with me,' said Hunter.

Magnus shot him a look of panic. Learning to control and develop his powers had been the happiest he's ever felt in his entire life. He felt like he could finally have a purpose in this world if he could master his telekinesis. There was no way he could possibly give up on his progress now.

'Absolutely not,' Magnus said with complete conviction, 'if anything, I want to practice even harder. I stupidly thought I'd be able to make it out there in the world by myself, but tonight has proven how wrong I was.'

Hunter smiled at him and gave him a nod.

'Very well, we'll continue tomorrow,' he replied. 'Oh, and I'm sorry I missed our lesson today.'

'It's okay. I understand,' Magnus interjected. 'Jethro told me about your mother.'

Hunter gave him an appreciative nod, grateful that he didn't have to go into further detail.

Magnus was beyond relieved Hunter wasn't angry with him and still wanted to continue with his lessons. He walked over to the bed and sat down on the chair opposite his mentor.

'I'm really sorry I disobeyed you, Hunter. I should never have gone down to the Underworld.'

'Now you understand why it's off-limits,' Hunter replied, raising his eyebrows.

Magnus nodded ashamedly.

'My father isn't the most tactful man; it's got to be said. Since my mother died, he locked himself away from the world and became something of a recluse. Having said that, we rarely saw much of him before she died either. But he definitely had better social skills back then, and when he did show his face, he was a great father.'

Magnus noticed a faint but fleeting smile appear on Hunter's lips.

'Now he's become a shadow of his former self, obsessed with righting the wrongs of his past. I barely recognise him anymore.'

'He misses you. He says you hardly come to visit him anymore,' said Magnus.

Hunter took a deep breath as he tried to conceal his emotion.

'I know. It's just... It's hard seeing the man you once admired slowly deteriorating as he grows old. I should go and visit him more often. Kayla's always telling me to do so.'

'He mentioned you, and he used to live in Arcadia.'

'We did,' Hunter replied.

'What was it like there?' asked Magnus, unable to fight his curiosity.

'It was a paradise. It had beautiful scenery, tall buildings, plentiful food for everyone to enjoy. My family and I had a great life there.'

Magnus suddenly felt a warm feeling inside. It seemed Hunter was enjoying reminiscing about his time living in the city in the sky.

'In fact, we enjoyed our lives so much that we were blissfully ignorant to the tremendous suffering of those who lived outside the city walls. It seems that privilege is invisible to those who are born with it. It was only once we had been banished from Arcadia that we were made aware of the true horror people in this country were suffering on a daily basis. When I saw all those people on the verge of death, with no food, no supplies, unable to decide whether to carry on living or end the agony, it brought me to the brink of despair.'

'What stopped it?' asked Magnus curiously.

'Kayla,' he replied, looking lovingly at his sleeping wife, 'she was one of the first people we rescued. Her parents had died of the virus several years prior, and she'd stayed in isolation until she heard our call and braved the streets to find us. She had as much reason as anybody to give up hope and end it all. But she refused. She taught me that life is always worth fighting for, no matter how hopeless the future looks.'

Magnus looked down at the floor. He remembered the despair he felt a few hours ago when he impulsively dashed from the base and onto the streets of London, endangering himself and the lives of the people trying to save him. The intense feeling of guilt was starting to return in the pit of his stomach. Hunter looked at him and instantly noticed his discomfort.

'It's getting late. You best get some rest if we're going to start training again tomorrow. We'll resume after breakfast, okay?'

He sounded noticeably more upbeat. Magnus smiled gratefully and nodded to his teacher. He got up off his chair and left Hunter alone with Kayla.

The next morning Magnus was up bright and early for breakfast. As expected, he'd gotten very little sleep after the previous evenings little fiasco and decided to spend most of the early hours of the morning practising with Flip, trying his best not to wake up Andro in the process. He still felt racked with guilt over what happened to Kayla, but he was determined not to let his emotions get the better of him while busy mastering his powers.

As he was eating his porridge with Amelia and Tom in the Great Hall, he noticed whispering and fleeting glances coming from the tables nearby. It seemed word had already gotten out about what had happened last night, and the looks of disapproval were starting to grow. It had been a long time since Magnus had attracted this sort of behaviour amongst the people of Ground Zero; however, he wasn't going to let it get to him. He had a job to do, and his mind was entirely fixated on completing it.

Before he had even swallowed his last mouthful of porridge, Magnus marched straight over to the training arena where Hunter was patiently waiting for him. In preparation for their lesson, Hunter had set up a giant obstacle course, which covered the entirety of the room.

On the floor in front of him was an armoured suit with red lights similar to the ones the Shadow Squad wore, but this one was smaller in size.

Magnus stepped into the middle of the room, and they both bowed to each other.

'Good morning, Magnus,' said Hunter.

'Morning, Hunter, how's Kayla doing?' asked Magnus tentatively.

'She's doing fine. A few days' rest, and she'll be right as rain. In the meantime, I hope you're ready to take your training to the next level.'

Magnus nodded determinedly.

'I've been going easy on you up until now, but after last night I believe you're ready to take things up a notch.'

Magnus felt a mixture of excitement and nerves as he anxiously pondered what Hunter had in store for him this time.

Hunter bent down and lifted up the suit.

'This is your new body armour. You're going to need it for this particular exercise.'

Magnus stared at the suit in utter disbelief. He'd had dreams about wearing a suit such as this and one day doing battle alongside the Shadow Squad, but he never believed it would ever actually happen. He was entirely beside himself with feelings of absolute elation and joy.

'Here, try it on,' Hunter said as he passed the armour to the excited teen.

Magnus stared at the Shadow Squad crest on his chest plate. Was this really happening? He didn't wait a moment to find out. He didn't want to take a chance that this might all be a dream that he could wake up from at any moment. As he slipped on the suit, he was amazed at how easily it all stayed in place. Every part of it was a perfect fit for his body, and the teenager had a massive grin on his face as he proudly strode around the arena.

'It looks great on you,' said Hunter enthusiastically, 'now let's see how you cope against these.'

He pressed a switch on the remote he was holding, and five battle drones came to life and started circling around them in a threatening manner.

'You've practised how to control multiple objects mid-flight, but now you need to learn how to do so whilst avoiding incoming laser fire. In this exercise, you're going to focus on the drone's position and anticipate its laser's trajectory. Are you ready?'

Magnus nodded. After struggling to defend himself against the drones last night, this was exactly what he needed to concentrate all his attention on. His mind was entirely focused, and his body was poised. Hunter knelt down and bowed his head to his student. Magnus bent his leg and was about to bow his head, but before he could fully lower himself, Hunter pressed a button on the remote, and the drones suddenly turned and began firing in his direction. Magnus leapt out of the way and started hurtling around the arena, ducking and diving as fast as he could. He felt a bit annoyed that Hunter had started before he was ready, but there wasn't any time to dwell on it as he tumbled around the obstacle course at a great pace. He suddenly noticed he could feel the presence of two of the drones that were coming up behind him. He held out his arm, and the drones smashed into each other and instantly fell to the floor. He jumped up a wall and kicked off it in a completely new direction. The remaining drones seemed bedazzled by the teenager as they struggled to keep up with his dizzying speed and agility. Finally, they got a lock on the boy and began firing at him. However, Magnus quickly jumped out of the way of the blasts and held both his hands out in front of him. The three drones instantly crumpled into tiny metal balls and fell lifelessly to the ground.

Magnus breathed a sigh of relief at the ease with which he'd dispatched the drones. He took a swig of water and gave himself a second to catch his breath. However, Hunter wasn't finished with this exercise yet.

'There's no time for resting,' he said as he pressed the button once again, and ten more drones came flying into view. Magnus rolled his eyes and resumed running again. The drones were firing at a commensurate rate, but Magnus was doing a good job of dodging the blasts. He was also getting the hang of focusing on the drones' position whilst on the move. He suddenly discovered he could make the drones implode without moving his arms, which proved incredibly advantageous whilst ducking and diving through the obstacle course. One by one, the drones were imploding in quick succession until there were only four left intact. However, in all the commotion, Magnus failed to notice Hunter had thrown Flip into the mix. The small robot whizzed past Magnus extremely quickly, knocking him off balance, and he fell to the floor with a thud. He suddenly experienced several sharp pains in his back that felt like he was getting kicked by multiple steel-capped boots all at the same time. He was, in fact, being bombarded with laser fire from all possible angles,

222

but luckily, he had a mental grasp of the location of each individual drone. He stuck out his arms and lifted them up high above his head. The drones each flew into the concrete ceiling and fell to the floor in bits. Magnus closed his eyes and thrust his hand out once again. Suddenly, Flip stopped in his tracks, unable to move.

A powerful hush fell upon the room as Hunter looked at him, stunned. After months of non-stop work, Magnus had finally achieved his goal of apprehending that pesky little flying robot. Hunter immediately threw his hands in the air and started clapping. Magnus opened his eyes in disbelief.

'Absolutely fantastic, Magnus! Well done!' his mentor exclaimed with immeasurable joy.

Magnus could feel tears welling up in his eyes. The sheer emotional delight he'd just experienced from capturing Flip for the first time was beyond anything he'd ever felt before in his life.

'Can you do that again?' asked Hunter, eager to check it wasn't a fluke.

Magnus let go of the robot as it started whizzing around the room again. He closed his eyes and shut off his senses. He could feel Flip's presence much clearer than he ever had before. He stuck out his arm, and Flip once again stopped in the air, completely immobilized.

Hunter raised his fists into the air in celebration and ran over to Magnus. He threw his arms around his student and pulled him in for a tight hug. Magnus was taken aback. He'd never expected a reaction like that, especially from his typically stoic mentor. However, he was enjoying this moment far too much to question it further.

'This is a very special achievement, Magnus,' said Hunter as he unhooked him from his muscular arms. He sounded like an excited child. 'You've just passed one of the hardest tests ever created for this program. I think you might be ready to take this into the field.'

Magnus suddenly felt a sharp sting in his chest. Sure, he was elated about what he'd just achieved, but the thought of doing the same thing in a real life-or-death situation like the one he experienced last night made him severely doubt himself.

'I think that'll be all for now. Get some rest and meet me back here at four o'clock. I have a surprise in store for you.

- CHAPTER 17 -
THE SURPRISE EVENT

As Magnus made his way back to his room, he had a mixture of emotions after the lesson he had just had with Hunter. On the one hand, he felt a great sense of achievement and fulfilment, having just completed a task he once thought was impossible. On the other hand, he couldn't shake off a feeling of anxiety about the prospect of applying those skills in a real combat situation. It hadn't worked out too well for him thus far, and he would hate to have a repeat of last night's perilous proceedings. Did Hunter really think Magnus was ready to take this out into the field? Or was he simply being impatient about getting his so-called 'revolution' underway? Whatever the answer to that question, only time would tell.

As he walked down the corridor towards his room, Magnus felt a wave of excitement about telling Andro about the amazing progress he'd just made. He hadn't seen or spoken to him since everything kicked off last night, and he hoped this would be a good icebreaker for them. However, upon opening his bedroom door, he noticed Andro was gone, and so was his docking station

'That's strange!' Magnus thought. Andro very rarely wakes up unless someone switches him on, and he certainly never took his power station anywhere with him. Had someone come into his room and swiped him?

Magnus quickly made his way to the Great Hall, where he saw Amelia and George sitting at a dining table reading. Amelia looked up from her book and saw Magnus with a slightly perturbed expression on his face.

'Magnus, is everything okay?' she asked cautiously. She didn't want to say anything that might spark a reaction similar to last night's debacle.

'Has anyone seen Andro?' asked Magnus, 'he's not in my room, and his docking station's disappeared.'

Amelia shook her head.

'I've not seen him since last night,' she replied, 'perhaps Sam's playing with him.'

Magnus hoped not for Andro's sake. He'd kicked up that much of a fuss about spending all day playing with Sam yesterday he didn't think Andro could cope with very much more of him.

'Everyone's missing in action this morning,' said George looking up from his book, 'Tom hasn't been down for breakfast yet.'

Magnus looked at both of them, completely baffled. There was definitely something strange going on today.

'Come on; let's have a look in the Sanctum. One of the kids in there is bound to know where Andro is,' said Amelia as she grabbed his hand and pulled him towards the exit.

'If you see your brother....' George called out, but the two teenagers had already disappeared from view. The old man gave a sigh of resignation and shook his head as his eyes wandered back to his book.

Magnus and Amelia made their way down the corridor and knocked on the Sanctum door. It promptly opened, and Magnus was shocked by what he could see inside. There was an unusually long line of children, which stretched almost the entire length of the play area. At the front of the queue, Magnus could see Sam with Andro perched on his head and playing with the robot's joysticks. The small boy suddenly cried out in anguish.

'NOOOO!' he exclaimed.

'Better luck next time, Sam. NEXT!' shouted Andro.

'Just one more go,' Sam pleaded, 'I've nearly killed the final boss.'

'Sorry, Sam, but the rule is one turn per person,' said Andro sternly, 'otherwise it's not fair on the other kids.'

'Yeah, stop hogging Andro,' came several voices from behind him. Sam reluctantly removed Andro from on top of his head and made his way to the back of the queue, eager to await his next turn. Magnus and Amelia approached Andro before the next kid had attached him to their head.

'Andro, what's going on?' asked Magnus in a confused tone.

Andro looked up and saw Magnus and Amelia staring at him with equally confounded expressions.

'Hi guys,' he said enthusiastically.

'Hey, no pushing in,' said the girl who was next in line, 'I've been waiting nearly an hour to play with Andro.'

'It's okay, Agnes, I can do two things at once. Hop in,' said Andro. The girl's pout disappeared instantly as she placed him on top of her head and began playing.

'So what's going on, guys?' said the robot nonchalantly.

Magnus thought it a bit strange to be talking to Andro whilst he was attached to a young girl's head but decided to try and look past it. He glanced over at the seemingly endless line of children waiting for a turn with the robot.

'How long has this been going on?' Magnus asked in disbelief.

'I've been here about five hours now. The kids just can't seem to get enough of my games,' said Andro gleefully.

'That's a long time. Are you not getting tired?' asked Amelia.

'I was starting to lose power about an hour ago, but one of the kids was kind enough to retrieve my power bank from your bedroom,' said the robot whilst pointing at the docking station plugged into the wall, 'now I should be able to go all day with this as long as the kids want to play.'

'But won't you get sick of it?' asked Magnus.

'Are you kidding? I finally feel useful again,' Andro replied, 'you've got your training with Hunter and Battleball practice with your friends. You don't really need me to entertain you anymore. I'm happy I can now provide a bit of joy to these young whippersnappers.'

Magnus felt a sting of guilt wash over him. The past few months, he'd been so wrapped up in the progress he was making in his own life, he didn't realise he was neglecting the needs of his oldest companion.

'I'm sorry, Andro. I haven't been a very good friend to you recently, have I?'

'It's fine, Magnus, really. I'm happy that you're growing up and embracing this new life, and I'm proud of what you have accomplished since you came here. We will always remain friends no matter what, but now I've found a new way to help others that makes me feel a real sense of purpose again.'

Magnus paused for a second before giving his robot friend a warm smile.

'Well, as long as you're happy, then I'm happy for you,' he said sincerely.

'I am,' Andro replied.

'That's terrific, Andro,' said Amelia, 'we'll leave you to it then.'

She grabbed Magnus' hand and started pulling him towards the door. Magnus looked back at his robot friend, who was ushering the next kid to come and play with him. In a sense, it felt like the teenager was finally saying goodbye to his childhood and embracing his future.

Magnus and Amelia spent most of the rest of the day sitting in the Great Hall with George, sipping hot beverages and playing a quick game of 'Arcadian Deception'. The rest of the hall was utterly rife with gossip, as rumours had started to spread that Hunter was planning some kind of grand event in the training arena at four o'clock and that everyone was invited to attend. This was highly unorthodox, according to George, and theories started flying around about what the so-called event could possibly be about.

'Hopefully, he's going to do a speech about the importance of personal hygiene. Gerald's body odour is really beginning to stink the place out,' said George gesturing to the grumpy old man sitting in a chair fast asleep. Magnus laughed, and Amelia shook her head.

'He wouldn't need to hold a meeting in the training arena for that,' said Amelia dismissively, 'he could just do it in here.'

'Alright then, what's your grand theory Miss Smarty Knickers?' George said, overly defensive.

'I've no idea, but I bet it's got something to do with the fact we haven't seen Tom this morning,' Amelia surmised.

Magnus threw her a confused look.

'What do you mean by that?' he asked.

'Tom never misses breakfast under any circumstances. Always says it's the most important meal of the day, especially for Battleball practice. All of a sudden, he disappears on the one day that Hunter organises a super-secret surprise event in the training arena. I highly doubt it's a coincidence.'

Magnus nodded in agreement. He remembered Hunter had said something about a 'surprise' during their lesson this morning. He wondered if the two things were connected in some way.

'Anyway, it's your turn to bet, Dad,' said Amelia drawing everyone's attention back to the game at hand. George grabbed three tokens and placed them into the centre of the table. He looked deep into his daughter's eyes and smirked.

'I think you have two Arcadian Knights, three battle drones and two hover buggies,' he said with confidence. Magnus looked at Amelia's face with intense concentration in an attempt to read any sort of reaction from her. She was avidly shaking her head, but Magnus noticed the twitch in her left eye when her father was predicting her hand, something she only did when she felt noticeably uncomfortable. He grabbed three of his tokens and threw them into the centre of the table with complete conviction.

'I'll go with that too,' he said with obvious self-assurance. Amelia looked both Magnus and George in the eyes and then back at her cards. She was tempted to try and bluff her way out of it, but that hadn't worked out too well for her thus far.

'DAMNATION!' she exclaimed with resignation as she threw her cards face up in the centre of the table. George had predicted her hand right to the very last card. 'How do you always get a read on me?'

'You've always been terrible at lying, Amelia,' George said with a laugh as he started taking six of his daughter's last remaining tokens. 'Your brother's exactly the same. Your mother and I clearly did too good a job on your upbringing.'

Magnus started laughing, and Amelia folded her arms and slouched back in her chair in a huff.

Eventually, four o'clock came around, and hordes of people began making their way to the training arena.

Magnus started getting butterflies in his stomach in anticipation of what this surprise could possibly be. He figured it had to be something to do with the Shadow Squad; otherwise, the use of the training arena would be pointless.

As Magnus and Amelia arrived on the fourth floor, they noticed the training arena had been laid out differently from how it usually was. There were no weapons, obstacle courses or flying drones anywhere in sight, and several rows of benches had been set up around the room as if they had arrived at some kind of professional sports competition.

Magnus looked around, and through the crowd of people taking their seats, he noticed Kayla sitting on a bench on the top row with a bandage wrapped around her waist. He looked at her in shock. He'd certainly not expected to see her out of bed so soon after what happened last night, but he felt a great sense of relief that she was strong enough to do so. She caught his eye and waved as he and Amelia both dashed over to see her. Magnus was still very eager to apologise for his behaviour the previous evening.

'Hi, Kayla,' said Amelia in her usual enthusiastic tone.

'Hello, Amelia,' Kayla responded with a warm smile.

'We were so worried about you. We weren't sure if you were going to make it. Wait, aren't you supposed to be resting?'

'You sound like Hunter,' she scoffed, 'I'm absolutely fine. It'll take a lot more than one puny battle drone to finish me off, don't you worry. Why don't you come and have a seat next to me?'

Amelia didn't need to be asked twice. She sat down instantly and looked up in admiration at her lifelong hero. Kayla turned to face Magnus, who was looking at the ground rather sheepishly.

'Hello, Magnus,' she said in a friendly tone. Magnus finally looked her in the eyes.

'I'm so sorry about what happened last night, Kayla,' he blurted out somewhat faster than expected, 'it was stupid and selfish of me and....'

Kayla held up her hand to stop him mid-sentence.

'It's forgotten, Magnus, okay? Come here.'

She held out her hands, and Magnus moved in for a warm embrace. He was beyond relieved that she didn't hate him for what he put her through last night. Kayla finally broke the hug and Magnus sat down on the other side of her.

'Any idea what this is about?' he asked curiously.

'You'll see shortly,' Kayla replied, failing to hide a noticeable grin.

After waiting for several minutes for everyone to find their seats, the elevator doors finally opened, and ten members of the Shadow Squad walked into the arena. A huge roar of applause erupted from the crowd as each Squad member wearing their armoured suits made their way to the centre of the room. Magnus noticed that half of them were wearing a blue band around their left arm, and the other half was wearing red bands. Of those he knew the names of, Magnus could make out Hunter in the middle, Toro and Max either side of him and Carter and Taylor behind them. Right at the very back of the group, he noticed Billy and Tom holding the training bats they practised with in Battleball.

Magnus and Amelia both looked at each other in bewilderment.

'What's Tom doing out there?' asked Magnus in a whisper.

'No idea,' Amelia replied with a blank expression.

'He's not been recruited into the Shadow Squad in secret, has he?'

'No way,' Amelia laughed, 'If there's one thing my brother wouldn't be able to keep secret, it's being recruited into the Shadow Squad!'

Suddenly Hunter started to speak in a raised voice so the whole room could hear. Magnus and Amelia automatically faced forward and began listening intently.

'Good afternoon everyone, I thank you all for joining us in here for this meeting. I apologise for all the secrecy surrounding this, but I didn't want to spoil the surprise. I understand that times have been rather tough recently for everybody, and I decided we needed to do something fun to keep our spirits high.'

He paused for a moment as the crowd began to murmur.

'Today, my team and I are going to treat you all to a friendly game of Battleball. As is tradition, the team that loses has to wash everyone's underwear for a week.'

A huge laugh broke out in the crowd, and Magnus started grinning from ear to ear.

'Oh, this is going to be absolutely mega!' he thought to himself.

'So, without further ado, let the match begin.'

The crowd cheered with delight as the group separated into their teams and got into position. Tom took his place at the back of the blue team, which appeared to be captained by Hunter. Billy positioned himself at the other end, with Toro as captain of the red team. Both teams knelt down and bowed their heads to their opponents.

Magnus couldn't believe he was about to witness a game of Battleball played by members of the Shadow Squad. The only thing that could make it even better would be if he were able to participate in the game alongside them.

Within a few seconds, a whistle was blown, and the rubber ball was thrown into play. The crowd instantly started cheering as the players leapt to their feet and began knocking the ball back and forth across the arena.

Magnus' heart was racing with sheer elation. The games he played with the kids in the Sanctum were a far cry from this. This was proper Battleball! The level of acrobatic skill and ball control on display from the Shadow Squad was far superior in every way, and within just a few minutes, Taylor had scored the first goal for the blue team resulting in screams of delight from the crowd. Not wishing to be outshone by his twin sister; however, Carter promptly scored the next goal for the reds. Both teams were evenly matched in all departments, having trained rigorously together for so many years. It was an utter joy to behold.

Magnus felt a boost of excitement when he saw Hunter gain possession of the ball. He wondered what tricks his mentor had up his sleeve for this game. As Hunter was running, he saw Toro approach for an interception just ahead of him. He bounced the ball to Max and did a spectacular front flip manoeuvre over Toro's head. Toro looked back in confusion as Max returned the ball to Hunter, who punched it past Billy's bat and into the red team's basket. A huge cheer erupted once again as the blue team sprang into the lead.

It didn't last long, however, as the reds managed to gain the advantage after scoring three goals in a row to make the score 4-2. Magnus felt bad for Tom, who seemed to be having a tough time defending his basket against his highly skilled opponents. He knew how important it was for Tom to be able to prove his worth to Hunter for a potential position in the Shadow Squad.

Suddenly, Taylor was violently tackled by her brother, causing her to spin rapidly in the air. There were synchronized gasps from the audience as Taylor fell to the ground in a heap. The referee blew the whistle, and the game momentarily ground to a halt.

'Why is it always you that falls on your face when we play this game?' Carter joked as he pulled his sister up off the floor.

'Maybe because your fat ass is always getting in my way,' Taylor quipped back. Carter laughed and returned to his side of the court. The referee announced that it was a free hit to the blues, and the ball was promptly passed to Tom, who looked noticeably apprehensive.

Magnus and Amelia both waited anxiously to see how this would pan out. They'd seen first-hand how much Tom had practised in recent weeks and knew what he was capable of. This was his moment to shine. Tom took a deep breath. His heart was pumping wildly inside his chest as he anticipated that familiar high-pitched sound. After what felt like an eternity, the referee finally blew the whistle, and Tom chucked the ball into the air without hesitation. Magnus' heart stopped as Tom drew back his bat and hit the ball directly in the centre of its face. It hurtled towards the open hoop and, without even touching the sides, fell straight through and landed in the mesh. He'd scored the winning goal for the blue team.

The roar from the crowd was deafening. Magnus and Amelia both rose to their feet and began jumping for joy on their benches. Taylor and Max lifted Tom up onto their shoulders and started running around the arena in hysterics. Magnus looked over at the red team and was surprised to see Billy clapping on the other side of the court.

'He evidently only gets angry when playing with kids,' Magnus thought to himself.

Hunter and Toro both shook hands.

'Good game! Looks like we have our next recruit for Shadow Squad training,' said Hunter smugly.

'He got lucky,' Toro scoffed, 'next time, make sure he's on my team,' he said under his breath.

Hunter laughed.

'Fat chance of that.'

The crowd were making such a ruckus; no one noticed the sharp rumble that momentarily sent a shock wave through the walls. Suddenly a loud siren could be heard echoing around the training arena, followed by a deafening bang from the floor above. Dust began to fall from the ceiling as Hunter looked around in a panic. Suddenly the doors of the training ground blew off their hinges and hit Tom, knocking him to the ground.

The arena instantly filled with smoke as the frightened crowd began scrambling to their feet. Magnus saw a slew of laser fire through the cloud of smoke as soldiers wearing white armour began filling the room and attacking the Shadow Squad. Hunter and his team began fighting back; however, without the use of their weapons, it was a losing battle.

Magnus noticed Billy incapacitating several intruders by hitting them repeatedly with his bat. One of the soldiers ducked his swing and swept his legs, knocking him to the floor. The soldier aimed his gun directly at Billy's face, but Magnus stuck out his arm and, using his powers, lifted the soldier high into the air. The intruder's body slammed hard into the ceiling and crashed to the floor in front of Billy, who looked up at Magnus in shock. A nearby soldier saw what had just happened and pointed straight at Magnus.

'ASSET AT TWELVE O'CLOCK! he yelled at the top of his voice.

Kayla grabbed Magnus by the shoulders and pulled him out of view.

'Magnus, you have to get out of here right now,' she said urgently.

'I can help,' he replied.

'No. They're here for you. If they capture you, then it's all over, do you understand?' Magnus nodded frantically as Kayla turned to face Amelia.

'Take him to the Sanctum. Don't look back,' she commanded.

Amelia nodded and yanked on Magnus' arm, pulling him towards a trap door Magnus never even knew existed. One of the attackers noticed the two teens escaping through the door and gestured to his soldiers to follow them. Kayla stood blocking the exit, and roundhouse kicked one of the pursuing soldiers in the head. She took down two more soldiers with equal ease by sweeping both their legs. However, she suddenly received a hard kick to her wounded abdomen. She cried out in pain and fell to the floor before getting stunned in the chest. Once the pathway was clear, the soldiers quickly departed from the training arena and chased after the sprinting teens.

Magnus and Amelia dashed down the steps at lightning speed as they headed for the third floor.

'Where are we going?' Magnus cried, out of breath.

'The Sanctum. If we can get you inside there, then there's no way they can get to you,' she replied as they turned a sharp corner and darted down the hallway. They finally reached the Sanctum door, and Amelia quickly did the secret knock. The door swiftly opened, and she pushed Magnus inside without hesitation. But before she could follow him, Amelia was hit in the arm by a laser blast. She instantly went limp and fell to the floor.

'AMELIA!' Magnus cried as he scrambled back towards the door, but it was too late. The doors of the Sanctum closed, leaving Magnus trapped inside. He suddenly heard gasps of fear from behind him as he looked around and noticed Andro and a group of frightened children hiding in a corner. The robot flew over to his friend.

'What's going on, Magnus?' he asked in a panic.

'We're under attack,' Magnus replied, 'look after the kids.'

His heartbeat was going a million miles a second as he heard laser fire from the other side of the door. He really wanted to get out and help Amelia, but he knew that he couldn't.

Suddenly there was a large bang, which shook the Sanctum walls and made everyone inside jump out of their skin. The intruders were trying to blast the door open, but it didn't budge. The children started crying, and Andro flew back over to try to comfort them.

'Don't worry, they can't get inside,' he said in an attempt to sound calm, but it didn't seem to be having the desired effect.

Suddenly there was another loud bang, but once again, the door remained closed. Then there was complete silence. Magnus tried to listen carefully to see if he could make out what was happening outside the room. Then a voice could be heard from behind the door.

'We have your friend here, boy. The little girl,' the voice was Colonel Braxton's.

Magnus' heart dropped upon realising they had Amelia and were likely to use her as leverage.

'If you want her to live, you'd better open the door within the next five seconds. FIVE...'

Magnus had no idea what he was going to do.

'FOUR...'

He couldn't allow them inside and potentially put more lives in danger.

'THREE...'

But at the same time, he couldn't sit back and let his best friend be killed.

'TWO...'

He desperately hoped something would come along in the next nanosecond to save him from having to make this choice.

'ONE.'

Without thinking, Magnus instinctively thrust out his arm.

'MAGNUS, NO!' cried Andro, but it was too late. The door swung open, and Braxton and his team began rushing inside. Andro flew over to the entrance and began attacking the soldiers with his red-hot laser. He managed to incapacitate several of them before suddenly receiving a violent blast to his face. Andro fell to the floor in a heap, and smoke began emanating from the hole in his visor.

'ANDRO!' Magnus cried in terror as soldiers continued bounding into the room.

Seething with rage, Magnus outstretched both of his hands, and the ground began to shake. Braxton lost his balance and stumbled to the floor, dropping his gun. Bricks started coming loose from the walls, and Magnus began firing them through the air at the incoming soldiers. Many of them suffered major blows to their bodies as the endless onslaught of flying bricks cascaded in their direction. Magnus had tears streaming down his cheeks as the walls began collapsing around them. He had one job now, stopping the soldiers at all costs and protecting the frightened children behind him.

Suddenly, Braxton steadied himself and was able to pick up his gun and aim it in Magnus' direction. He pulled the trigger, and a laser blast hit the teenager directly in the chest. The bricks instantly fell to the floor, and the room stopped shaking. Magnus had been stunned. He was suddenly reminded of the numbing sensation he experienced the night he escaped from prison. His body was starting to go limp, and his vision went blurry as he collapsed on the floor. He could just about make out Braxton's silhouette standing over him before everything once again fell into complete darkness.

- CHAPTER 18 -

AFTERMATH

Hunter awoke in a daze. He was lying on the floor of the training arena surrounded by rubble and hundreds of lifeless bodies. He tried to lift himself up but his arms felt shaky and the pain in his head was throbbing. His memory of the battle with the Arcadian intruders was hazy at best, but he did recall being hit in the side of the head by a blunt weapon moments before falling to the ground. He must have been stunned after that as he currently had no feeling in his legs, and that familiar sense of nausea was beginning to set in. However, when he looked up at the clock on the wall and checked the time and date, he noticed only two hours had passed since the attack. This confused him considerably. Usually, getting stunned would knock someone out for at least a couple of days. Why was this different?

Hunter lifted himself so that he was sitting upright. He scanned the room and noticed Jethro sitting on a stool in the corner examining a weapon dropped by an Arcadian soldier.

'Dad?' said Hunter in a disconcerted voice. He wasn't used to seeing his father out of his workstation, let alone twice in two days. Jethro turned to face his son.

'Oh, you're awake,' he replied, 'don't worry, that nauseous feeling goes pretty quickly.'

'What happened?' Hunter asked whilst rubbing his sore head.

'These Arcadian weapons are remarkable,' Jethro continued as if in his own world, 'for years, I tried to come up with a formula that would temporarily stun people for less than a few hours, but I could never get it right. Whoever they've got in charge of the engineering department in Arcadia clearly knows their stuff.'

'Dad,' Hunter interrupted, irritated by his father's incessant enthusiasm, 'can you stop admiring the enemy's weapon for a second and tell me what's going on. What happened to Magnus?'

'Your guess is as good as mine; I'm afraid, son,' Jethro replied, shrugging his shoulders.

Hunter tried to lift himself off the ground as he slowly started to get feeling back in his legs. However, they were still too weak to support his weight, and he fell back to the floor.

'We have to look for him,' said Hunter in a flustered voice.

'Slow down, son; you're in no state to move anywhere just yet. Give your muscles enough time to regain their strength,' said Jethro as he continued casually examining the firearm in his hands.

'We could have really used your help during the ambush, Dad.'

Jethro shot his son a cold look.

'Who did you think sounded the alert?' he replied, a little offended, 'I saw the enemy approaching on my monitor while you and everyone else were up here having your little Battleball party. I notice I wasn't invited to that, by the way.'

Jethro had a juvenile pout plastered on his face, which Hunter didn't appreciate at all.

'I rushed up the stairs to try and cut them off using my sonic cannon, but I wasn't fast enough, and they stunned me before I reached the top floor. I only woke up about ten minutes before you did.'

Hunter didn't respond. He was still mad at his father but felt it was best not to rise to it. He scanned the general area where he was sitting and was relieved to see several people were gradually starting to regain consciousness. He noticed Kayla was shifting her body weight as she struggled to sit upright. He crawled over towards her and suddenly spotted the bandage wrapped around her waist was covered in blood.

'Kayla, your wound,' said Hunter in a panic.

'I'll be fine. I think a few stitches have come out, that's all,' Kayla replied, shaking off the pain she was feeling.

Suddenly the door to the training arena opened, and Amelia stepped inside, holding a lifeless Andro in her arms. She was followed by a large group of very frightened children. They all glanced around the room in shock at the devastation that befell their eyes. Amelia searched the crowd of writhing bodies on the floor and found her father attempting to lift himself up. Without hesitation, she sprinted over and wrapped her arms around him as tightly as she could.

'Dad!' she exclaimed with relief.

'Oh, Amelia, thank God you're all right; I was worried sick when you ran off,' said George as he just about mustered the strength to lift his arms around his daughter.

Sam ran over to Billy, who was shaking off the numbness in his legs and gave his brother a huge embrace.

'Hey, Squirt,' said Billy breathing a sigh of relief.

'Billy, they took Magnus,' Sam uttered in a frantic panic.

Hunter rose to his feet and put his arms on the little boy's shoulders.

'Did you see Magnus get taken, Sam?' he asked urgently.

Sam nodded at Hunter with a fearful look in his eyes.

'He was put into a brown sack and carried out by a big bad man. There was nothing we could do to stop it,' said the small boy, almost on the verge of tears.

Hunter took a step backwards and fell to his knees. His worst fears had suddenly been realised.

'I failed him,' said Hunter in a shaken voice. He closed his eyes and hung his head in shame.

Jethro stood up from his stool and placed his hand on Hunter's shoulder.

'Don't blame yourself, Son,' he said in a calm voice, 'the boy gave away our location. It was only a matter of time before they found us and came for him.'

Hunter suddenly felt a wave of rage wash over him as he swiftly leapt to his feet.

'His name is MAGNUS!' Hunter snapped angrily as he batted his father's hand away. 'Don't you dare try to blame any of this on him. He wouldn't have run off if not for you.'

Hunter pointed at his father accusingly.

'Not this again,' said Jethro rolling his eyes. 'Listen, Son; I'm not blaming anyone, okay? This is no time for us to lose our heads.'

Jethro was trying his best to keep the situation as calm as he could; however, it seemed to be making matters worse.

'This is the perfect time to lose our heads, old man. Our base has been compromised, the enemy has Magnus in their possession, and they're going to torture him until he can't take the pain any longer, potentially starting a new world war. WHAT PART OF ANYTHING I'VE JUST SAID IS NOT WORTH LOSING OUR HEADS OVER?'

Hunter sounded furious, and Jethro was struggling to maintain his calm composure.

'All I'm saying is that we need to start thinking clearly about how we're going to progress further.'

'How we're going to progress further?' Hunter repeated in outrage. 'You're unbelievable, Dad.'

He started laughing in disbelief.

'I don't know why I'm surprised. You showed no emotion when Mum died either. This is just another inconvenience for you, isn't it? Another blip in your journey towards 'progress' because that's the only thing you've ever really cared about.'

Jethro looked at his son in shock. He couldn't believe the hateful words that were coming out of his mouth.

'Do you honestly believe that?' asked Jethro, anger growing in his voice.

'Admit it, Dad. You've never cared about your family. You've never cared about anyone but yourself and your precious inventions.'

Without thinking, Jethro lunged at his son and punched him hard in the face. Hunter fell back in shock, and Kayla jumped up to try and support his body weight.

'STOP IT, BOTH OF YOU!' she yelled in anger. 'This isn't helping Magnus.'

Hunter looked up at his father, who had tears in his eyes and was breathing heavily. This was the first time any of them had seen the old man lose control in such a manner.

'I loved your mother more than anything in the world,' said Jethro with a lump growing in his throat, 'watching her die in my arms was the single worst experience of my entire life. It tore my soul apart in ways you could never imagine.'

Jethro had an intense look of guilt and sadness painted on his face as he stared deep into his son's eyes. This was more emotion than Hunter had ever seen from his father. The pain he'd been suppressing all these years had finally boiled up to the surface.

'I'm truly sorry I haven't been the greatest father in the world to you, Hunter, but never try to tell me that I don't care. I care more than anything.'

The atmosphere in the room fell sombre and silent. It seemed Hunter was lost for words after the sudden outburst of emotion from his father.

Jethro turned around to try and calm himself down and noticed Andro looking a bit worse for wear in Amelia's arms.

'What happened to him?' he asked in a much more subdued voice.

'One of the intruders shot him in the face. I've not been able to revive him,' Amelia replied sombrely.

'Let me have a look at him.'

Amelia passed the robot to Jethro, who opened the casing on his back.

'Do you think you can fix him?' asked Amelia, with a predictably hopeful glint in her eyes.

'I'll see what I can do,' Jethro replied. He perched himself on his little stool and began tinkering with Andro's control panel.

Amelia suddenly noticed a hand sticking out from beneath some rubble near the doorway. She recognised who it belonged to instantly.

'TOM!' she cried at the top of her lungs as she rushed over to clear the debris that was on top of her brother. George rose to his feet immediately and began helping his daughter lift the door that was covering his son. Finally, Tom's dust-covered face came into the light, and George lifted him up and put his ear to the boy's chest.

'Is he alive?' asked Amelia, tears forming in her eyes.

To George's relief, he could hear a faint heartbeat coming from his son's chest.

'Yes, but his heart rate is slow. I think his airway might be blocked with dust. Pass me that water bottle behind you.'

Amelia quickly picked up a discarded water bottle from the floor and passed it to her father. George poured a few large drops into his son's mouth, and Tom instantly sprung to life in a mad coughing fit. Amelia and George both breathed an immense sigh of relief, and Tom hugged his father tighter than he had ever hugged him before.

Hunter put his hand on George's shoulder and turned to face the crowd of people. He looked into the eyes of his teammates Max, Toro, Taylor, Carter and the rest of the group, who were looking to him to provide some comforting words for them. But the fear and doubt in Hunter's mind were too much for him to bear.

'Everyone listen to me. A great tragedy has befallen us this day. The enemy has kidnapped Magnus and will try to use him as a weapon to start another war. Survival is now our top priority. The Shadow Squad and I will go out in search of a new base far away from here and hope the Arcadians don't discover our location.

Kayla shot him a look of incredulity.

'Hunter, what about Magnus? We can't just leave him to a fate worse than death.'

Hunter looked at her, defeated.

'I failed to protect him. It's over, Kayla.'

'It's not over while we're still alive,' Kayla said, trying to knock some sense into her husband, 'we have to figure out a way to try and help him.'

'It's impossible. Even if we could find a way to break into Arcadia, which we can't, we don't have the strength in numbers to battle their army.'

'So we just leave him to a life of torture while we run and hide, is that what you're saying?'

'WE LOST, KAYLA!' Hunter yelled aggressively.

The room suddenly went completely silent as the tension rose to boiling point.

'The mission failed. Magnus is beyond our help now. The best thing we can do is try and find a suitable location to lay low before the Arcadian soldiers come looking for us again. It's the only way to guarantee the survival of Ground Zero.'

Hunter turned and started walking away.

'I never realised I was married to such a coward,' Kayla said spitefully.

Hunter froze to the spot but didn't turn around. There were gasps and murmurs from the crowd as they waited anxiously to see what would happen next. After a few seconds, Hunter continued walking away, leaving Kayla shaking her head in disappointment.

Suddenly, an Arcadian soldier wearing a white suit could be seen walking over the rubble at the entrance of the training area. Hunter immediately stopped in his tracks, and the soldier put his hands in the air in a non-threatening manner. Jethro picked up the gun he was examining earlier and pointed it directly at the soldier's head.

'I'm unarmed. Listen to me, I'm not a threat to you,' said the soldier, in a surprisingly pathetic voice.

Hunter lunged at the Arcadian and pinned him against the wall by his throat. The soldier tried to wriggle free, but Hunter's grip was far too strong for him.

'Please, Hunter, stop! I come in peace,' the soldier cried out in a breathless whisper. Hunter loosened his grip the second he heard his name. This man knew who he was. He pulled the soldier's mask off and instantly recognised his face.

'Tobias?' he said, unable to believe his eyes. 'What the hell?'

'Good to see you, Hunter, it's… it's been a long time,' Tobias replied, rather awkwardly.

Jethro's eyes bulged, and he lunged forward, positioning his gun straight at Tobias' temple.

'Ah, Jethro, good to see you too, old friend,' Tobias said with not so subtle sarcasm.

'What would a pompous little weasel like you be doing all the way out here, Tobias?' Jethro hissed, trying with all his might to resist the urge to pull the trigger.

'Well, it's funny you should ask that question, Jethro,' Tobias said as he started laughing to himself, 'you remember that boy we locked away fifteen years ago to prevent the outcome of the next world war? Well, you people decided it was a good idea to break him out of prison, thus alerting the Master to his existence. Now he has the most destructive weapon in the world at his disposal and has banished me from the city for insubordination.'

'You deserve worse,' said Jethro with utter contempt.

'Well, now there's no one on the inside that has the power to stop him, thanks to you. Excellent job, guys!'

Tobias started clapping sarcastically.

'Don't you dare try and pin this on us, you little snake,' said Jethro fiercely, 'if it wasn't for your weakness, we wouldn't be in this mess in the first place, and my wife would still be alive.

Tobias paused for a moment and looked down at the ground.

'Look, I know you've suffered, all of you. I'm sorry about that; I truly am. This wasn't what I wanted to happen,' he said, trying his best to sound sincere.

'You didn't exactly do much to prevent it, though, did you?' said Hunter. 'Taking responsibility for your actions has never been one of your strengths, has it, Tobias?'

'What was I supposed to do, Hunter? You know the power the Master possesses, and now thanks to you, he has the most dangerous weapon of all.'

'Right, that's it, I've heard enough,' said Jethro, taking the stun off his weapon, 'stand back, Son.'

Hunter eased his grip on Tobias and stepped out of the way.

'Wait, I can help you,' Tobias spoke frantically as he cowered to the floor in fear.

'Help us? You can't even help yourself. You're no use to anyone anymore,' Jethro said condescendingly, 'it's time you finally got what you deserve.'

He was seconds away from pulling the trigger when Kayla put her hand on his gun.

'JETHRO, STOP!' she commanded.

He immediately released his finger from the trigger.

'Killing him won't bring Maria back!'

'It's not just about my wife. This man is responsible for the suffering of countless innocent people.'

'Yes, and right now, he might be the only person who can help us save Magnus. Let's hear what he's got to say before you blow him to halfway to hell.'

'Kayla, I know this man. You cannot trust a word he says. He's just telling us what we want to hear in order to save his own skin. It's what he's always done,' said Jethro scornfully.

'You'll want to hear what I have to say if you wish to save the boy,' said Tobias looking up from the floor.

'SHUT UP!' Jethro shouted.

'DROP THE GUN, JETHRO AND LET HIM SPEAK!' Kayla yelled.

Jethro looked into the eyes of his daughter-in-law. He knew this was a fight he wasn't going to win. After a few seconds of hesitation, he reluctantly dropped his weapon and stepped out of the way.

'Fine, speak!' he said, throwing Tobias a look of pure hatred.

Tobias took a deep breath in order to collect his thoughts before divulging his plan.

'The gates to Arcadia have an access code only certain elite officials know the combination to. Now, given that I've just been banished from the city, it's likely my passcode has been erased from the database. However, in the likely event I ever forgot my passcode, I made sure I always kept the override code on me at all times. Resetting this particular combination requires a full system reboot, which is unlikely to have been carried out

254

in the time since my absence. If you can get me to the gate before they have a chance to reboot the system, then I'll be able to get you inside the city. But we have to hurry.'

Hunter and Kayla exchanged a look of curious interest.

'If what you say is true, why didn't you use the code to get back inside the city before now?' asked Hunter suspiciously.

'Do you really think they'd let me simply stroll back in? I'd have been apprehended the second the gate closed behind me. I thought it would be a much smarter plan to return with some muscle by my side.'

Tobias looked specifically at Max standing nearby.

'Why do you even want to get back in there?' asked Kayla in a bemused tone.

'Because my family is still inside, I fear for their safety,' Tobias replied, unable to hide his vulnerability.

Hunter thought about this for a long time. He knew Tobias was untrustworthy, but at this very moment, they had very few options available to them.

'We need to discuss this,' he said, looking at Kayla, 'Max, watch him. Make sure he doesn't move.'

Max nodded and pressed his humongous foot on Tobias' shoulder, pinning him down.

'Oh, by all means, let's talk it through. It's not as if time is of the essence or anything,' said Tobias sarcastically.

'Shut up, Scumbag!' Max jeered, pressing his full body weight down on the ex-commander's shoulder, making him cry out in agony, 'things aren't as hoity-toity here as they are where you come from.'

Hunter and Kayla moved to one side, away from the crowd. He kissed her lovingly on the lips.

'I'm sorry for my despair earlier. I should never have shouted at you. I was frightened,' Hunter apologised.

'I know. I'm sorry I said you were a coward,' Kayla replied.

'You were right. I was being a coward. We can't allow Magnus to suffer at the hands of that monster. I think we're going to have to take Tobias up on his offer.'

'Do you think we can trust him?'

'Absolutely not!' Hunter replied, shaking his head and laughing under his breath, 'there's every likelihood he's leading us into some sort of trap, but it doesn't look like we have much choice. From the sounds of it, he seems to be as desperate as we are to get back in there.'

They both nodded to each other and exchanged a knowing look.

'Max, release him,' Hunter commanded. Max promptly lifted his foot off Tobias, and Hunter grabbed him by the shoulders and pulled him upright.

'All right, Tobias. You have a deal.'

Hunter extended his hand, which Tobias shook instantly. Jethro shot his son a look of deep concern.

'Excellent,' Tobias replied in a jovial tone.

'But if I get any indication that you're trying to sabotage this mission in any way, even for a second, then Max has permission to re-sculpt your face using both of his fists. Do I make myself clear?'

Tobias glanced over at Max, who seemed to be relishing that particular prospect.

'Very clear,' he replied, taking a large gulp.

Jethro turned away, shaking his head disapprovingly, and Hunter turned to address the room.

'Shadow Squad, prepare yourselves. The time has come to execute the mission we've been planning for fifteen years. There may be no coming back from this, but we cannot leave Magnus to a life of torture and slavery. Let's take these bastards down once and for all.'

A cheer erupted from the Squad as each member turned to go grab his or her weapons. Amelia stood to attention and tapped Kayla on the back.

'Kayla, I'd like to volunteer my services in this rescue mission.'

'No, Amelia. It's too dangerous,' Kayla replied, shaking her head.

'Kayla's right Amelia,' said George, putting his hand on his daughter's shoulders, 'it's too dangerous for you.'

'Dad, Magnus is my friend. I want to help bring him back.'

'This is not a game, Amelia. We nearly lost your brother tonight; I'm not about to allow you to walk into a war zone to save your friend. I'm sorry!'

'Listen to your Dad, Amelia,' said Kayla. 'Leave the fighting to the experts.'

Amelia shook her head and turned to face her father.

'What if it was Mum? What if there was a chance we could bring her back? Wouldn't you want to do anything within your power to help make that happen?'

Amelia stared deeply into her father's tear-filled eyes as she allowed her words to sink in.

'I'm not a little girl anymore, Dad. You have to let me go.'

George paused for a moment. He could see how important this was to his daughter.

'If you really feel you have to go, then I'm coming with you,' he said.

'Dad, you're the only doctor in this place. You need to tend to the people here,' Amelia replied.

In that moment, Billy stepped forward and bowed his head to George. Everyone stared at him with shocked expressions due to this sudden uncharacteristic display of manners.

'She can ride with me, Mr Hart. I know how much Magnus means to Amelia. I'll make sure nothing bad happens to her, I promise,' he said, giving Amelia a nod.

Amelia didn't know how to react. This was the first time Billy had ever shown anything resembling kindness towards her since they'd met.

George looked deep into his daughter's pleading eyes before finally and reluctantly giving his nod of approval. Amelia smiled and swung her arms tightly around her father's waist.

'Thanks, Dad, I knew you'd understand,' she said lovingly.

'You make sure you come back in one piece; do you understand me, Amelia?' he said, trying to resist the urge to break down and cry.

'I will, Dad.'

Hunter turned to address the young girl.

'You're a brave kid, Amelia. If you're coming with us, then you'll need a suit.'

He looked over at Jethro.

'Let's see if we can find one that fits you.'

- CHAPTER 19 -
MEETING THE MASTER

Magnus opened his eyes suddenly as if waking from a bad dream. He felt weak and disoriented and was shocked to notice that his arms and legs were bound in metal cuffs, and his body was stretched out wide like a starfish. He looked around in horror at the thick glass walls that surrounded him. He seemed to be encased in some sort of transparent chamber. He tried with all his might to wrestle free from his metal bonds, but it was no use. He was trapped. His heart rate began to increase as panic set in, and a million questions whirled around in his head:

'Where am I? Who brought me here? How do I get out of this?' were just a few that came instantly to mind.

Magnus looked around the room outside his glass tomb to see if he could find anything that might help ameliorate his current situation, but it was completely encased in darkness. He could only see a few feet in front of him. Suddenly he heard a deep, booming voice echo from every possible angle, which sent a cold shiver down his spine.

'It's good to see you awake, boy! I hope my soldiers weren't too rough with you.'

Magnus was trying to determine where the voice was coming from. His eyes darted in all directions, but he couldn't see anything or anybody through the darkness.

'Who said that?' he said in a shaky voice.

'Someone who has been very much looking forward to meeting you. Someone who until quite recently believed you to be dead.'

Suddenly, Magnus noticed an ominous cloaked figure emerge from the shadows, floating towards him on some sort of hovering chair. His black mask and breathing apparatus resembled something from a gothic nightmare. Magnus looked at him in horror as he edged closer to the glass wall that divided them.

'My name is Calvin Mortifer, but you can call me Master. I am the ruler of Arcadia.'

Magnus' heart sank. He had heard many stories about the Master over the past couple of months, but he never imagined he would look and sound so menacing.

'What should I call you?' asked the Master in a calm voice.

'Magnus,' the teenager replied, trying not to reveal how utterly terrified he was.

'Magnus? An appropriate name for one as powerful as you.'

The dark figure tilted his head to the side as he gazed at the teenager in front of him.

'I must say you look different to what I was expecting. My memory must not be what it once was.'

Magnus looked at him, confused. Had they somehow met before? None of this was making any sense to him.

'Why did you kidnap me?' asked Magnus, finding some courage from somewhere deep inside him.

'I brought you home,' the Master responded with palpable glee.

Magnus looked at him in utter disbelief.

'You must have spent your entire life wondering where you came from. What your purpose was. It all started here, Magnus, and I have all the answers you've been waiting for. Let me take you back to the beginning.'

Magnus braced himself. The Master was right; he had spent every waking hour of his life contemplating the reasons for his existence. However, now that he was finally about to learn the truth, he wasn't sure he wanted to know.

The Master pressed a button on his chair, and a hologram appeared of a man in his mid-thirties with a bald head, similar in appearance to Magnus. The boy looked at the hologram in complete shock. It was as if he was watching footage of himself twenty years in the future.

'When the Andromeda virus first hit all those years ago, I was one of the first to be volunteered, against my will, to test out a new vaccine the government had approved for human trials.'

The footage started to show the man being forcibly strapped to a hospital bed and injected in the arm with the vaccine.

'However, it didn't have the effect they were hoping for. It mutated my cells and gave me abilities far beyond anyone else's control.'

The footage then showed the man using his powers to attack the doctors who inflicted this suffering upon him. Magnus winced as he saw people being thrown hundreds of feet and ripped apart in front of his eyes.

'From that moment on, I realised I had the power to bend anything and anyone to my will. After a lifetime of struggle and hardship living in complete poverty, I finally had control of my destiny. I knew that my rise to power would be inevitable. However, as the years passed, my declining health and old age made me vulnerable, and I knew I needed an heir if I was to maintain dominance over my land. Using highly advanced, state of the art technology, I ordered my scientists to begin work on cell duplication to see if they could create new life using my DNA. However, the results were a disaster.'

The hologram started showing babies being born with monstrous deformities. Some had limbs growing out of their faces. Some had no limbs at all. Some of them reminded Magnus of the grotesque demons in his old video games. It was truly the stuff of nightmares.

'None of the experiments survived... until you, Magnus!'

Magnus suddenly looked up at the Master in shock. He shook his head in disbelief at what he had just heard.

'That's right, Magnus,' the Master said with relish. 'You are my one surviving clone.'

As he said those words, he removed his mask to reveal the pasty, wrinkled face of an old, decrepit man who was struggling to breathe on his own. Magnus could clearly see the fire-bolt shaped birthmark over his left eye that was identical to his own.

He felt instantly sick. He wasn't prepared for a revelation like this. It couldn't possibly be true.

'YOU'RE LYING!' Magnus shouted at the top of his lungs as tears began to roll down his cheeks.

'Did you ever wonder why you could never grow hair on any part of your body? It's because of a rare auto-immune disorder called Alopecia Universalis, something I've suffered from since birth.'

Magnus shook his head. He refused to believe it.

'Take a look for yourself....'

Footage popped up on the hologram of Calvin as a young boy, living rough on the streets of London. Another clip then popped up of his recruitment into the army as a teenager. Then another clip showed him fighting in the war with a young Jethro by his side.

Magnus noticed the resemblance to himself immediately. There could be no denying it. Ten feet away from him, behind the thick glass wall that divided them, sat the man he would one day become.

The Master began coughing and sputtering and promptly put his mask back on to assist with his breathing.

'You see, Magnus. You were meant to return to me. We are one and the same.'

'I'M NOTHING LIKE YOU!' Magnus screamed, tears streaming down his face, 'YOU'RE EVIL!'

'I used to think the same way about those who were in power. But trust me, once you join me and see the things we can do together to build a stronger empire for our people, you'll change your outlook.'

Magnus shook his head.

'I'LL NEVER JOIN YOU!'

He lifted his hands in an attempt to break the glass surrounding him using his powers, but nothing happened. He tried again with all his strength and concentration, but the glass didn't even wobble. He glanced at Calvin, who seemed to be chuckling maniacally to himself.

'Your powers won't work inside this chamber, boy! You see that box above your head?'

Magnus looked up to see a hexagonal box with a blinking green light attached to the top of his chamber, identical in appearance to the one he used to stare at in his old prison cell.

'It's the exact same telekinetic inhibitor you had in your room at Periculo Prison, created by the very people who locked you away all those years ago. I had my soldiers pick it up before the raid on the rebels base. They call it an immobiliser. A genius invention, I must admit. It could have put me in a lot of bother fifteen years ago, but they were too weak and cowardly to use it, and I was far too clever. I thought about destroying it once we'd captured you, but then I realised I could use it to my advantage. As long as it surrounds your chamber, your powers will be useless.'

Magnus felt completely helpless as he hung his head in defeat.

'You see, Magnus. You really don't have any other option but to become the weapon you were made for. There isn't any point in trying to resist.'

'You can't make me fight for you,' Magnus said aggressively, but Calvin just laughed.

'If there's one thing I've learnt over my many years as ruler of this country, it's that I can make people do anything I want them to do.'

The Master pushed a button on his chair, and suddenly a surge of electricity rushed through Magnus' body, causing his muscles to seize violently. Magnus cried out in terror as the pain in his body reached a level he'd never experienced before. He thought at that moment he was going to die.

After several seconds, Calvin released his finger from the button, and the electrical surge came to a stop. Magnus' body went limp, and his breathing became rapid, desperate to get oxygen back into his lungs. His heart was pumping in his chest faster than ever before as if it was trying to catch up on the beats it had just missed.

'You see, boy, it's hopeless for you. If you refuse to cooperate with me, you'll see first-hand to what level I relish inflicting pain on others.'

The Master pressed the button once again, and another surge of electricity shot through Magnus' body. Somehow the pain was even worse this time, and he could feel his wrists and his ankles burning against his metal bindings. Magnus' cries echoed through the void of the Master's chambers. All he could do was pray for a miracle that would save him from this excruciating torture.

Back at the base, Hunter and the Shadow Squad were suited up and ready to board the jet. Tobias boarded first, followed closely by Max, who was holding a gun to his back. Kayla and Billy helped Amelia onto the aircraft, and the others followed in behind them.

Hunter was the last to exit Ground Zero. However, he suddenly noticed his father had gotten his suit on and was heading towards the entrance to the plane carrying Andro under his arm and a large bag on his back.

'Hold it there, Dad,' he said as if disciplining a naughty child.

Jethro instantly stopped in his tracks.

'You don't think I'm going to let you come on this mission, do you?'

'I'd like to see you try and stop me, Son,' he replied, turning to face Hunter.

'Dad, come on. You know you're too old for this fight,'

'Nonsense,' Jethro said dismissively, 'I may not be as nimble as I used to be, but I've still got it where it counts.'

'I need you to stay here and look after the others in case we don't make it back.'

Jethro got right up close to his son's face antagonistically.

'Listen to me, Hunter. I've waited fifteen years to finally take my revenge, and I'm not going to spend it babysitting while you and your team take all the glory.'

He turned back around and began to board the plane. However, Hunter suddenly grabbed him and pulled him back.

'Dad, stop!' he commanded. Jethro pushed his son's arm away in anger.

'Remember who you're talking to, boy!' Jethro said with the condescending authority only a father could possess, 'I'm not one of your lackeys you get to order around. I'm your father, and there's nothing you can say or do that will stop me from getting on this plane.'

'Dad, you don't understand....'

'I do understand, Son. I've understood since the very beginning. I know you blame me for your mother's death. Don't worry; I've blamed myself every moment since the day it happened. But this is my chance to try and put things right once and for all. Don't take that away from me.'

Hunter started shaking his head.

'I can't afford to lose you, Dad,' he said with a lump growing in his throat. Jethro took a deep breath.

'Son, if you don't let me do this, then you may as well have lost me,' he replied, looking deep into his son's eyes, 'I'll never be able to rest, do you understand? Don't tell me you wouldn't do the same for Kayla.'

Hunter hung his head. His father was absolutely right. If the boot were on the other foot, he'd be doing the exact same thing his father was. Jethro put his hand on his son's shoulder.

'Don't worry, Son. Everything will work out if we stick together as a unit.'

In that moment, Hunter did something he hadn't done in very a long time. He lunged at his father and wrapped his arms around him in a tight embrace. Jethro had tears in his eyes as he wrapped his hands around Hunter for the first time in fifteen years. He finally felt like he had his son back.

Kayla smiled as she looked out the window of the jet to see her husband and his father sharing a loving embrace.

After a few seconds, the two men finally broke the hug and stepped apart.

'Come on. Let's get this done,' said Jethro.

Hunter nodded, and they both climbed aboard the plane.

Jethro took a seat next to Kayla, and Hunter stood at the front of the jet to address his team.

'Shadow Squad. This is the fight of our lives. We all know our missions. Tobias will break us into the city using his access codes. Once we're inside, we head straight to the Capitol building, where Magnus is being held prisoner. After Jethro gives the signal, Billy and Amelia will sneak into the Capitol building and break into the Master's chamber to rescue Magnus while the rest of us keep the Arcadian guards at bay. Everyone clear?'

'YES, CAPTAIN!' the squad replied in unison.

'Failure is not an option on this mission. Everyone strap yourselves in. Let's go rescue Magnus,' Hunter said with a glint of excitement and determination in his eyes.

The Shadow Squad cheered with delight as the plane began to rise into the air and turned its trajectory in the direction of the city in the sky.

- CHAPTER 20 -
RESCUE MISSION

After two hours of flying in torrential rain, the jet finally reached its destination at the Arcadian border. It landed on the helipad in front of the gateway, and battle drones were dispatched to attack within seconds.

Hunter suddenly leapt to his feet, and his mask folded over his face.

'Let's move,' he said with urgency as the team followed him towards the doorway at the end of the plane.

Amelia suddenly felt a wave of nerves wash over her body. This was the furthest she'd ever been out of the Southern province, and she was about to step outside into a barrage of laser fire. She rubbed her hands together to stop herself from trembling. Kayla glanced over at the young girl and could see the blatant fear in her eyes.

'Come on, Amelia, put your mask on. Let's go get Magnus back.'

Amelia smiled and nodded determinedly. The mere mention of Magnus' name was all she needed to summon the courage from deep within her to fight. She pressed the button on her suit, and her mask folded out over her face.

Hunter looked over at his father, who'd spent the majority of the flight casually tinkering with Andro's mechanical insides.

'Dad, we're here. Get your mask on,' the captain commanded impatiently.

'One second, Son, I'm almost finished,' Jethro replied, twisting his screwdriver deep into Andro's metal skull.

'Quick question,' said Kayla. 'How's Andro supposed to survive the EMP?'

'He's fitted with a backup power bank which will kick in when the EMP goes off,' explained Jethro. 'None of the Arcadian drones have such a feature, which will give us the advantage.'

Suddenly, a spark flew out of Andro's side panel, and the robot sprung to life, holding out his arms in a fisticuffs manner.

'Alright, who wants some of this?' the robot exclaimed as if in some sort of bar room brawl. He suddenly noticed he was no longer in the Sanctum beating up Arcadian thugs. He was, in fact, hovering in front of several very confused looking members of the Shadow Squad.

'Have I missed something?' the robot asked, looking around in bewilderment. 'Where's Magnus?'

'He got captured during the raid,' replied Amelia, 'we've flown all the way to Arcadia to rescue him.'

'WHAT?' Andro yelled out in terror.

Suddenly, the plane shook violently from a sharp blast to its side, and Andro fell from the air into Carter's arms.

'Don't worry, little buddy, we won't let anyone short circuit you,' he joked, but Andro didn't see the funny side. Taylor gave her brother a hard punch to the arm.

'You two, stop messing about,' said Toro, cocking his gun.

The plane took another big hit to the side, which seemed to shake Tobias to his core. He suddenly felt a rush of adrenaline pump through his body upon the realisation that any minute he would have to walk into a potentially deadly combat situation – something he'd spent his entire life trying to avoid. Hunter grabbed him by the shoulders and pulled him up to his feet. He ignited his shock-absorbent shield and wrapped it around the ex-commander.

'This thing deflects laser fire, right?' asked Tobias nervously.

'You'd better hope so,' replied Hunter in an apathetic tone, 'remember, no funny business. You stick with us until Magnus is safe. Understood?'

Tobias looked over at Max, who was cracking his knuckles and smiling at him sadistically.

'Understood,' Tobias replied, nodding vigorously, 'just make sure you keep that big meat sack away from me.'

Max simply laughed.

Billy turned to Amelia and passed her a small laser gun concealed in his pocket.

'You might need this when we head out there. Make sure you stay close to me,' he said protectively.

Amelia nodded and prepared herself for what was to come.

Hunter braced Tobias and turned to address the group.

'Shadow Squad, get ready. Doors open in three, two, one.'

The captain pressed a button, and the door swung open. Lasers immediately began shooting through the open door and bouncing off the walls inside the plane. Hunter pushed Tobias out onto the helipad with a great deal of force, straight into the thrashing down rain. The Shadow Squad followed behind their leader and split up into small groups around the hanger. This made it difficult for the drones to lock on to a specific target.

The attack was intense but predictably brief, as the drones were clearly still no match for the shooting prowess of the Shadow Squad.

Hunter and Tobias reached the front gate with relative ease, and Tobias opened the keypad on the wall in front of him. He took out a small piece of parchment he had stashed in his inside pocket and began typing in the override code written inside:

1815191_12213119_1315121225

As he was typing, he realised his hand was shaking uncontrollably, and his vision was blurred due to the rain splashing against his visor. He wasn't entirely sure he was pressing the right buttons, and to complicate matters further, the rain was causing the ink on the piece of parchment to run. He typed in the last number, and a red warning sign started flashing on the screen in front of his face:

'Access Denied.'

Tobias suddenly felt a rush of fear. They couldn't possibly have rebooted the system already, could they?

If he didn't get the Shadow Squad inside the city walls, there's no telling what that brute Max was going to do to him. To make matters worse, more drones had been dispatched and started firing directly at Hunter and Tobias. Hunter's shield was taking a royal pounding as Tobias attempted to type the number in a second time.

'What's taking so long?' Hunter shouted.

'Patience is a virtue, Hunter,' replied Tobias flippantly.

'Not right now it isn't!'

Tobias keyed in the last number once again, and this time, a green screen flashed up in front of them.

'Access Granted.'

Tobias breathed a huge sigh of relief that the old system was still in operation, and the gateway began to open in front of them.

'Everybody inside!' Hunter called to his team as they all flew through the circular doorway. Once everyone was inside, Tobias typed in his code again, and the doors slammed shut, locking out the remaining battle drones.

'Everyone hold out your arms and legs,' Jethro instructed. The team adopted the starfish position as hot air began pumping round the decontamination chamber. After a few seconds, the air pumps turned off, and a voice echoed through the chamber.

'*Decontamination process complete.*'

The doors to the city opened, and the team rushed inside before they got locked in the chamber. The gate closed behind them, and the Squad retracted their masks. The first stage of their mission was complete, and

Hunter decided this would be a good opportunity for a short breather.

For many members of the team, this was their first time inside the city walls. Amelia was absolutely mesmerised by the sight she saw ahead of her. The beautiful night sky was lit up by hundreds of flying vehicles gliding through the gaps between massive skyscrapers. It was truly a wonder to behold. In fact, she'd gotten so caught up in the city's beauty she almost forgot the purpose they were there in the first place. However, she quickly snapped out of it when she noticed Tobias trying to make a sneaky getaway.

'Where's he going?' Amelia yelled.

Hunter looked round in shock to see Tobias sprinting in the opposite direction.

'TOBIAS!' he shouted at the top of his lungs, but there was no response. Hunter activated the boosters on his suit, but Kayla held him back.

'Leave him, Hunter. He's no longer any use to us. He'd only slow us down anyway.'

Kayla was right. Tobias had served his purpose. Hunter only wished to keep him on a leash so that he could have the satisfaction of making the ex-commander's life a living hell once this was all over. He took a moment to compose himself and then turned back to face the team again.

'Right, everyone, regroup. The Capitol building is two miles North East from here,' he said, gesturing in the direction they needed to head, 'it'll be quicker if we fly. Everyone follow my lead.'

He activated his boosters and started to levitate off the ground. The others did the same as they each flew off in unison, trying to keep up with the captain. Amelia felt a bit unsteady in her suit, as this was the first experience flying in one. However, she was soon starting to get the hang of it.

They flew up alongside an Arcadian pod that had two children pressing their faces against the glass. Amelia waved at them, and they waved back, exchanging looks of innocent wonder. Their mother pulled them away from the pod window and gazed out in shock as the Shadow Squad flew past.

The Squad weaved in and out of oncoming traffic with immense skill and precision. However, they were suddenly set upon by another barrage of laser fire. Arcadian guards had been made aware of the Shadow Squad's infiltration of the city, and their hover buggies were in full speed pursuit as they tried to knock them out of the sky. The team ignited their shields to deflect the lasers; however, they ricocheted off in all directions and caused substantial damage to some nearby buildings. Billy noticed one of the guards firing at Amelia, who was struggling to fend him off. He flew over and kicked the guard's buggy extremely hard, sending it hurtling towards the ground at an almighty speed.

'Thanks,' said Amelia gratefully.

Billy nodded and flew out ahead of her.

The Squad rounded a corner, and the towering Capitol building came into view ahead of them. Hunter gave a signal for the Squad to begin their descent to the ground.

However, the second they landed, a huge swarm of battle drones escaped from the Capitol building, followed by a small army of Arcadian soldiers marching in precise formation. Leading the army was Colonel Braxton, and they were all armed to the teeth with state of the art weapons, ready to do battle.

Amelia looked out in shock at the sheer size of the army in front of them. The Squad was severely outnumbered and massively outgunned.

'This is where the real fun begins,' said Taylor excitedly.

'Whoever takes out the least soldiers buys the drinks tonight,' said Carter. He and his sister high-fived and assumed their battle stance.

Braxton raised his fist in the air, and the army immediately stopped marching.

'You are trespassing on Arcadian land,' he shouted, 'rebellious actions such as this will not be tolerated by this government. Surrender your weapons now, or they will be taken by force.'

'Fat chance of that,' said Toro gripping his gun tightly.

'Give us back the boy, and we will leave in peace!' Hunter yelled to the colonel.

'This is not a negotiation,' Braxton replied. 'Drop your weapons now or suffer the consequences.'

Both sides were poised and ready to fight; the slightest pin drop would have been enough to set the battle in motion. Without warning, Hunter moved for his gun and shot Braxton directly in the shoulder. The colonel fell to the floor, clutching his burning wound.

'GET THEM!' Braxton yelled at the top of his lungs as his army began to race forward and attack.

'FOR MAGNUS!' Hunter cried as the Shadow Squad jeered and assumed battle formation. Drones began firing from the sky above as the Squad ignited their shields and held them over their heads. Andro flew out and began shooting his laser at the drones up above. The Squad banded together in a cluster in order to create the best attack and defence strategy. Each member on the right would act as a shield to those on the left whilst using their weapons to fight back against the soldiers. Several Arcadians broke free of their ranks and started attacking them from all angles. Amelia was almost hit in the face by an electrically charged metal staff, but Billy deflected it with his sword thanks to his fast reactions. She raised her laser gun and pointed it at the soldier's groin. She fired the weapon, and the soldier fell to the floor, clutching his tender regions as his legs slowly turned to jelly.

'Nice one!' exclaimed Billy as he continued fending off more soldiers.

The fight increased in intensity, and on Hunter's command, the Squad broke formation in order to cover more ground. Each member had a different method of fighting or skill that was effective in its own right. Hunter had his speed. Kayla had her agility. Max and Toro had their brute strength and stamina. Carter and Taylor had their acrobatic prowess, and Jethro had his gadgets and gizmos. Together they made a formidable team, competently holding their own against the sizable Arcadian army.

Jethro hurled his backpack onto the floor and opened it to reveal his EMP machine.

'EVERYONE TAKE COVER!' he yelled as he pulled the lever on the machine, and huge sparks flew out in all directions. Hundreds of drones immediately fell out of the sky as all the electrical power in the immediate vicinity instantly died. That was the signal for Amelia, Billy and Andro to sneak into the Capitol building and descend towards the Master's Chamber.

At the same time the battle was happening at the Capitol, Tobias finally reached his home and keyed in his combination to unlock the door.

'Welcome home, Tobias,' said Electra. Tobias felt surprisingly comforted by the voice of his home security system. However, after taking only one step into his giant hallway, he heard euphoric laughter coming from his living room. He slowly walked inside to see Rosa and Grant sitting on his sofa with their arms around each other, drinking wine and laughing hysterically.

'What's going on here?' asked Tobias, unable to comprehend what he was seeing.

Rosa and Grant turned in shock and immediately leapt off the couch as if it was on fire.

'Tobias?' exclaimed Grant.

'This isn't what it looks like,' said Rosa, trying to sound as convincing as she could.

Tobias was seething. He couldn't believe his wife and friend could have betrayed him in this way. He was so enraged that he failed to notice Grant pressing a panic button on a remote in his pocket. Tobias grabbed a gun from inside a compartment of his suit and pointed it at them both.

'And what exactly does it look like, Rosa? Like my friend and my wife having an affair behind my back?' Tobias yelled in outrage.

'I heard that you'd been banished from the city... Grant simply came over to... to make sure that me and the kids were all right,' said Rosa, struggling to form the words to explain herself.

'Well, you seemed to be handling the news pretty well a moment ago,' Tobias said resentfully. Rosa started crying.

'How did you get back into the city?' asked Grant.

'I joined forces with the rebels,' Tobias replied smugly, 'they've broken into the city, and they're storming the Capitol as we speak.'

Grant looked at him in shock. He reached into his pocket to take out his phone, but Tobias pointed the gun directly at his face.

'Don't even think about it... friend!'

It pained him to say it.

'Drop the phone.'

Grant did as he was told and raised his hands into the air.

'So tell me. How long has this been going on?' Tobias asked, glaring at his wife, but she couldn't respond. She could barely look him in the eye.

'It's been two years,' said Grant ashamedly.

'TWO YEARS?' Tobias screamed furiously. 'Are you kidding me?'

Suddenly a revelation occurred to him.

'It WAS you who was feeding information to the Master all this time, wasn't it? All so you could get me out of the picture and be with my wife.'

Grant didn't need to answer; Tobias could see it in his face. He looked back at Rosa.

'How could you do this to me?'

'It just happened, Tobias. We didn't plan it. For years I tried so hard to make our family work while you were away running the country, but I got so lonely, and I knew deep down you didn't really care,' Rosa explained.

'Do you think running the country is an easy job, Rosa? Do you think I didn't wish every second of every day that I could just come home and be with you and the kids? I sacrificed everything to make sure you had a perfect life, and it still wasn't enough for you.'

Suddenly Lucas and Molly poked their little heads around the corner of the room.

'DADDY!' they both exclaimed in unison. Tobias turned to face them, and they ran over to give him a big hug.

'Oh, I've missed you two so much,' he said, pulling them closer and kissing them on the forehead.

'Mummy said we'd never see you again,' said Molly on the verge of tears.

Tobias looked up at his deceitful wife. The intense hatred in his eyes was enough to turn her heart to stone.

'Don't worry, Molly,' Tobias whispered in his daughter's ear, 'Mummy was severely mistaken.'

Rosa looked into her husband's eyes with intense remorse for her actions. She wished more than anything she could have taken it all back.

All of a sudden, the front door burst open, and several armed guards flooded into the living room.

'Arrest him!' Grant shouted to his men. Tobias stood up and aimed his gun in Grant's direction, but before he could pull the trigger, two guards grabbed him by the arms and slammed him face-first against the wall, pinning him in place. The kids screamed and ran over to their mother.

'Don't hurt him,' shouted Rosa hysterically.

'Take him to the Capitol,' Grant commanded, 'there's a prison cell in the Master's chamber with his name on it.'

The guards bowed their heads, wrenched Tobias away from the wall and dragged him towards the front door. Grant picked up his briefcase and coat.

'Where are you going?' asked Rosa.

'Rebels are attacking the city. I need to go warn the Master. Wait here until I get back,' said Grant. He went to kiss her on the lips, but she turned her face away from him. He kissed her on the cheek and headed to the front door.

Rosa stood with Lucas and Molly, looking out of the window at the men dragging her husband away. Tobias looked back through the window at his wife and children. Rosa felt a sharp sting of regret in the pit of her stomach.

'How did it come to this?' she asked herself.

- CHAPTER 21 -
FIGHT TO THE DEATH

Magnus' screams echoed deep into the Master's chamber. He'd spent the last few hours in complete and utter agony after continually refusing to give in to the Master's demands. The pain he experienced was so intense he thought he would likely pass out at any moment. Calvin didn't seem to care. He took extreme pleasure in torturing helpless victims and knew it was only a matter of time before the teenager would crack under pressure. They always did.

Suddenly a blue hologram of Grant Boswell's head appeared in front of the Master's chair. He released his hand from the button, and the electrocution momentarily stopped.

'Begging your pardon, my Lord,' said Grant sounding panicked.

'NOT NOW!' Calvin barked, feeling extremely irritated by the untimely interruption.

'My Lord, we are under attack. Rebels have broken into the city and are storming the Capitol....'

Suddenly the hologram disappeared, and the lights in the chamber died, thrusting the room into complete darkness. The Master's hoverchair fell to the ground with a crash. Something had killed all the power to the building.

Calvin gazed around in confusion.

'Activate back up power,' he said as the lights instantly flickered back on and his chair rose from the ground again.

'Show me the security footage from outside the Capitol building.'

A new hologram appeared, and the Master watched in horror at the carnage happening outside. The Shadow Squad were dispatching his soldiers with unprecedented efficiency, and their numbers seemed to be dwindling at a rapid pace.

Calvin glanced up at Magnus, who was slumped forward with smoke coming off his clothes. It was clear the boy was approaching the end of his tether.

'It looks like your troublesome friends have come to rescue you, boy. I'm going to leave this footage on so that you can watch me slaughter every single one of them.'

The Master's chair turned 180 degrees and started floating towards the exit. On his way out, Calvin passed two of his guards standing in the doorway.

'Watch him until I get back,' he said commandingly. Both guards nodded as the Master made his way out of the chamber.

Amelia, Billy and Andro descended down the steps of the Capitol building until they reached a hallway on the bottom floor. Suddenly they noticed a door in front of them open as the Master hovered into the room. Luckily, due to the poor lighting and Calvin's restricted eyesight, they were able to leap behind a large nearby cabinet before he could detect their presence. He floated right past them and made his way up the steps towards the exit of the building. As soon as the coast was clear, the trio ran down the hallway towards the chamber at the end of the room, praying they weren't too late.

The guards on the other side of the door heard a strange knocking sound. One of the guards opened the door, assuming the Master was having issues and needed assistance. However, he immediately got hit in the face by Billy's fist. The other guard reached for his staff, but he too got a large thwack to the head. Both guards collapsed in a heap on the floor, and Billy gave them another couple of hard kicks for good measure.

'I think they're knocked out, Billy,' said Amelia, implying he should probably stop before he did some serious damage.

'Just making sure,' Billy replied, giving them one last kick and stepping over their lifeless bodies.

Andro flew straight over to Magnus' cell, where he stood hanging from his bindings. He didn't seem entirely conscious.

'MAGNUS!' Amelia cried, running over to him. She started banging on the glass, trying her hardest to wake him up.

Magnus heard the faint sound of his voice being called from the other side of the glass wall. He tilted his head up using all the strength he could muster and saw Amelia and Andro's worried faces looking straight back at him.

'Magnus, are you okay?' she asked with huge concern. However, he didn't have the strength to reply. He barely had the strength to hold his head up.

'Don't worry; we're going to get you out of there. How do we open this damn thing?' Amelia asked. She looked to her right and noticed a combination lock. She started pressing random buttons on the keypad, hoping she would somehow get lucky and guess the code.

'There's no way you're going to work out the number like that, Amelia,' said Billy dismissively whilst walking up behind her. 'Stand back, both of you.'

Amelia and Andro both took a step back from the glass as Billy reached into his pocket and pulled out a ring-shaped object. He stuck it to the glass and turned it anti-clockwise. The ring began burning a hole in the glass. It edged its way through to the other side, where it fell on the floor next to Magnus' feet.

'Magnus, shield your eyes,' Billy instructed as he took a couple of large steps back. Magnus placed his head into his arm to cover his eyes, and Billy suddenly lunged forward with great speed towards the thick glass. He kicked at the ring-shaped hole, which made a huge crack in the pane surrounding it. Billy kicked it another few times until it finally gave way and shattered into a million pieces.

Andro flew straight into the cell and activated his red laser to cut Magnus' bindings. Magnus fell to the floor, and Amelia ran over to lift him up.

'Magnus, are you alright?' she cried with deep concern.

'I'm okay,' he whispered in a raspy voice. He wrapped his arms around his friend. 'Thank you.'

Amelia smiled from ear to ear as she pulled him in closer to her. She was so relieved that no serious harm had come to her best friend.

Magnus looked up and noticed his robot floating nearby.

'Andro!' he exclaimed, throwing his arms around him, 'I thought I'd lost you.'

'You almost did. Jethro fixed me on the way here. You can't get rid of me that easily,' Andro replied with a chuckle.

Magnus finally turned to Billy, who, he had to admit, was the last person he was expecting to see on this rescue mission. They both looked at each other, unsure of what to say or do.

'Glad you're okay, Maggie,' said Billy, breaking the tension.

'Thanks for coming to save me,' Magnus replied.

'Well, I owed you one for saving me before. Now we're square.'

He held out his fist, and Magnus fist-bumped him. This was the first moment of mutual respect between the two of them, and Magnus wanted to savour it. Unfortunately, time was against them.

'Come on, we have to help the others,' said Billy urgently.

The ferocity of the fight outside continued to escalate as the Shadow Squad got closer to victory. Hunter and Toro were fighting side by side, Kayla had picked a fight with a female Arcadian soldier of equal strength and speed, and the twins were busy keeping score of the number of soldiers they'd dispatched. Max had picked out Braxton, who seemed to have shaken off his wounded shoulder. He lunged at the colonel with his axe, but Braxton saw it coming and blocked it with his sword. The force from the axe caused shards of metal from Braxton's weapon to ping off in all directions as the fight grew in intensity. Unfortunately, the weight of Max's axe was beginning to affect his speed, and Braxton took full advantage, successfully landing several clean slashes to his legs and torso. Noticing that Max was struggling, Hunter lunged towards them and intervened in the fight. Max limped off, letting the two swordsmen battle it out.

Hunter and Braxton were incredibly evenly matched, both having been trained to fight by Jethro; however, Hunter's acrobatic prowess was on a different level and seemed to throw Braxton off balance a fair few times. Suddenly the colonel landed a blow to Hunter's hand, causing him to drop his weapon. However, Hunter's quick thinking allowed him to sweep Braxton's legs before he could take another swing of his sword. The colonel fell to the ground, and his weapon flew out of his hands and landed several metres out of reach.

Both men were now unarmed. Braxton lunged once again at the captain, and they continued to fight hand to hand. Braxton wasn't nearly as proficient as Hunter without his sword, and the captain successfully landed several hard blows to the colonel's face. It looked like Hunter was close to winning the fight when suddenly he started levitating off the ground, unable to move his muscles. He looked around to see what was going on and noticed that the same thing had happened to the rest of the Shadow Squad. This could only mean one thing; The Master had arrived.

The old man floated in his hoverchair down the steps of the Capitol building and made his way towards the rebels suspended twenty feet in the air. He looked up at them, noticing a few familiar faces he'd not seen in a long time.

'Jethro?' he said with extreme surprise. 'So you're responsible for this pathetic excuse of a rebellion. What a pleasant surprise. I must be honest; I never expected I'd ever see your face again, old friend.'

'It'll be the last face you ever see on this earth, Calvin,' barked Jethro.

The Master began laughing maniacally.

'I highly doubt that.'

'Where's Magnus?' asked Hunter, feeling his arms and legs getting stretched out wider.

'The boy is where he belongs. I really should be thanking you, rebels. If you hadn't have broken him out of prison, I'd have had no knowledge of my own clone's existence.'

'Give him back to us, you filth!' shouted Jethro.

Calvin clasped his hand shut, and Jethro's voice box closed, cutting off air to his lungs.

'I think I'll enjoy killing you the most, old friend.'

'LET HIM GO!' cried Hunter.

Calvin then turned his attention to the captain as he too started choking uncontrollably. The blood was starting to drain from Jethro and Hunter's faces as they continued to gasp for air.

Suddenly Calvin's mask was violently ripped from his face as if of its own accord. He looked around in surprise as his body began floating several feet off his chair and was suddenly slammed down on the ground with a great deal of force. The Shadow Squad fell out of the sky at the same time and hit the floor with a thud.

Calvin looked behind him and saw Magnus with his arms stretched out, exiting the Capitol building with his friends. He grimaced in anger as he lifted himself up off the ground. He raised his hands into the air, and numerous flying vehicles began dropping out of the sky in the direction of the Shadow Squad. Magnus lifted his hands to try and guide the pods to a safe landing, but there were too many of them for him to stop. Several vehicles spun out of control and crashed to the ground with incredible force, one of which landed on Colonel Braxton, fatally crushing his body.

Calvin outstretched his hand and lifted Magnus off his feet. The teenager let out a sharp cry of anguish as his arms and legs started to stretch beyond their limits. It felt like his limbs were about to be ripped from his torso. He suddenly heard a loud crack as his right shoulder popped out of its joint. Magnus screamed as the intensity of the pain overwhelmed his body.

Amelia quickly took the immobiliser she'd swiped from Magnus' cell out of her pocket and threw it over to Billy. With a huge swing of his sword's sheath, he swatted the immobiliser towards the Master as if he was scoring the winning goal of a Battleball match. It latched itself onto Calvin's chest, and Magnus immediately fell out of the sky. The boy was seconds from hitting the ground when Andro flew in and caught him just in time.

Calvin stretched out his arm in an attempt to use his powers again, but nothing happened. His telekinesis wasn't working with the immobiliser stuck to his chest.

Hunter nodded to his father and threw his sword to him. Jethro lunged at Calvin with great speed and stabbed him from behind, straight through his heart.

Calvin cried out in pain as Jethro moved in closer to speak into his mortal enemy's ear.

'This is for Maria!' Jethro whispered with hateful malice. He pulled the sword sharply, ripping it from the Master's back.

Calvin slumped to the floor, and Jethro stood over his body as he watched the light leave his enemy's eyes. He breathed a huge sigh of relief and fell to his knees. After fifteen years of waiting, Jethro had finally gotten his revenge.

Kayla ran over to Magnus, who was clutching his dislocated shoulder.

'Magnus, thank God! Are you okay?' she cried.

'I'm okay,' he said with a wince.

'I need to pop your shoulder back in.'

She helped him to his feet and took hold of his arm.

'This is going to hurt,' she warned him.

Magnus braced himself as Kayla pushed his arm against the joint. With a sharp snap, his shoulder popped back into place. Unfortunately, the pain was excruciating, and a numb, tingling sensation rushed through his arm.

'Brave boy! I'm so glad we got to you in time.'

She pulled him close and held him in a warm embrace.

'Give your arm a few weeks to heal, and it should be back to normal in no time.'

Magnus sank into her body, relieved that the fighting was finally finished.

'Thanks, Kayla,' he said genuinely.

Suddenly, a pod pulled up at the Capitol, and several guards stepped out of the vehicle brandishing their weapons. Grant jumped out, holding Tobias by the scruff of the neck. He surveyed the aftermath of the battle that just took place and noticed the Master lying dead on the ground as well as hundreds of lifeless soldiers. He fished into his pocket, pulled a gun out and held it to Tobias' head.

'Everyone drop your weapons. By order of Arcadian decree, you're all under arrest,' he yelled, trying his best to sound like a man who was in charge. However, the Squad barely responded.

'I said drop your weapons NOW, or I'll shoot your comrade right where he stands.'

Jethro and Hunter looked at each other and exchanged a wry smirk.

'Go ahead,' said Hunter shrugging his shoulders.

Tobias had a panicked look in his eyes. Was Grant actually going to shoot him?

Before he got the chance, however, Magnus held out his good arm and the barrel of Grant's gun collapsed in his hand. Grant pulled the trigger, but nothing happened. Magnus then turned his attention to the pod they arrived in. The guards couldn't believe their eyes as their vehicle began folding in on itself until it became nothing more than a crumpled up metal cube.

Grant looked at the Squad in dismay. He knew this was a fight he and his guards were unlikely to win. There was only one thing left to do. He lifted his hands above his head in surrender and nodded at his men to do the same. Carter and Taylor disarmed the guards and took the opportunity to pocket their many weapons. Max walked over to Tobias and grabbed him by the scruff of the neck.

'Remember me?' he said with tremendous delight. Tobias took a sharp intake of breath as he and Grant were dutifully escorted away by the muscular mercenary.

Amelia swung her arms around Magnus.

'We did it!' she said, overwhelmed with joy. 'We won.'

Magnus looked deep into his friend's eyes.

'Thank you for coming to rescue me,' he said with heartfelt gratitude. Amelia smiled and hugged him once again. She never wanted to let him go.

Kayla limped over to Hunter and kissed him in sheer relief.

'Now what?' She asked with an exhausted chuckle.

Hunter gave himself a moment to think. He honestly didn't expect they would ever get this far. He looked over to the announcement podium at the front of the entrance to the Capitol building. He'd seen it many times before on news broadcasts when he was young. It would appear on his television screen every time the

Commander-in-Chief of Arcadia had an announcement to make to the public. The podium was hardwired to every household in the city the moment the microphone was switched on.

'We need to tell the people of Arcadia what happened here today. They deserve to know the truth.'

Kayla nodded and stepped out of his way. The other Squad members looked on in awe as they watched their leader march over to the podium and turn on the microphone.

Silence swallowed the city of Arcadia as every TV monitor and hologram in the city popped up with Hunter's face on it. He suddenly wished he'd prepared some kind of speech. He paused for a moment to collect his thoughts before finally leaning forward to speak into the microphone.

'Citizens of Arcadia, please listen to me. Your Master, Calvin Mortifer, is dead, and his corrupted politicians have been taken into custody. Today a rebellion took place with the objective to overthrow the tyrannical government that has abandoned the needs of its country in order to serve itself. I am the leader of that rebellion. My name is Hunter Beckett. I was once an Arcadian just like you until I finally had my eyes opened to the horrors the citizens who live outside these walls face every single day. People are dying in their homes and on the streets, unable to get the essential supplies necessary for their families' survival. As human beings, we have a moral obligation and responsibility to share our wealth and

resources with those most in need of our help. This suffering cannot continue anymore. From this day on, Arcadia will no longer be a home exclusively for the rich and the privileged. Instead, it'll become what it was created to be - a sanctuary for each and every human being desperately fighting for their lives. We must band together and throw open our doors. I implore you all to join us in our mission to make the future brighter for everyone. Today is a day of new beginnings. Thank you for listening.'

Hunter stepped away from the podium and looked over towards his enervated, battle-scarred mercenaries. Each and every one of them had taken a knee and was bowing their heads in respect and admiration for their honourable leader.

- CHAPTER 22 -
NEW BEGINNINGS

Twelve weeks later, Magnus and Amelia looked out over the balcony of the Capitol building at the city they now called home. They were completely overwhelmed by the beauty of the early morning sunrise, which painted the tall buildings and picturesque scenery in beautiful yellows and oranges. Neither one of them had witnessed anything so majestic or serene in their entire lives, and they were determined to appreciate every single moment of it for as long as they possibly could.

Since moving to Arcadia, Magnus and the Shadow Squad had spent most of their days rescuing people from their slums and bringing them to safety at the city in the sky. Thanks to Arcadia's superior tracking technology, the Squad were able to cover far more ground than ever before, and Magnus' determination to save as many people in the country as possible was unrivalled.

He had to admit, though, he was shocked by the overwhelming support they had received from Arcadia's inhabitants after Hunter's speech at the Capitol. He felt for sure there would be at least some resistance from them regarding opening their doors to non-Arcadian folk, but most people welcomed them with open arms. Many were of the opinion that it was about time the city did more to help the poor and needy, but they were too frightened to protest against the tyrannical government. Such generosity restored Magnus' faith in humanity, and it seemed there was finally some hope of a brighter future for those who felt they had none.

Among those first to be rescued were the remaining inhabitants of Ground Zero. Magnus was very pleased to be reunited with his good friends George, Tom, Sam and the rest of the gang. He was even happy to see Gerald's grumpy old face again.

Magnus reflected on how much his life had changed over the past few months and how much he'd grown as a person. From being little more than an anxious teenager scared of his own shadow to a determined young freedom fighter, he had definitely come a long way in such a short space of time. He'd also discovered something new about himself thanks to blood tests conducted by Jethro. Calvin never knew, but the power they both possessed had unlocked immunity to the virus within their cells, which meant Magnus was able to breathe the air outside the city without the need for a mask. This created the exciting possibility that a new vaccine was on the horizon that had the potential to immunise the entire country. However, they were a long way off that outcome. For the time being, the teenager was more than happy standing guard in his tower and waiting for the call to go out and rescue those in need.

As Magnus stood admiring the view, Amelia was busy explaining how far she'd gotten on the game 'Magnificent Warlords'.

'So we've almost reached Lord Foltran's castle, right? But then a horde of demons converge on us before we can get inside.'

'Let me guess; Andro finds some pathetic way to get himself killed before you get a chance to destroy all the demons.'

'Every time!'

Magnus started laughing.

'We get to the exact same point, and he always gets killed. He never seems to learn from his mistakes. I reckon he's doing it on purpose,' said Amelia in a sceptical tone.

'No, it's because he insists on playing as Lariel. I keep telling him she's the worst character, but he refuses to listen. He's fascinated by the colour of her hair for some strange reason.'

Amelia chuckled.

'She does have pretty hair, to be fair. Maybe I should become a redhead.'

Magnus just looked at her, puzzled.

'Do you not think it would suit me?' she asked, hoping he would agree.

'No,' he answered bluntly.

Amelia grew a pout on her face as Magnus started laughing.

They heard the door open behind them, and Hunter walked onto the balcony overlooking the city.

'Hello, you two, a beautiful morning, isn't it?' he said, unusually upbeat.

'It sure is,' said Amelia. 'I've never seen anything so striking in my whole life,'

She had an immense sense of wonder and awe in her voice as she looked out over the horizon.

'It certainly makes a nice change from your leaking bedroom at Ground Zero, doesn't it, Magnus?' Hunter said, patting the teenage boy on the back.

Magnus nodded but looked contemplative.

'What's the matter?' asked Hunter inquisitively. He'd have thought this would be a dream come true for a boy who's spent his whole life locked away from the world in one tiny room.

'Oh, nothing,' Magnus responded flippantly. 'It's stupid, really. My life has changed so much for the better in the past few months since you rescued me. However there's a part of me that still misses my old prison cell. The world seemed so much smaller and simpler back then.'

'That's all part of growing up,' Hunter replied, like a father educating his son. 'You have a new purpose now, and there's no greater gift in life than that.'

Magnus nodded in agreement. However, there still seemed to be something praying on his mind.

'Can I ask you a question?'

'Of course.'

'Did you always know I was... you know...' Magnus stuttered, trying to get his words out. It still pained him to admit it to himself... 'A clone?'

Hunter paused for a moment before responding.

'Yes,' he replied definitively. 'My father knew the moment he laid eyes on you as a baby. That birthmark around your eye is unmistakable. I'm sorry I didn't tell you the truth, Magnus. I didn't want you to feel ashamed of who you are.'

'It's okay; I don't blame you. But did you not ever worry I might start acting like him?'

'No. Never!' Hunter replied without an ounce of doubt.

'Sometimes it worries me,' Magnus admitted. 'Sometimes I get so angry that I completely lose all control.'

'That happens to all of us, Magnus.'

'But what if I turn into him when I'm older?'

Magnus had a look of deep consternation in his eyes. The thought of growing up to become the evilest man in the free world filled him with immeasurable dread.

'Now you listen to me, Magnus,' said Hunter, putting his hands on the boy's shoulders and looking him straight in the eyes. 'I want you to really listen carefully, okay? You are not him! Calvin was selfish and cruel beyond measure because he felt like the world owed him something for his lifelong misfortune. When you have power, it's much easier to bully people into getting what you want than to actually work hard for it. He never had any desire to use his powers to help people; he only used them to serve his own needs. But in all my years on this Earth, I've never met anyone as hard working and compassionate towards other people as you, Magnus.'

The boy smiled. The compliment made him feel a lot better about himself.

'You may have the same blood flowing through your veins, but you will never be the monster that he was. You're far too good-natured.'

Amelia put her hand on his shoulder and nodded in concurrence.

'It's true, Magnus. I knew the moment I met you that you had a good soul, and I'm an excellent judge of character,' she said boastfully.

'You can't argue with logic like that, can you, Magnus?' said Hunter jokingly. Magnus just rolled his eyes and smirked.

Suddenly an alarm could be heard, which echoed around the Capitol building. Andro burst through the door to the balcony with incredible haste.

'What is it, Andro?' asked Hunter urgently.

'There's been a sighting of a family seeking asylum in the North. Do you want to see their coordinates?'

'Show me on the way. Time to go to work, Magnus,' said Hunter as he and Andro turned to leave straight away. Magnus moved to follow them but was yanked back by Amelia grabbing his arm.

'What are you....' but before he could finish his sentence, she leaned forward and kissed him on the lips. Magnus' heart stopped, and his mind went fuzzy. He certainly wasn't expecting this to happen. Amelia broke the kiss and smiled directly into his eyes.

'Go get 'em,' she said encouragingly. Magnus smiled warmly and, with a spring in his step, headed off the balcony to suit up.

As Magnus stood on the edge of the Arcadian hanger with the other members of the Shadow Squad by his side, he thought about how truly lucky he was at that moment.

For most of his life, he had nobody except Andro and the four walls of his prison cell for company. Now he had everything a young boy could ever dream of – a family, good friends, an amazing home and a true sense of purpose to his life. He looked over at his comrades, Hunter, Kayla, Max, Toro, Carter, Taylor, Billy and Andro, and his heart swelled with the utmost gratitude. He finally realised that for the first time in his life, he was truly happy in every possible way, and he hoped to be able to provide the same level of happiness to whoever needed rescuing.

Hunter gave the signal, and each member of the Shadow Squad leapt off the edge of the helipad in unison and plummeted to the city below, ready to rescue every last survivor in their path.